A MAIDEN OF SNAKES

BY JANE MCGARRY

A Maiden of Snakes
by Jane McGarry
Published by JM Books

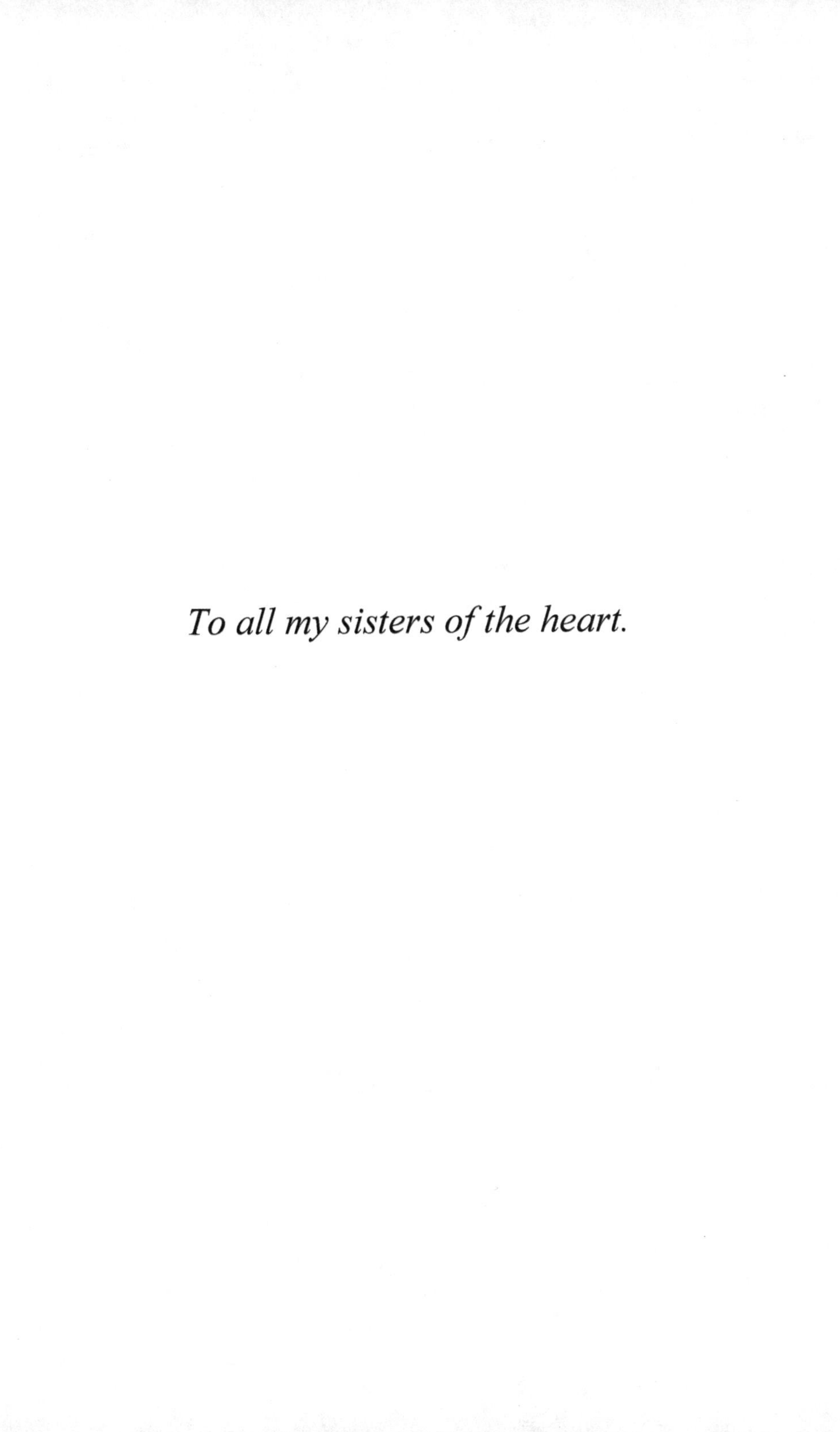

To all my sisters of the heart.

CHAPTER ONE

The day was perfect, a warm spring sun in a cloudless sky. Yet from the castle balcony, Marchioness Lamberico stared at the city below with a heavy heart. Rays of light reflected off the buildings which stood in orderly fashion down the hillside, red-tiled roofs like well-placed bricks aligned by a child. Off to the north, against the backdrop of the white-capped Alps, the cathedral steeple soared proudly, a tall sentry against the imposing peaks. In the shadow of these majestic mountains, the city's inhabitants made their way through the everyday tasks of provincial Italian life.

Voices buzzed from the markets, its stalls a riot of color against the dull gray stones of the square. The earthy smell of overturned soil from newly plowed fields lingered across the air. In the higher pastures, cows and sheep lowed, eating their fill of the tall grass while their shepherds lazed under the nearby trees. The neatly lined vineyards blossomed with tiny fragrant flowers destined to ripen into fat juicy grapes. Monferrato burst with life, the beckon of spring calling forth bud and grass. All around her, the fruitfulness of the season grew. In every place except her own womb. With a sigh, Adeleta returned to her chambers, leaving the cityscape and its accusatory fecundity behind. She dropped into a chair and rubbed her forehead. Three years had passed since her marriage to the Marquis of Monferrato. Three long years where every sliver of hope for a pregnancy had been snuffed like the flame of a candle. Her two sisters, one younger than herself, had already delivered multiple offspring to their husbands. Though her spouse held the most authority of these men, the rank of marchioness did nothing to assist her with the production of an heir.

The marquis tried his best to encourage the marchioness and keep her filled with purpose on the mission to conceive, visiting her bed nightly. Although considered cold by many who knew him, Marquis Lamberico's heart ached for the misery of his wife and no words of praise or gift of gems healed her sense of despair. Many days she went to sit in her private garden alone with her thoughts, only to return with red-rimmed eyes while the couple sat through an uncomfortably silent supper. The entirety of her failure tormented her mind; an agony sleep did not alleviate but magnified with taunting dreams of babies in her arms. A heart ready to burst with happiness, merely to awaken to cruel reality.

Whispers filled the castle and the whole city, no doubt, of the marquis' need to cast Adeleta aside for a more fertile partner. The laundry maids murmured behind their hands each month when her lack of conception became apparent on soiled sheets. Whether they thought the marchioness did not notice or they did not care if she did, only added to her suffering. After all, her primary job was to provide Nardo with a son. His nephew, Piero, birthed by his brother's wife, waited in the wings to grab the title of Marquis. How she hated the smug expression the boy's father always wore in her presence. Sadly, the boy's mother passed in childbirth.

Adeleta, with the assistance of her head maid, Tessina, tried a number of herbs and elixirs, none of which brought about the desired outcome. Tessina, the only confidante of the marchioness, felt the pain of her mistress each time she crossed a failed attempt off a list of suggestions to induce a pregnancy. Today, the maid put a line through the last entry on a piece of paper once filled on each side with ideas. Every possible option Tessina ever heard of had been exhausted, with nothing to show for it. Every option—except one. She shuddered at the unpleasant thought and buried the idea, adamant not to mention it to the marchioness. In the end, her silence was for naught. Adeleta suggested it on her own.

"Your hair looks so lovely after the infusion of oils in tonight's bath," Tessina said, stroking a brush through Adeleta's chestnut tresses one evening.

Another servant wiped down the tub and picked up the wet towels from the dressing room floor. Once gathered in a tight bundle across her chest, she left maid and mistress alone.

The marchioness stared at her fingers, deep in thought, while her hair was braided. A warm breezed flowed in from the open balcony doors and crickets chirped their nightly serenade. She looked up and met eyes with Tessina in the mirror's reflection.

"I bet they will all be mocking me in the laundry when those towels arrive." Her voice held such sorrow, the maid put down the brush and took her hand.

"Don't worry about what any of them say. I'm sure more time is all that is needed. One day soon, you will be holding your own baby, and all this petty chatter will be but a distant memory." This was the same assurance she gave her friend each month, and by now the words rang hollow.

"Tessina, I need your help," she declared, a resolute expression on her face.

"Anything, my lady." Tessina had no power to deny any request from her mistress, but their close friendship made it unlikely she would ever wish to, whatever the demand.

"I must visit with Imelda as soon as possible." Her voice was soft, but still determined.

"Are you certain that is . . . wise?" The same sense of dread that arose whenever Tessina considered this alternative consumed her, and the marchioness tightened her grip.

"I have run out of choices. You know this as well as I. The meeting must be done with all secrecy. Can I count on you to help me?"

The maid saw the pleading in Adeleta's eyes. Though Tessina feared this avenue, she did not have the heart to refuse the woman who had been so kind and generous to her since the moment they met three years ago. Almost the same age, they each had been sent from their respective homes to a strange city when the marquis married, one to be a lady, the other a servant, but true friendship had formed. In truth, the maid's heart ached nearly as much as her lady's, who deserved to experience the joy of motherhood, not this constant life of disappointment. She had aided Adeleta in every other attempt and would not leave the marchioness on her own despite the dire lengths this course of action required.

The stories of Imelda were legend. Some called her a witch, others a sylph. Only the most desperate sought her help for if given, it came with a catch—an outcome the asker did not foresee, perhaps for the better or perhaps not. No one spoke of receiving help from Imelda, but gossip spread in Monferrato as noxiously as any other populated area of the globe. If all went well, heads were turned in the other direction. However, if misfortune occurred, retribution followed.

Two springs ago, a woman went to Imelda for pus spots on her face. Whatever remedy she was given, the boils cleared almost immediately. Not a week later, the city was beset with grape berry moth larva. The pests destroyed nearly the entire vineyard production of the city, a serious financial blow. Rumors circulated it was because of Imelda's witchcraft. Citizens burned down the house of the woman who received the witch's medicine before they chased her out of town. She barely escaped with her life. No vengeance was ever carried out on Imelda for fear of her powers.

Secrecy of their visit would be imperative. If word spread, the marchioness visited Imelda and some sort of calamity followed, Adeleta would take the brunt of the punishment. A tingle ran down the maid's spine, but she straightened up tall and, with a squeeze of her mistress' hand, said, "I will do whatever you ask of me, my lady."

"So be it," Adeleta proclaimed, hope forming anew in her heart.

CHAPTER TWO

The sunrise was just a thought in the steely pre-dawn sky when Tessina, awake for the last hour, woke her mistress as instructed. Adeleta rubbed the traces of restless sleep from her eyes. She rose and donned the plain servant's dress her maid obtained, the unfamiliar fabric rough against her royal skin, and adjusted her braid, messy from sleep. Not a sound could be heard except a rogue rooster, up far earlier than his companions. Adeleta's hands shook as she straightened out the front of her dress.

"Here is a cloak," Tessina whispered, holding out one that matched her own.

The marchioness wrapped it around her shoulders before they crept from her chambers like twin shadows. In front of them, an empty hallway unfolded. Candles flickered in sconces every few feet, casting wavy outlines on the wall. Their silk-slippered steps were all but noiseless on the stone floor, attracting only the attention of a fat cat, who sat with a dead mouse in its mouth. It watched them pass before consuming its quarry. A circular flight of steps deposited the ladies at a servant's door, where they exited into morning air still crisp with the last vestiges of winter.

From there they slunk across a few main streets, careful to hug the edges of walls with heads down. Seedier parts of the city engulfed them, places the marchioness never visited, yet Tessina seemed to know somehow. Ducking into a dark alley, the stench of urine filled the air, and the marchioness pulled her cloak even further around her face to cover her nose. They saw no one, though prying eyes peering from any window remained a possibility. Halfway down the city's hill, they cut across to a dirt road where the houses now sat farther apart, growing more dilapidated as they went. No sound emerged from the ramshackle buildings. The only living creature they saw was a lone goat near a broken fence, so thin ribs protruded from its sides while it chewed on the overgrown grass. At the end of the road, they crossed a stream where a forlorn wooden bridge sagged underfoot. Soon after, they entered the edge of a forest. Though not yet in full leaf, the trees provided cover from any onlookers. A squirrel raced off at the sight of them, scattering the carpet of dead leaves.

"How far into the woods must we go?" Adeleta asked, pushing the hood of her cloak onto her shoulders and inhaling a breath of fresh air.

"About a mile from what I can figure." The maid pulled out a scrap of paper with rudimentary directions and landmarks. "I wrote this from memory, putting down all the information that I've overheard over the years."

The marchioness smiled at the woman's discretion. *A trustworthy soul*, she thought, *so difficult to find in this world.*

When Adeleta first arrive in Monferrato, a scared girl of sixteen, Nardo assigned Tessina to be her head maid. Only a year younger than her mistress, the maid was anxious to perform her job as properly as the new marchioness hoped to do hers. This common sense of apprehension bonded the two despite the differences in their station. Adeleta knew her failure to conceive over the past three years distressed Tessina as if it was her own affliction and loved her all the more for it.

"Do you know if anyone else has asked Imelda for help with this particular problem before?" the marchioness asked, stepping over the trunk of a downed tree. Her cloak snagged on a knotty lump and she stooped to tear it free.

"Yes. I've heard rumors of three women in the city. Two bore a child, one did not."

"And did anything . . . bad happen to them?" she asked, a dismissive glance at the small tear now in the hem of her wrap.

Tessina hesitated, the disquiet in her mistress' voice palpable. For a moment, only the crunch of leaves and plaintive cry of an owl filled the silence.

The maid gave a carefully worded reply, "The one who did not give birth passed away suddenly, not long after her visit. Some people blamed Imelda's antidote," she quickly added, "but there is no proof to think such a thing."

"Well, that is a bit disconcerting. And what of the others? The two who gave birth?" Adeleta pulled Tessina to a stop and stared into her eyes.

"One had a perfect baby boy, who is one of the delights of the servant village," she answered, a large smile at the thought of his golden head and sky-blue eyes which never failed to enchant adults and children alike. "He is both smart and good-natured,"

"And the other?" the marchioness pressed, her murmur filled with anxiety.

"She is a sickly child, small for her age and some gossips whisper . . ." she trailed off, but a hard look from her mistress drew out the rest, "well, they say she has . . . a tail."

"A tail!" the marchioness blanched, her certainty in this mission fading fast. She lowered herself onto a large rock, put her head in her hands, and wept.

Tessina knelt beside her to stroke her arm. "Do not despair, my lady. You are the worthiest woman I know. Fate will look kindly on you. I am sure of it."

"Is it worth the risk? What if something horrible happens?" she croaked between tears.

"It won't. It simply can't. You deserve to be a mother more than anyone I know," Tessina consoled, wiping Adeleta's tears with the sleeve of her dress. "Besides, the tail story is only a rumor. I've seen the girl myself and there is no evidence of one. I'm sure it's just the petty gossip of those who have nothing better to do with their time. But this is *your* decision and I will support you either way."

The marchioness steeled her resolve, wiping her tears on the cloak. She stood and smoothed out her garments with brisk movements, brushing the dirt at the hem onto the ground. "Thank you, Tessina. I don't know what I would do without you. Let's at least go hear what Imelda has to say."

They joined hands and walked farther into the forest. Though hidden from their view, the sun rose slowly over the horizon, turning the sky overhead pink. Birdsong started in the trees, the woods awakening around them. Tessina consulted her map a few times and steered their course accordingly past whatever specified rock or tree served as a marker. A light mist swirled around the forest floor, dampening their slippers. Though they said no more, Tessina felt the return of Adeleta's determination.

Amid a small clearing, a cabin carved into the bole of an enormous oak came into view, its base resting on the outstretched arms of the roots. In the structure's center sat an oval-topped door of bright green, its surface adorned with carvings of snakes, birds, and fairies. A roof of mossy thatch sat atop like a tuft of unkempt hair. The dwelling merged into the massive tree trunk which loomed high into the sky where boughs created a natural umbrella of protection around it.

The women crossed the clearing, hands still clasped tightly. Adeleta rose her free hand to knock just as the door swung open. A tall figure with gray eyes regarded them with an enigmatic expression.

"Welcome, Marchioness Lamberico. Please come in."

CHAPTER THREE

The morning sun did not yet reach into the darkness of the cabin, a single candle on a large table was not enough to expose the recesses of the room. Imelda gestured for them to sit, the pale cascade of her hair flowing with every movement. Despite the whiteness of her tresses, her age could not be guessed. Her eyes were deep with knowledge, yet her smile bright and youthful with but a trace of fine lines. Rumors of her existence had circulated for ages, lending to the speculation she was an otherworldly being untouched by the passing of years.

"How may I help you?" she asked, sitting on the opposite side of the table from where the women waited, the very question belied by a knowing smile.

Adeleta slid into a chair at the round table with Tessina at her side. Silence followed; the marchioness studied her folded hands for a moment and the maid worried her nerve had failed. Tessina took one of her patroness' shaky hands in her own. A halo of light from the lone candle flickered onto Imelda's face creating an ethereal glow. She patiently waited for a reply. Tessina felt something rub against her leg and looked to see the yellow eyes of a cat staring up at her. It brushed against her skirt again and disappeared into the gloom.

"I have tried to conceive for three years," Adeleta stated, her voice growing stronger with each word, "but to no avail."

"I see," the witch said. "And you would like me to give you something to help in that endeavor?"

"Yes." The marchioness leveled her eyes with Imelda, her tone strong despite her trembling frame.

"I see." The witch paused, her gray eyes boring into Adeleta, who would swear she saw a glint of calculation in them. "I have something to help."

Imelda rose and walked to a worktable; its edges still hidden in shadow. She pulled down two flasks from disorganized shelves, filled with bottles and other decanters. She poured them into a bowl, where the combination created a light smoke that plumed in a slow coil from the container. Tessina shared a concerned look with her mistress. The witch paid them no mind. After careful contemplation, she pulled some dried herbs from sprigs hanging haphazardly from the rafters and, after crushing them with a mortar and pestle, added the amalgamation to the liquid. A bright green glow emanated from the bowl. Happy with the outcome, Imelda poured the contents into a small vial, pushing the stopper down firmly. She returned to the table and placed the vial of vibrant green mixture on the surface between her and the ladies. The vessel shone brighter than the candle.

"That will fix the problem?" Tessina asked, noticing a hint of movement in the gloom cast beneath the worktable and the unmistakable waver of a cat's tail.

"Yes. However," Imelda hesitated, enjoying the uncomfortable silence that followed. "Magic is a fickle master. There is always a consequence connected to its use for good or evil. You must be prepared for this if you wish to use the potion."

"But how does one know if the consequence will be good or evil?" Adeleta exclaimed, her face ashen in the unnatural green light.

"There is no way to tell. What happens, happens. Though, I get an odd sense from you," the witch ventured at the exact moment a black cat hopped onto the table. Both visitors started with fright. "That is just Oscar. He helps me analyze situations."

Imelda pointed toward the marchioness, and the cat crossed the table. He sniffed around her hands, then her neck, his whiskers tickled against her skin. With a sudden move, the cat pushed the marchioness with its head until she was forced to back up her chair. Leaping into Adeleta's lap, it placed his head against her lower stomach. For a few moments, it remained still before jumping back on the table. The animal returned to the witch, who lowered her head while it rubbed across her face several times with his nose. At last, it jumped off the table and vanished into the dark edges of the room.

"Interesting," murmured the witch, her arms crossed over her chest.

The two women stared perplexed, unsure what to say. Oscar meowed from some shadowy hiding spot and the hair on Tessina's neck rose.

"There is a reason you could not conceive. Something magical needs to escape with any pregnancy of yours. This will help release it." Imelda nodded at the vial still laying on the table.

"Something magical? What does that mean?" Tessina demanded, tired of all the mysterious talk and half-explanations.

"I do not know for sure," the witch replied with a shrug. "The child may be blessed with certain gifts."

"But there will definitely be a child?" Adeleta asked and hope sprang into her heart.

"Yes."

The simple pronouncement brought joy to the marchioness, a feeling she had long forgotten. Her eyes glowed with wonder, moistness rising in them. Next to her, the maid's mind filled with concern. She wished to see her mistress pregnant—but at what cost? Thoughts of babies with tails or other such horrors flashed through her mind.

"What do I need to do?" Adeleta's question brought Tessina back to the present.

"On the fourteenth day after your last monthly courses, drink this precisely at midnight and then go lie with your husband. If you do exactly this, your wish will be granted, but only do so with the full awareness of what we have spoken of today," the witch proclaimed.

Abruptly, the marchioness stood, taking the vial, and stuffing it into the pocket of her dress.

Tessina rose on hesitant feet, eyes fixed to the spot where the vial had been which still glowed despite the container's absence. She leveled her eyes with Imelda, whose expression remained unreadable.

"I thank you for your help and your discretion." Adeleta laid a generous handful of gold coins on the table. "We must return now."

"Of course." Imelda bowed her head in acknowledgement of the payment.

The women hurried out the door without so much as a glance back. Their pace through the woods so swift, Tessina did not have the breath to say anything of the visit or the potential ramifications of the potion. In her heart, she knew any words would be futile. Her mistress' sole goal was to have a child. There would be no talking her out of it. The maid watched the faint light of day creep into the darkness of the forest with a sense of foreboding.

Back in the city, the women crept to the palace, hooded once more. The servant's entrance was busier now with the official arrival of dawn. They took a circuitous route to the library and entered with no one to witness. A bookshelf on the wall of a little used aisle opened to reveal a hidden door back into the chambers of the marchioness.

Tessina remained silent as her mistress changed out of the servant's cloak and dress. Adeleta fingered the vial in her hands for a moment before storing it in a secret compartment in her vanity table.

"You think I shouldn't take it," the mistress said in a defensive tone, while she pulled her nightgown over her head.

The maid removed her own cloak, laying it on a chair with the used servant's outfit. She contemplated her words, her sisterly love for this woman welling in her heart. "I think you should carefully weigh the decision."

"Ha! You talk in the same circles Imelda did," Adeleta chided. "But don't worry, all will be well once I am pregnant."

A rap on the door from the adjoining room silenced any reply. Marquis Lamberico strolled in, newly shaven, and dressed for the day.

"Good morning, love." He crossed the room to kiss his wife's cheek. "Just woke up?"

"Yes," Adeleta said, stretching her arms for effect.

"Tessina, have breakfast brought up. My wife and I will enjoy it together on her terrace this morning."

"Yes, sir." The maid gathered the contraband clothes from the chair, relieved he had not noticed. When she turned to close the door, Adeleta beamed at her husband in a way the maid had not seen since the early days of their marriage. A pit filled Tessina's stomach as the latch clicked shut.

CHAPTER FOUR

The marchioness dutifully counted down the time in anticipation of the designated night. Thirteen days, three hundred and twelve hours to be exact, during which she hurtled from glorious highs to dreadful lows. The vial remained hidden in her vanity among her perfumes and oils. A safe enough spot for, besides herself, only Tessina ever opened the drawer, a good thing given the eerie green glow the object emitted.

The maid, for her part, did not mention the potion, the secret meeting, or any of the possible consequences that may lie ahead. Only shared glances of either joy or fear, depending on her mistress' mood, bespoke of that fateful visit to Imelda. Tessina knew her patron's obstinate nature enough where this issue was concerned to realize any words of warning would fall on deaf ears. She decided all she could do was support her friend through whatever fate brought in the end.

Adeleta spent afternoons in her private garden. Discovered not long after she arrived in Monferrato, she saw potential in the small, enclosed space. After previous years of neglect, workers followed her instructions on what to plant and where, gardening a passion from her youth. Soon, ivies climbed the wall, spilling over the outside like an unconfined green waterfall. Once inside the scrolled gate, one could stroll along meandering paths, among beds bursting with roses, lavender, wisteria, and delphinium. Benches sat tucked away here and there with clumps of lady's mantle standing guard around them, their waxy leaves bright in the sun. In the center, a small fountain of a cherub with water flowing down from his pitcher, lent a relaxing tinkle to the air.

For three years, she tended this garden; now an eruption of green splashed with color as vivid as a painter's palette. Adeleta had taken comfort in the chaotic overgrowth, such a contrast to the neatly ordered city with its methodical red rooftops lining the hill amongst the perfect squares of well-tended pastures and vineyards. For some reason, the garden's disarray made her mind focus in a way she could not in the systematic establishment of the city. Until now, she concentrated on the garden's beauty, on her ability to bring something to life while her womb lay bare, but now, in the lush bounty of spring, it was a place to dwell on the happiness that lay ahead.

This afternoon, she roamed the paths; the sun playing hide and seek with the clouds. Tonight was *the* night. The required days had passed, somehow both swiftly and with agonizing sluggishness all at once. It was finally time to act . . . or not. Her heart decided to take the potion the moment the vial was offered, but her mind, a more prudent source, warned her of the possible ramifications. Tessina, she knew, thought the choice was made. However, these past two weeks her heart and mind grappled to find unity with one another, until the marchioness conceded just today that there could be none. In the end, the sense of pure joy brought when picturing an infant in her arms overthrew any intellectual doubts. She would take the potion and accept whatever destiny followed.

The decision, once made, took all burdens off her shoulders, and a bright hope filled her. That evening, she dined with her husband and a table of noble citizens, all of whom remarked on her glowing beauty. Marquis Lamberico noticed himself and did not hide his enthusiasm when his wife privately made clear to him her intention to visit his chambers that night.

Dinner ended late, as is so often the case when people enjoy a sense of importance, and who would not in the company of such hosts. It was after eleven when the marquis bid his last guest farewell. Though his wife disappeared some minutes earlier, he returned to his room satisfied with how the evening went and what was to come. His worries for the marchioness, who seemed filled with contemplation these last few weeks, dissipated when she whispered at dinner her wish to be with him. Whatever she mused over in her garden earlier today, he was grateful it led to this.

Meanwhile, in that very garden, the marchioness sat alone on the edge of the fountain, potion in hand. Her ears strained to hear the clock tower which sat atop the cathedral in the center of the city. Its chime would be her signal. Her heart pounded against her ribs, every moment an eternity, until a gentle bong floated across the air, followed by another. Midnight. With shaking hands, she uncapped the vial and before she could hesitate, raised it to her lips. The liquid held a sweet sensation as it slithered down her throat in a thick trail. She swallowed every drop and waited for some type of reaction, but there was nothing. Not a tingle, or a shiver, or a spasm of any kind went through her body. Adeleta assumed magic would have an immediate effect. A slight sense of disappointment filled her, but the first step was done and now she must fulfill the rest of the instructions and trust the witch told her the truth.

Hastily, she corked the vial and placed it in a hole she dug earlier under some hollyhock across from the fountain. After a quick stop in her room to freshen up, she went to join her husband in his chambers. He eagerly completed the deed, happy with a passion shown by his wife which he had not seen in some time.

When they finished, he watched her sleep, her face illuminated by the moonlight pouring in through the open window, a satisfied smile on her lips.

Under the hollyhock in the garden, the ground stirred. A shoot pushed from the soil, a circle of dirt fanning around it. The growth thickened to the trunk of a small sandalwood tree, a variety only found in far warmer climates. Small branches formed, spreading in delicate tendrils from the sapling. Tiny green leaves burst forth intermingled with the buds of miniature white and red flowers. Beneath the earth, the roots wrapped around a hollow in the soil, forming the walls of a den. Eight diminutive eggs materialized, a bright green glow emanating from them. They expanded in size until a head emerged from each and eight snakes coiled around each other in the darkness of the nest.

The next few weeks were anguish for the marchioness, the doubt piling up like bricks each day, the calm brought on by the decision, replaced with the complete upheaval of her senses. Her temper was short with Tessina, who walked a balance beam between showing the proper concern and not mentioning the whole situation. Adeleta spent the afternoons pacing her garden, praying to whoever may be listening for the success of her endeavor. So intent were her ministrations, she never noticed the small sandalwood tree which sprung up where she buried the potion vial. Marquis Lamberico, flustered by his wife's ever-changing demeanor, did not know how to help, and took to giving her a wide berth by claiming any number of business distractions.

The two-week mark passed with no sign of her monthly courses. By the end of the third week, the maids who did the laundry, began to whisper about the lack of soiled clothing and sheets. Once the fourth week came and went, the physician was summoned. After a brief exam and a number of questions, he proclaimed his diagnosis.

"The marchioness is with child," he stoically informed the marquis, whose stunned silence was his only reply. "It will be born at the beginning of next year."

CHAPTER FIVE

Once the initial shock wore off, Marquis Lamberico's excitement was matched by the citizens of Monferrato, who saw it as a good omen for their families and lands. The mild summer weather spoke of an abundant harvest come fall. Of course, an official announcement regarding the pregnancy was not made until after the twelfth week had passed, by which time the information had already filtered down to the lowliest peasants. Betting pools on the date of birth and gender ran at nearly every tavern, even amongst the palace staff. To Tessina's great relief, she heard no rumors of Imelda connected with the long-awaited pregnancy of the marchioness.

Adeleta's smile broadened with her belly, enchanted by the flutters of life inside her, which brought her even more joy than she ever imagined possible. Her main occupation became the design of the nursery. Certain she carried a daughter, the room exploded with pink bedding, draperies, and tapestries, all threaded through with gold. The servants muttered about the gender-specific room, worried the baby may be a son, but the marchioness, so certain in her prediction, barely noticed. She spent any free time in her garden, basking in the life around her. Heavy blossoms filled the space, vibrant bursts of purples and corals amid humid air thick with fragrance.

"Do you feel well today?" Tessina asked her on one such afternoon as they relaxed on a bench, a wisteria covered trellis providing them shade from the mid-July sun.

"Well enough, though my feet are sore." She removed her ever-tightening slippers to flex her swollen toes. She must talk to the staff about some larger pairs of shoes. "Such a mild infliction, I've no right to complain."

"Very common," the maid assured. "My mother birthed ten babies and her feet swelled with all of them. The heat makes it worse."

Tessina rose and took two towels to the fountain, the cherub's pitcher tinkling merrily while she dipped them in the cool water. Placing the wet clothes on her mistress' feet, she raised one to her lap to massage it, firm strokes through the chilled material. Birds flitted about, pecking up the last crumbs of bread the ladies brought for them. One took a dip in the fountain once the maid walked away. It hopped up to the edge and ruffled its feathers dry.

Adeleta leaned back against the bench with a sigh. "You spoil me too much, Tessina."

"Not at all." The maid continued her soothing treatment, remembering how much her mother appreciated the foot rubs. "Have you and the marquis spoken about any names yet?"

"He says the choice should be mine since it's a girl." Her husband remained most indulgent with his wife's insistence of the gender. After another sigh of contentment, Adeleta joked, "Perhaps I should speak to your mother—she named ten of you, after all."

"By the time I came along and then my last sister, her patience on name picking drew thin," laughed the maid. "I'm surprised she managed to . . . oh my goodness!"

Tessina shrieked and jumped up, alarming the marchioness, who sat up with a start. She followed the maid's gaze to the grass where a slender, green snake sat next to Adeleta's slippers. Head slightly raised, it regarded the women, a delicate forked tongue flicking in and out, and the maid swore it looked ready to speak to them.

"Shoo!" Tessina cried and threw a stone at it. Swiftly, it slithered away back into the cover of the bushes. "Are you all right, mistress?"

"Yes, though you startled me with your scream. After all, it was only a common garden snake not an asp from Egypt." She leaned back to rest a hand on her belly as though to soothe the occupant inside.

"My apologies. I never saw one that close before," the maid stated, returning to her foot rubbing duty. "It took me by surprise."

Neither lady mentioned the snake again, it seemed so trivial a matter. Two days later, Adeleta again sought refuge in her garden. This time she was alone, tired from a morning of interacting with some townswomen at a monthly breakfast where nobles dined with her to discuss the affairs of the city. Normally, the meals were just glorified gossip sessions, but today most of the talk centered around the expected child, every attendee a spate of suggestions and advice about motherhood. Afterwards, the marchioness craved some peace.

She strolled the rambling paths which wove around the secluded space. The sun was high in the sky, but the air pleasant, yesterday's humidity chased away by thunderstorms the night before. Beads of water still shone on every petal and leaf, lending an enchanted shine to the garden. At the fountain, she eased down onto the edge to enjoy the rainbow that shimmered through the cherub's waterspout. His full cheeks, though carved in gray stone, warmed her heart with the thought of her future infant's rosy face.

An oddity caught her eye—a sapling grew where no tree had been before. She got up to inspect where it rose out of the hollyhock, dwarfing the colorful blossoms. Fingering the bark, she detected a scent and rose her hand to her nose. Sandalwood. A tree not native to this mountain climate. Her father had one in his conservatory when she was a child, its aromatic flowers always a favorite of hers. *I wonder who planted this*, she thought. With a start, she realized it grew in the exact spot she buried the vial of potion all those months ago.

She returned to the ledge, a wary look at the tree, but perhaps the fact that of a beloved reminder of her childhood now thrived in this unlikely spot was a symbol of good luck. As if to comment, the baby inside gave a subtle kick. With a smile, she closed her eyes and turned her face to the sun, its rays a perfect contrast to the cool mist of the fountain.

After a few moments, she lowered her head. Spots danced in her eyes as they adjusted, so at first, she thought she imagined it. But once clarity settled in, she could not deny it. On the path directly in front of her sat the garden snake. Somehow, she knew it was the same creature she had seen with Tessina. Its head raised off the ground, amber eyes inspecting her. While she stared back bewildered, a second snake slithered next to the first, followed by two more. In the time it took her to blink, four more joined the group, duplicates of each other but for the varied color of their eyes. They each drew themselves up in a way reminiscent of the charmed snakes of the east she heard tales about. Though the snakes remained where they were and made no threatening movements, a sudden dread filled the marchioness, especially when she noticed they issued from under the strange sandalwood tree. Clutching her stomach protectively, she fled the garden.

Her distraction at dinner that evening concerned the marquis, but she told him it was only fatigue. Later, Tessina brushed out her hair with long, even strokes, a routine which usually calmed her, but she remained on edge.

"Is everything all right?" the maid, who missed nothing when it came to Adeleta's moods, questioned, meeting her eyes in the mirror.

Adeleta paused, but knew the maid was the only person she could trust. She stood, took the brush from Tessina, and led her to the bed where they sat together, hands entwined. "I went to the garden today. I saw the snake again, only this time seven more joined it. They were watching me."

A brief flicker of fear crossed the maid's face at the thought of Imelda and the potion. Neither lady ever spoke of that auspicious night, content to pretend as though it never happened now that the desired outcome was achieved.

"It's probably just a coincidence, right? Just a family of snakes who reside in the garden this year," the marchioness said with a convincing nod.

"I'm sure that is all there is to it," Tessina conceded, though her heart hammered against her ribs. "You should rest now."

She tucked Adeleta beneath the blankets and kissed her forehead. Once the candles were snuffed, the maid retired to her adjoining chamber. Though the women never mentioned the subject again, from that day forth, the marchioness ceased all visits to her garden.

CHAPTER SIX

By the time autumn ended, Adeleta's stomach had grown increasingly ungainly. Festive gatherings filled December leading up to Christmas, an extra special season for the expectant mother. By New Year's Day, the marchioness endured the discomfort of pregnancy's final stage and longed for her infant's arrival. Still, happiness filled her mind, most of the time. Checking that all was ready in the nursery, she smiled while fingering a small hat or new blanket, at the thought of the baby in her arms after so long a wait. However, there were moments of disquiet. Every so often, she dreamt of the snakes in the garden. In the visions, they grew large and attacked her to get her baby. Waking in a cold sweat on these nights, the dread only fully passed with the light of dawn.

Tessina, who shared the marchioness' secret, was also haunted by thoughts of what exactly might happen at the birth. She stole glances at the rounded belly of her mistress and prayed an ordinary baby waited inside, or if not ordinary, with some affliction which could be easily hidden. Certainly, scandal must be avoided at all costs. To that end, she convinced Adeleta to only allow herself and the mid-wife in the room for the actual delivery, forgoing the usual use of additional servants. The fact that her mistress agreed to this request with very little persuasion, made clear their mutual anxiety on the matter.

So, on a wintry morning in mid-January when Adeleta complained of pains, the mid-wife was summoned and everyone else excused. The old woman entered the room, a small satchel tucked under her arm. She ordered extra towels and saw to a large vat of water over the fire with all composure. Zebina's movements, developed from years of routine, flowed naturally. One of her first deliveries had been Marquis Lamberico himself. Well into her sixties, her tiny yet robust presence brought confidence into the room that the birth would be routine, and both Adeleta and her maid relaxed in her presence.

"You must track the contractions. Write down the time and duration," she ordered Tessina, handing her a piece of parchment and quill. "Now I will examine the patient."

She tied a kerchief around her head, a few wisps of gray peeking out from the edges, rolled up her sleeves, and administered a brief check of the marchioness. "You are on your way, but long hours lay ahead. Save your strength for the end."

"Thank you, Zebina. It is a comfort to have you here," Adeleta said, readjusting the blanket around herself.

"Nothing to eat, only water or broth. Keep her on her feet and moving as much as possible. I'll be back shortly." Once the door closed behind her, Adeleta and her maid shared a smile. Zebina, well-prized for her skill with delivery, was known for a curt bedside manner.

"Let's get you up and walking." Tessina helped the patient from the bed.

After a few turns around the chamber, a pain seized Adeleta and she doubled forward. The maid dutifully recorded the time and length of the contraction. Once her breath recovered, the marchioness stood straight and continued walking.

"Only hours to go," she tried to joke, but groaned with another spasm.

"Keep faith, my lady. By this time tomorrow, your baby will be safe in your arms," Tessina encouraged.

Time passed slowly, as it does for most in this condition. Zebina examined Adeleta every hour, nodding her head in approval each time, but providing no details. As the day wore on, the mid-wife dozed on a pallet brought in for her, a cloud of gray hair spread across her back. The marchioness walked as much as she could but needed more and more breaks as the afternoon wore on. Tessina never left her side. The room grew hot from the boiling vat on the fire and the mid-wife cracked the window. Cold air rushed in with flurry of dancing white snowflakes which sprinkled the floor. Tessina mopped Adeleta's brow where she lay in bed. The pains came swift and hard now. The moment was at hand.

Zebina rose, tightened her kerchief, and washed her hands. She positioned pillows as bolsters around the expectant mother. "Hold her knees apart for me," she ordered the maid. "It's time to push."

Whether she pushed for ten minutes or ten hours, Adeleta could never say. Such is the way of birth that once the infant makes its appearance, all time before is forgotten. When she felt the last throng of agony, followed by a wave of relief and then a tiny cry, her heart filled with joy. Zebina adeptly sutured the cord and lay the newborn on the mother's chest to clean. When she wiped the muck of birth from the baby, all three women gasped. A tiny green snake coiled three times around the infant's neck. Its amber eyes opened as it unwound and before anyone could react, it slithered across the bed onto the floor before disappearing into a hole in the stone wall. For a moment, there was complete silence until the baby let out a tiny mewl, redirecting their attention.

"A daughter as you predicted," the mid-wife said, as though nothing unusual had passed, swaddling the girl. "She looks perfect to me. And look, her friend even left a mark."

She pointed to the baby's neck where a spiral of gold glimmered ever so slightly in the spot where the snake had been. Adeleta traced the three swirls with her finger, entranced by their beauty. Even Tessina stared in awe at the shimmering skin. *Far more beautiful than a tail*, the new mother thought.

"Now, feed her while I finish up here," Zebina ordered, pulling some salve from her sack.

Tessina helped her mistress get the baby to suckle while the mid-wife finished tending to Adeleta. While the infant nursed, Adeleta stroked her tiny head, a golden crown of soft hair against fair skin. Utter contentment filled every pore of her body, whatever pleasure she imagined motherhood would bring far eclipsed by the actuality of holding her newborn.

"What will you name her?" Tessina asked.

"Biancabella," the marchioness replied.

"*Fair beauty*—well-fitting," Zebina stated. Done with her work, she helped Adeleta clean up and change while the maid cradled the girl in her arms. "I will take my leave now. Call for me if any problems arise. I will be back to check on you tomorrow."

"Zebina . . ." the marchioness began, and the mid-wife turned at the door, satchel in hand. "I hope that what occurred here stays in our confidence."

Zebina gave Adeleta a knowing smile. "Yours is not the first baby I have delivered where Imelda has intervened. I have seen strange events in my time, more extraordinary than even this. But you have my word, what happened here will go with me to my grave."

"Thank you," Adeleta whispered.

The mid-wife had barely gone when the marquis burst into the room. One look at mother and daughter and his eyes filled with tears. He sat on the bed, arm around his wife's shoulder staring at the tiny bundle in her arms, so touching a family moment, Tessina could not help but smile.

Yet, later, as mistress and infant lie sleeping, the maid's eyes kept returning to the hole in the stones where the snake disappeared.

The womb had been dark and warm; the baby nestled contentedly underneath her body, a place of pure comfort. An explosion of light and sound broke her tranquility. The infant screamed before being placed in someone's arms. Rough strokes wiped over her scales clearing away the moisture from the womb and a rush of icy air raced across her. She opened her eyes to three women staring at her, jaws agape. Beneath her, the child squirmed, familiar movements the creature barely noticed, her attention focused on the sheer size of the room and panic seized her.

Fear not, all will be well, a voice sounded from somewhere—perhaps inside her head, *leave the baby and come to us.*

With all the strength her tiny form could muster, she uncoiled from the infant, a pang at the separation, and slid across the soft bed and down to the cold floor. The voice rang out again, and she slithered toward it through a crevice in the bottom of the wall. Down dark passages, dusty with cobwebs, she persisted always in the direction of the voice. The air grew frigid the farther she went until she popped out of another hole into the snow.

A large snake looked down at her, kindness in her golden eyes. "I am Ulani. Long have we anticipated your arrival."

"Who are you? What about the baby? Shouldn't I be with her?" the tiny snake asked in confusion.

"My sister's and I live in a garden. We will teach you about your gifts. You will reunite with your sister in time. For now, she is too small to interact with. Now follow me."

The order left no room for questions so the young reptile trailed after her larger counterpart across the palace grounds, now under a thick blanket of white. Gray clouds dropped a steady fall of flakes, which swirled in the chilly wind like miniature cyclones. Eventually, they came to stone that walled in an area of the property. Under it, they glided into an overgrown garden, its naked branches and stalks sagging under piles of snow.

Ulani's scales glimmered like emeralds against the pristine white. "Come, we will get warm."

They approached a small tree, which stood next to a fountain. Untouched by winter, it stood in full leaf, tiny red and white flowers gracing its limbs. No snow sat beneath it, only green grass. Ulani indicated a gap near the base of the slender trunk before she disappeared inside. With a hesitant peek into the dark opening, the young snake followed.

Deep into the ground they descended in a tunnel of rich soil, far more comforting than the bitter snow. The baby snake smelled the earthy aroma as her tongue darted in and out. Blinded in the darkness, she relied on the vibrations in front of her as proof Ulani remained ahead. The passageway widened and opened into a round cavern of tightly packed dirt. Inside, seven other snakes roused at their entry. The newcomer's eyes adjusted to the pale, green light which emanated from the bodies of the serpents, filling the space with a soft glow.

"At last, she is here!" a snake with gray eyes cried in delight.

As one, the seven slithered toward the new arrival, who cowered amid their entwined forms still acclimating to life in the outside world, so full of noise, light, and novelty. Inborn instincts helped her understand some of what was going on, but not all. The stares of the fellow snakes penetrated her and, coupled with the strong aroma of the sandalwood's roots, which made up the cavern's ceiling, overwhelmed the young snake.

"Back up," Ulani commanded, clearly the leader among them. "Samaritana has only sprung from the womb; do not bombard her."

"Samaritana?" the infant repeated, the sound of the name a recollection in the recesses of her mind.

"That is your name, dear one. You are special, your birth long foreseen."

All the others, now backed up a bit, nodded their heads in agreement while Samaritana looked on in bewilderment. *How am I special? How did they know of my imminent arrival? What does the baby have to do with any of it?*

Ulani, as if sensing her questions, said, "Come, have something to eat, and we will explain everything."

She directed Samaritana to the middle of the cave where a bed of leaves covered an indented space. The gray-eyed snake, who introduced herself as Oda, produced several grubs. Samaritana ate them with all haste, hunger consuming her at the sight of the food. While she swallowed them, the others settled into a woven pile of scales around her. It was difficult to determine where one creature ended and another began. A patient silence filled the air until the meal was complete.

"The stars have predicted signs of your birth for some time now," Oda said, her tone as soft as a mother's caress.

"What signs?" Samaritana asked. Now warm with a full stomach, she found it easier to concentrate.

"We are enchanted beings of the earth," Ulani explained, "bestowers of fertility and holders of wisdom. Every few generations, our magic must emit a buildup of extra power into a human, who is coupled with a special snake. This pairing enhances our bond with the energy that flows through the earth so we can continue to use our gifts for the benefit of mankind."

"So, the baby is my twin?" Samaritana queried, with a deep longing to return to the cozy folds of her neck.

"Yes, you both contain the energy of both human and snake," Ulani told her. "Someday, you will each possess the capability to shift from one form to the other."

"But that is only a trifling matter," Oda interjected.

This comment earned her a withering stare from their leader, who continued, "The stars have shown the inherent goodness of the girl, a trait which could lead her to danger. Her soul is so pure, she will have trouble distinguishing evil. Her trusting heart, unable to understand malice, will leave her vulnerable to those with wicked intent. Your main priority is to protect her with the innate wisdom you possess, knowledge you will pass on to her."

At Ulani's description, a primal urge pervaded Samaritana, her entire essence burning to be reunited with her sister.

"I must go to her now," she exclaimed and moved toward the hole in the cavern wall.

"No!" Ulani commanded. "Now is not the time. The infant is well protected for the time being, and you have much to learn. You will remain in the hibernacula with us. We must hibernate until warmer weather returns."

Gently, she nudged Samaritana into the indentation where she intertwined in the conglomeration of snakes. The comfort of the bodies and the sweet smell of sandalwood overcame Samaritana, who gave into her fatigue. One by one, the snakes around her drifted to sleep and the green light gradually faded, leaving the space in darkness.

CHAPTER SEVEN

As the years of Biancabella's infancy and childhood passed, she grew in beauty and grace. The darling of the kingdom, her name was a balm on the tongue of any who spoke it. The marquis and his wife brought her proudly in their company to all public events where necks craned to glimpse the special child. Indeed, since her birth the city saw years of prosperity as it had never known.

Lost in the pure joy of motherhood, Adeleta never mentioned the snake, but kept her daughter close, never out of her sight for long just in case. For the first few years, dreadful thoughts lingered in the back of Tessina's mind as well, but time elapsed without incident and both women relaxed. When Biancabella showed signs of both a kind heart and a loyal spirit, the maid's misgivings of any wicked outcome faded. The golden marks around the girl's neck were barely visible, but those who did notice thought the girl was marked favorably by heaven and the marchioness could not help but agree. Biancabella was blessed.

Her beauty ripened from an early age along with a thirst for knowledge, a fountain of questions always tumbling from her lips. *How does a clock work? Why does a giraffe look the way it does? Where are the edges of the earth?* Every day brought a fresh batch of queries from her inquisitive mind. Her parents, delighted by her sharp brain, hired tutors and scholars to instruct her in all manner of subjects and praised their young student's ability to absorb information. Biancabella reveled in the attention of the adults, but longed for a friend her own age, a circumstance that occurred with the arrival of her cousin when she was eight.

"Piero is coming today. He has been through a lot, Biancabella," her mother explained one day. "Imagine if you lost both your parents. This is to be his home now. Be kind to him."

The boy was the son of her father's sister, who had passed in childbirth. His father recently fell victim to a summer fever, leaving the boy an orphan. Sorrow filled Biancabella's heart at the thought of his loss and she welcomed her cousin warmly. A quiet child one year older than her, he studied alongside her, but without the enthusiasm she displayed. With time and gentleness, the girl befriended Piero, though an air of sadness clung to him. They were playmates with her usually leading the way, though always under the watchful eye of the marchioness and Piero's maid, Pomma.

At ten years old, tired of her mother's ever-present gaze, Biancabella insisted on more freedom to explore the grounds. Her mother agreed, the initial fears for the child subsiding with time. Thrilled, Biancabella wandered the palace with abandon, Tessina always in her wake. Oh, the fun of learning to knead dough from the baker, watching the farrier reshoe a horse in the stable, discovering an attic full of secret doors and hiding spots. The maid collapsed each night, weary from the girl's endless activity. Biancabella hoped her cousin would join her in these escapades, but the shy boy usually preferred to remain at his studies.

One fine spring day, Biancabella scampered across the grass of the formal gardens to a line of paving stones. Under the fair blue sky, she hopped from one to the next, pretending the grass was now treacherous waters whose depths she must avoid. Once safely across, she continued to a courtyard of stately topiaries cut in striking geometric shapes. A ladybug landed on her hand and she watched the insect crawl up to her fingertip before bursting into flight. It disappeared over the top of a stone wall choked with roses. For the first time, she noticed a rusted gate so hidden in the overgrowth it was nearly consumed.

"Where does this gate go?" Biancabella called back to Tessina, who was only just now catching up with her charge.

The hairs on the back of the maid's neck stood on end when she remembered the foot rub and the snake. "There used to be a small private garden in there."

"Used to be? You mean it is not there still?" Biancabella attempted to push some roses out of the way but pulled her hand back with a gasp. A thorn pierced her finger and a bright red dot of blood emerged.

"Whatever is there is completely overgrown and see, now you have wounded yourself." Tessina pulled a handkerchief from her pocket and handed it to the girl. "Press down so the bleeding stops."

Biancabella did as instructed, a red stain blotting the white fabric. The maid took her firmly by the arm and lead her back toward the palace, happy to put some distance between herself and the garden, hoping to change the subject.

"Everything else is kept so neat on the grounds. Why has that space been forgotten?" She pulled her arm from Tessina's and looked over her shoulder at the gate.

"That small garden was your mother's. She spent time in it before you were born. When she stopped going there, it became neglected, I guess," Tessina replied, cupping the girl's elbow to lead her away.

"Why did she stop going there?"

The maid sighed in exasperation at the infinite questions. She knelt to the girl's level and gently took her hand. "Your mother waited a long time for a baby. Once you were born, all her time was dedicated to you. Whatever joy the garden brought her, you bring so much more. Now let's just forget about it, shall we? I hear Cook plans to make your favorite chocolate pie for dessert tonight. If we pay her a visit, maybe we can get an early taste."

Biancabella smiled and nodded in agreement. She would go to the kitchen now to sneak a treat, but she certainly had no intention of forgetting about the garden; its secrets holding a special allure in her normally predictable life.

The kitchen staff was elated to see her, such was her magnetism with all who encountered her. Cook let her roll out the dough for the pie crust, her thick arms and hands over Biancabella's petite ones for support. "Do me a favor, precious one, go to the pantry and ask for some more sugar—I want this pie to be as sweet as you."

With a smile, Biancabella leapt from her stool to walk down a small hallway to the pantry. The door stood ajar, and lowered voices issued from the gap.

". . . it's just you look pale with fright. Are you all right?" an unfamiliar female voice asked.

"Yes. It's just the girl stumbled onto the entrance to her mother's garden." This voice belonged to Tessina.

"You didn't let her in?" gasped the stranger.

"No, of course not. It's too overgrown at this point, anyway. I don't know why it upset me so."

"Because of the bad rumors about that place," volunteered the other, "and how it's related to the marchioness' pregnancy."

"Isolde! You are never to mention that to me or anyone else again," Tessina scolded, her tone startling Biancabella.

"I am only repeating what is common gossip. Sooner or later, it will reach the girl's ears," retorted the first.

Another kitchen hand bumped past Biancabella on her way into the pantry. The two women inside quickly parted. Biancabella followed behind, a look of innocence painted on her face, and asked for sugar, which she brought back to the cook. While the aproned woman rattled on about the proper way to mix sugar in with eggs, the girl's head was full of other questions. *What happened in the garden? What did it have to do with her mother's pregnancy?* Questions piled onto questions.

That night, when the marchioness tucked the covers around her in bed, Biancabella seized the opportunity. "I came across a rusty gate on the grounds today. Tessina said it used to be your private garden, but now it is overgrown and forgotten. Why do you not go there anymore?"

For the briefest second, a shadow crossed her mother's face. *Fear?* Biancabella could not tell. A calm smile quickly replaced the emotion.

"It's a place I used to frequent for moments of happiness, but once you were born, I no longer needed it. You make me happier than I ever imagined." She embraced her child, kissing her on the forehead.

"That is what Tessina said. She also said I should just forget about the garden," Biancabella pressed.

"Then I think it would be wise to listen to Tessina," her mother said, a hint of authority in her tone. The girl must stay away from the garden. She rose to leave when a thought struck her, "How about tomorrow you and I have a picnic in the countryside?"

"Really? That would be so much fun!" the girl gushed as she settled under her blankets. *A day out of the castle grounds and time alone with her mother—what a treat.*

"Now get some sleep, my beautiful daughter." Confident her distraction worked, the marchioness extinguished the candle wicks and shut the door behind her.

Biancabella lay in the dark thinking of what food to bring the next day; however, soon her thoughts turned to the garden and all the information she heard that day. The reason for the garden's neglect and how it related to her mother's pregnancy remained a mystery. And she loved nothing more than a good mystery to solve.

∾〰 SAMARITANA 〰∾

Samaritana matured over the years as well. In the now neglected garden, Ulani and the others saw to her training. She spent the first few years learning about snake lore and their ability to channel energy from the earth. When she first practiced this skill, the drawing of the vital life force left her both exhilarated and exhausted. Lessons moved on to more difficult challenges which the young snake excelled at particularly healing.

"Your energy is special, Samaritana," Ulani explained one day while Samaritan tried to heal an injured fly. "Your snake energy is mixed with the human energy of your twin. This is a unique bond that seldom occurs. Each of you have special gifts, but she will have no teachers as you do, so you will have to help her cultivate her abilities."

"What will they be?" the younger one asked. Eager to learn anything of her sister, she forgot all about the wounded insect which floundered in front or her.

"That I do not know. When the time is right, you will assist in cleansing her with milk and rosewater which will awaken whatever her gifts turn out to be."

"And when will the time be right?" Samaritana pressed.

"Patience, my student, humans mature at a slower rate than we do. Biancabella is still too young to properly manage this magic."

"Biancabella," Samaritana repeated with wonder, the name stirring her heart. "I can't wait to meet her."

"And you will, but not yet. Now let us return to the lesson at hand." Ulani nodded at the fly and Samaritana concentrated on channeling healing energy once more.

Another winter passed in the warmth of the hibernacula, the ground always warm under the sandalwood tree. In the early spring, Samaritana sat under the tree with Oda, who told her stories of human/snake sisters. The garden waited to burst with life, trees and flowers in bud. The youth listened in rapt fascination at the tales of these rare types of twins, noting a special fate had been foretold in the stars of each which factored heavily in their lives and happiness.

"What do the stars say of Biancabella and me?" Samaritana asked.

"Well, that is really up to Ulani to discuss with you," Oda began, but at the crushed look in the young one's eyes, she added, "but I will tell you what I know if you promise not to tell her."

Samaritana nodded her head.

"All I know is you are meant to be your sister's protector. Evil things will befall her if you are ever separated from each other. You must always stay with her to avert disaster. If you remain together, all will be well."

"That sounds simple enough." Samaritana imagined never being parted from her sister.

"Ah, but humans can be fickle, which is why your task is of the utmost importance," Oda warned.

"What do you mean?" In the pleasant spring air of the garden, Samaritana could not fathom what could break her bond with Biancabella.

"I already have said too much, please wait for Ulani to explain further," the elder snake declared. "Now, back to the stories."

Samaritana took Oda's words to heart and vowed to protect her sister against any threat. As spring advanced, the garden bloomed lush with the overrun flowers, bushes, and trees. Weeds choked the fountain, the cherub's feet swallowed by a sea of green. One day, Samaritana slithered on the ledge where she noticed a crack in the pitcher. *How lovely this garden must have been when it was well tended*, she thought. Her elders had tried to describe its former beauty to her, but she knew it must surpass anything she could imagine.

Ulani glided to the fountain's edge with a snake named Elke at her side. "Samaritana, come down," the leader called. "I have a surprise for you."

Using a long flower stalk, Samaritana spiraled down to the ground where they waited. Elke resembled all the others except for her bright orange eyes. She had never instructed Samaritana in anything, so the young snake was eager to learn what the day held.

"Today, Elke will show you some of the grounds and inside of the castle. You may even get a glimpse of your sister," Ulani said, but seeing Samaritana's uncontained delight, she added, "You are to keep hidden at all costs. No one is to see you yet, especially Biancabella. Do you understand?"

Samaritana nodded obediently and followed Elke through a gap in the wall. She knew the others left the garden on occasion and wondered what lay outside its walls. Now she finally had a chance to see for herself. The vast palace grounds unfolded before her. Never had she seen such splendor—manicured hedges, gleaming marble statues, and exquisite topiaries lined their path, a stark contrast to the unkempt garden. Elke pointed out various areas and the best places to remain out of the sight of all the human inhabitants. Her knowledge came in handy as they hid under a bush while several groundskeepers walked past, shovels and shears in hand.

On their way again, the castle rose in front of them, the travertine courtyard aglow in the late spring sun. Scents of people, food, and soap, blended with unrecognizable odors, came to her with every flick of her tongue. A fat gray cat lounged in the sun on the stones. It yawned, stretching its front paws, before their movement caught its eye and it sank into hunting mode. Elke, unbothered by the threat, darted through a gap in the wall, Samaritana right behind her, heart pounding.

"Always be on your guard when you are outside the garden," the older serpent warned. "People and animals are a constant threat."

Elke showed her the kitchens, where they each had a mouse for a snack. The receiving room was next, empty of anyone. Samaritana wondered at its size, almost as large as the garden. Then, Elke took her to the marquis' study. He sat behind a desk reading a stack of papers. In some ways, he was her father, both him and magic. Samaritana watched him with interest. Even screwed up in concentration, his face held something kindly in it. A knock on the door brought in the marchioness, all aflutter that rain may ruin a tea party she planned for Biancabella.

Her voice was familiar, heard by Samaritana while in the womb. The woman's motherly concern made Samaritana smile.

The marquis calmed his wife, telling her they would figure out something to keep Biancabella happy if the weather did not cooperate. The love shared between them and for their daughter was evident. Her human parents facilitated magic's creation of her and though they would never raise her as they did her sister, she could not imagine two better people to call family.

"They are wonderful parents to Biancabella," Elke confirmed once hidden inside the wall again. "Would you like to try to find your sister now?

Samaritana nodded and trailed after Elke up some beams and across some dusty rafters. Elke moved with the ease of a creature quite familiar with the layout of the building. A glimmer of light shone through a small hole and they slid into a bright room. Elke positioned them at the base of the drapes where they could remain unnoticed.

A woman sat at a desk in front of a child, whose small legs dangled off the floor. The smell of flowers permeated the air of the large but comfortable room, every inch of it decorated in pink threaded with gold. Several dolls sat against the pillows on a chair next to the window, freshly cut roses stood in vases on the dressing table, and a large, canopied bed dripped with silks and satins. Samaritana marveled at the magnificence of it.

"There," a tiny voice said.

"It's lovely, just like you. I'll hang it on the wall with the others," the woman said, and rose with a picture in hand to expose the girl who sat drawing. "Why don't you make another?"

"All right, Tessina." She furrowed her little brow and picked up her pencil to sketch.

Samaritana could not take her eyes off her sister, who was more beautiful than she ever envisioned. Her hair tumbled over her petite shoulders in golden curls, her sky-blue eyes sparkled with life, matching the smile on her pink bowed lips.

"In a little bit, we will go outside to play, then your mother will be ready for the tea party," Tessina said, hanging the picture on the wall next to several others.

"Ooh, I can't wait," Biancabella squealed.

Tessina came to stand behind the girl, stroking her hair while looking down at the next drawing. "My, my, five years old and already such a gifted artist."

Biancabella gazed up to smile at the maid. Sunlight glinted off the golden marks around her neck. Samaritana was seized with a primal urge to slither up the girl and fit around them. Just as she moved forward, Elke coiled around her and pulled her back through the hole in the stones.

"The time is not yet right for you to meet your sister," she admonished. "She is still too young. Come, we must return to the garden."

With a wistful glance back, Samaritana left, anxious to be with her sister again soon, but happy to have had the chance to see her. The image of the beautiful girl now engraved in her mind would have to be enough to see her through the next few years until they could reunite.

CHAPTER EIGHT

Over the next few days, Biancabella waited for an opportunity to slip away unnoticed, a difficult task since Tessina seemed more watchful than ever. At last, one afternoon in late spring she played with Piero by the stables. Tessina and Pomma sat on a bench in the shade of a wall while the children ran on the cobblestones in front of them. Each child had a long stick with the likeness of a horse head on top, thick yarn hanging down as manes.

Though only a year older than Biancabella, Piero was a small, timid boy, happy to live in the shadow of his much beloved cousin. A mop of dark curls framed his large brown eyes and his pale skin spoke to a lack of outdoor activity. Thrilled to have his company, Biancabella orchestrated a game where they were opposing kings seeking to win a mighty battle. The echo of their galloping footsteps rang across the courtyard with their giggles.

In a bid to escape her reach, Piero leaned a little too far to his left. He fell face first onto the stones. With a howl, he stood, blood gushing from his nose and forehead. Both maids rushed over to his side. Pomma attempted to staunch the flow with her apron, but to no avail. Together, the ladies each grabbed an arm and led the shrieking boy back to the palace.

"Come, Biancabella," Tessina ordered over her shoulder.

For the first few steps, the girl followed until her maid's full distraction became clear. Now was her chance. With a quick step, she darted between two pillars and took off for the neglected garden. Once there, she thrust her hands through the roses to pull on the iron gate, but the rambling vines held it fast in place. On impulse, she used the plants to climb; the thorns scraping her hands and dress, and propelled herself over the top of the wall to the garden below.

Inside, flowers bloomed with wild abandon, so thick in some places they choked each other for space, their sweet scents floating across the air. Biancabella discerned the trace of a path, blooms and greenery spilling haphazardly across crumbling paving stones. She followed it to a fountain where a fat, moss-covered cherub stood, a crack running down his now dry pitcher. *How charming he must have been in the past*, she thought, and touched the cool stone of his arm.

"He was very charming in his prime," a soft voice answered.

Biancabella jumped, but looking all around saw no one. Her eyes drew back to the fountain where a swift movement on the ledge caught her attention. There sat a thin, green snake, eyes glued to hers. Never had she seen a real snake before and she thought she should be frightened. But she was not. Instead, she was oddly drawn to it, an urge to pick it up growing within her. Before she touched it, the snake spoke, "Though this entire garden looked much nicer when I first arrived."

Biancabella blinked twice. "How can you talk? What are you?"

"I am a snake. I can talk because I am special. You are special too, Biancabella."

"How do you know my name?" Though part of her instincts told her to run, curiosity kept her rooted to her spot.

"What made you come to this garden?" The snake lifted its head higher.

"I saw it the other day and wanted to come inside," the girl replied, sinking down onto the ledge next to the strange creature. She dearly wanted to touch it. "Also, I heard a rumor this place had something to do with my mother's pregnancy."

"The truth is we are sisters, you and I," the snake stated and rested its head in Biancabella's lap.

"That's not possible." Biancabella knew the idea sounded absurd, but a surge of familiarity filled her.

"Your birthmark symbolizes where I was wrapped around your neck three times when we came out of the womb."

Biancabella's hand flew to her throat to the mark she had admired so many times—her mark from God they had all said. If someone had told her this is what she would learn in the abandoned garden, she would have laughed at the ridiculousness of it, yet sitting here with this talking snake, she felt the truth of it flow through her, as if she had always known. The idea both thrilled and scared her.

"But how is that even possible?" she exclaimed, not sure any explanation would clarify the situation.

"May I?" the snake asked and wrapped itself around the girl's arm to climb. After a nod, it slithered up close to her face. "There is magic in us, Sister. Our mother needed the help of a witch to release us; she could not have given birth without it. Each of us has special gifts. And each of us will one day, with each other's help, be able to shift between woman and snake."

Biancabella stroked the snake's head with her fingers. She believed every word. "So, your gift is you can talk to people?"

"No. Only to you as of now. I don't think others will understand me until I learn to become a human. But I have other abilities as well. So will you when the magic is awakened."

"How do I awaken them?" The idea of being magical piqued her attention.

"I am the only one who can help but you must promise to obey any instructions I give you." The creature looked in her eyes sternly.

"I will," the girl swore, a solemn expression on her face.

"First, you must tell no one about me. Humans do not look kindly on magical creatures, especially snakes. Our mother has long kept her secret about the potion which made her pregnant with us. Telling anyone could put her life, your life, and mine in danger. I know it will be hard but you must never tell a soul before we are ready. Do you agree?"

"Yes, of course!" The thought of anything harmful befalling her beautiful mother was more than Biancabella could bear.

"To awaken your gifts, you must return here alone with milk and rose water."

"I will do as you say. I will keep you a secret and bring milk and rose water as soon as I can sneak away again. But it was hard enough for me to climb over the gate by myself, let alone holding two containers."

"Do not worry. I will place a spell on the gate. To all others it will remain shut with overgrowth, but for you, it will open with ease. But remember your promise, you must not tell anyone of this meeting," the snake declared.

"That is an easy promise to make. I won't tell a soul, not even Mother, and I will find a time to come back alone with the items you said," agreed the mesmerized girl. Already a fondness for this creature rose in her heart. A sister, even if she remained a secret, was still a sister. "Do you have a name?"

"Samaritana," her sibling replied, the sibilant ring of it pleasant to Biancabella's ears.

"Such a beautiful name. I cannot wait to see you again," the girl said happy to have found the confidante she yearned for.

"As am I, dear sister," Samaritana agreed with all affection.

They sat for a bit in the comfort of each other's presence, Samaritana coiled up in her sister's lap. Biancabella felt such a sense of contentment stroking the snake's smooth scales, she could have remained in the garden forever, but in the distance her name rang out. Tessina called for her.

"I must go before we are discovered. But I will be back as soon as I can, I promise."

She hurried to the gate. Just as Samaritana said, it opened easily. With one quick look back at the snake, she left the garden, the gate disappearing in a suffocating grip of roses behind her. As she hurried in the direction of the palace, Tessina's voice grew louder. Biancabella spied a large oak tree and sat down against its trunk, waiting to be found.

"There you are, you naughty girl," scolded the maid. "I've been scouring the grounds for you. What happened?" She nodded at the scrapes on the girl's hands and her ripped skirt.

"I was climbing this tree pretending it was a tall boat mast. It was more fun than watching Piero bleed all over himself," she said so convincingly, the maid just shook her head.

"Come, let's get you cleaned up for dinner."

Biancabella took her hand, and they walked away, a gentle breeze lifting her hair. "How is Piero?"

"He bloodied his nose and scraped his brow, but he will be fine. Though the way he carried on, you'd think it was much worse. His pride was wounded more than anything. Such a clumsy child," Tessina noted. "At least you found an interesting way to pass the afternoon."

An enigmatic smile filled the girl's face. "I certainly did."

Samaritana returned to the cavern overjoyed. She had finally talked to Biancabella. Since the first day she saw her sister five years ago, the longing to be close to her was an ever-present companion. The elder snakes had discussed the best way to orchestrate an encounter, but invariably disagreed on the process. Elke worried the child may be too frightened by the whole idea and they should wait until Biancabella was older, whereas Oda thought the sooner the sisters met, the better.

"After all," Oda complained, "how can Samaritana protect the girl unless the meet?"

Ulani contemplated their suggestions with care, seeing the merit of each argument. The leader searched for a way that Biancabella could be spoken to when no one else was around, a nearly impossible task as either the marchioness or Tessina stayed with the girl at all times. Another snake, Adriel, suggested Samaritana wake the girl at night, but others felt this method may startle the girl too much and cause a setback. Time passed and no clear strategy came to light.

Until today, when out of nowhere, Biancabella wandered into the garden on her own. When Samaritana saw her sister scramble over the wall, she almost slunk down to the cavern where the other snakes rested after a morning of channeling energy. She had been too restless to sleep and lolled under the sandalwood tree in the ever-warm grass. Though she knew she should check with Ulani first, the pull to speak to her sister was too intense to fight. Samaritana decided to forgo any permission and slithered out to introduce herself.

Now, she tumbled full speed into the den, sliding right over the huddled mound of scales in the center.

"What on earth?" Oda snapped, her head popping up from the tangle.

"Wake up, all of you! I have spoken to Biancabella!" Samaritana cried.

One by one the serpents peeled apart, a cascade of scales, and gave the young snake their full attention.

"She climbed over the wall into the garden. She was alone. I told her we were sisters and asked her to bring the rosewater and the milk, just like you said, Ulani," Samaritana puffed, nearly breathless.

"It's about time," Oda snorted, glad they could be finished deliberating the matter.

"She wasn't afraid of anything you told her?" Elke inquired, always worried how Biancabella would receive the news.

"No. She was excited to meet me and hear about her gifts. And she promised not to tell anyone about me or anything I said to her." Samaritana only realized at that moment how relieved she was that Biancabella accepted her story so willingly. "But don't worry, I didn't tell her about any of you."

"Just as well, for now," Adriel commented, settling back in the bed of leaves. The others followed except for Ulani who slithered over to Samaritana.

"You and I must speak alone," the leader ordered, a sharp look in her yellow eyes.

Samaritana trailed out of the den behind the elder. They emerged from under the sandalwood tree and continued across the garden. Rays of sun dappled the ground, patches of light dancing through breaks in the foliage. The two moved to a darker corner overhung with a clump of wisteria branches. Sensing their presence, a nearby bird flew to safety over the wall.

"You are angry with me," Samaritana said, "for being impulsive and speaking to her without telling you first."

"Not angry," Ulani clarified, "only concerned. Your impulsiveness worked out this time, but you need to work on controlling it. Had the girl been frightened, our job would have become more difficult."

Samaritana bent her head, the wise words of her elder ringing true. If she scared her sister, the girl may have cut off any future communication, or worse she may have had the snakes hunted down. She had dodged a possible catastrophe with her rash decision and the notion of it fell hard on her.

"Yet," Ulani continued, "I was not so worried Biancabella would be afraid of you. She sees only the good in everything. I was more concerned about anyone with her. It was a stroke of luck that brought her to you on her own, or perhaps—fate."

"Oda mentioned the foretelling in the stars once. She said I had to protect Biancabella from danger," Samaritana ventured, hoping to learn more.

"Yes, you and your sister are dyad, your energies are the most potent when you are together. You each have your own strengths and shortcomings which will balance each other out. Biancabella is blessed with abundant goodness, it is one of her gifts, but with it comes a certain blindness to harsh realities others see clearly. You must counsel her on these matters." Ulani slithered along the broken pathway to a spot in the sun where they both stopped.

"How?" Samaritana asked, awed by the magnitude of the responsibility.

"Tell me, on your trips around the castle grounds have you seen only kindness and compassion in all the people you have come across?"

"No," the young snake remembered. "I've seen a woman steal money from the pocket of another servant's coat. I've heard ladies speak disdainfully about another right after she left the room. I've even watched a man kick a dog for no other reason than pure meanness."

In fact, now that Samaritana thought about it, there were quite a few more examples she could add, but Ulani cut her off.

"Exactly. Biancabella's kind heart, though a blessing to many, leaves her vulnerable to the evil intents of others. You must act as an extra set of eyes and ears to protect her. Now the two of you can work together to enhance your connection. The stronger your bond, the more you can discern any danger and warn her."

"And the milk and rosewater will help?" Samaritana asked, as a parade of ants marched past, several carrying a large crumb of bread on their backs.

"They should stimulate her other gifts, whatever they may be. But be aware, these gifts could make her susceptible to greedy or unscrupulous people. You will need to teach her to control them as we have taught you to manage yours."

"Is that all that was foretold?" Samaritana questioned. Though the elder's explanation made sense, she had a nagging feeling something had been left out.

Ulani hesitated and watched the ants, who gave the snakes a wide berth. Her job, along with the rest of the snakes, was to prepare Samaritana for her role in Biancabella's life. The young pupil deserved to know the whole of what was predicted.

"As you know, you and your sister are rare twins. Understand that your life forces are joined—one cannot survive without the other. If evil befalls her or if you are separated, fate will turn against you both, but as long as you remain bonded and true to each other, all will be well. Remember that."

"I will," Samaritana promised, a fervency in her heart. "I will guide and protect her always."

"Good, my dear one," Ulani said. "Then all will be well."

CHAPTER NINE

Two days later, Biancabella prepared to carry out her mission. After careful consideration, the girl decided night would be the best time for her to escape the palace undetected, too many eyes watched her during the day. Samaritana consumed her thoughts, the idea of a magical sister beyond comprehension. She dearly wished to ask her mother about the story of her birth, but realized, her mother had chosen to keep it from her all these years for a reason. Biancabella knew people's fear of witchcraft. This secret, if exposed, could put her life and the lives of her mother and sister in jeopardy, so in the end, she saw the wisdom in concealing it.

Instead, she concentrated on the more practical matter of procuring the two items her sister requested. The rosewater was easy to come by, an endless supply of it waiting each evening to wash her hands before dinner. She stole a small pot from the garden supply shed and filled it to the brim. Yesterday, she hid it in the hollow of a tree trunk when her and Piero were out to play, pretending it was part of a game. He was none the wiser. The milk proved harder to obtain. Somehow, she had to steal it from the barn on her way to the secret garden.

The appointed night finally arrived. Her mother kissed Biancabella on the forehead when she tucked her in at bedtime. Tessina soon retired to her adjoining room. In the dark,

Biancabella watched the slim beam of candlelight that shone from the crack under the maid's door. Around eleven, the light went out. Just to be safe, the girl waited another hour before she tiptoed out of bed. In silence, she put on her slippers, ears ever alert for a noise from the maid's room. With her cloak around her shoulders, she crept onto the balcony. She stood for a moment, and after only hearing crickets, she swung her legs over the rail onto the limb of a birch. She shimmied down the tree trunk, where her nightgown caught on every errant branch, only freed with impatient tugs.

When she hit the ground, she waited in silence and watched for any movements while she caught her breath. Certain of her solitude, she edged along the shadow of the wall toward a pathway that led to the cowsheds. A bright moon lit her way to the large wooden structure. She squeezed through the cracked door into total darkness. The warmth of the cows filled the space together with their soft breaths. Biancabella wrinkled her nose at the odor of animals, hay, and manure. One step forward and her toe hit a metal pail with a loud clang, briefly startling herself and several of the shed's occupants. She stooped to retrieve the offending object, ears on high alert for the sound of any servant who may have heard the racket. All stayed quiet.

The area came into a faint focus as her eyes adjusted and she stepped next to the nearest cow, a darker shadow against the outline of the stalls. Placing the pail under the udder, she milked some warm liquid from the animal, who looked back at her, judging her clumsiness she surmised, but otherwise compliant. It took longer than she hoped for her unpracticed hands to fill the bucket even halfway, but it would have to do.

With the container in hand, she slithered back through the shed door into the moonlight, happy to take a deep breath of the fresh night air. At the tree, she retrieved the rosewater, its aroma as pleasant as the day before. She took a moment to glance back at her bedroom window in the palace. There were no lights on, a clear sign her escape remained unnoticed. Pleased with her progress so far, she carried the two receptacles to the garden. As promised, the gate opened easily for her. Once inside, it clamped back shut against all others. Unlike the refreshing evening outside the walls, the heavy air in the garden enfolded her in its grip, making her body as sticky as if she stood in the full summer sun.

Biancabella carried the requested items to the fountain where she deposited them on the ledge. The moss-covered cherub stood over her, an eerie glow on his face cast by the moonbeams. He seemed her only company in the garden and she scanned the ground for any signs of movement. Overgrown plants crept across the stones around her like menacing fingers waiting to drag her into the darkness. The dense atmosphere deafened all sound, not even a cricket could be heard in the otherworldly space. Fear spiraled up Biancabella, quelling some of the inherent warmth of the place.

"Samaritana, are you here? It's Biancabella. I've returned as you instructed." For two days she waited for this moment, telling no one and at times wondering if she imagined the entire encounter. Yet always, she felt a deep and abiding link to the serpent who claimed to be her sister. Now, she stood alone in the forgotten, unkempt space and prayed she had not erred in judgement. "Samaritana?"

"Biancabella, you are here." The snake appeared from under a lush lavender bush, its host of purple flowers reaching like tendrils toward the darkened sky.

"I have brought the milk and the rosewater as you asked," the girl confirmed, happy beyond measure at the sight of her magical sibling.

"Good, my sister. These will help reveal your gifts." Samaritana glided up to the fountain ledge, her head lifted high.

"What kind of gifts do you suppose I have?" Biancabella asked, entranced by the way the moonlight shone off the snake's scales in iridescent waves.

"We are special, you and I. Bonded since the womb. The golden necklace I left you is a sign of your magical abilities."

"Magic? I can do magic?" the girl whispered, a thrill rushing through her.

"It will seem like magic to all around you, but in truth it is a manifestation of your pure, sweet spirit."

Biancabella did not understand any of what her sister meant, but the profound connection she felt between them erased any misgivings. Without hesitation, she asked, "What do I need to do?"

"First remove your cloak and nightgown." Samaritana instructed. The girl did as told and shivered despite the warm air in the garden. "Now pour the milk over your head and rub it all over yourself."

The milk, despite still being warm from the cow, gave Biancabella goosebumps, but she diligently massaged the liquid into all corners of her pale skin, even working it through her pale tresses. When every last inch of her body was covered, Samaritana wound her way up Biancabella's leg and coiled her way around her sister's body to further imbue the milk. A delightful warmth filled Biancabella that radiated down to her fingertips. Samaritana finished and nodded approvingly.

"Now do the same with the rosewater," her serpent sister directed.

Where the milk brought heat, the rosewater sent cool tingles throughout her body. Her sister again rubbed the rosewater into every pore on the girl. Biancabella looked down, certain her whole being shimmered from the invigorating sensation, one so full of life as it emanated from deep within her.

"We are done," Samaritana proclaimed. "Your gifts are awoken."

"What are they?" the girl queried, happy to slip her nightgown and cape back on.

"Time will tell," her sister assured. "And I will be here to help you learn how to use them. Now return to your bed before your absence is detected."

Biancabella pulsed with a new exhilaration at being alive. She felt different, powerful in a way she could not explain. "I am so grateful to have found you, Samaritana. How can I thank you for helping me become what I truly am?"

Her sister slid up her arm to look her in the eye. "Our love, our bond, is more important than any other. You must promise never to leave me. If you obey, luck will follow you every day of your life. If not, an ill-fated future will follow you until the end of your days. Remain with me and all will be well."

"Of course! Anything you say, my dearest sister. I will stay with you always," Biancabella exclaimed, happier than ever and content in the sanctity of her promise.

Once more the gate opened easily on her departure. She crept back across the grounds and scaled the tree back to her balcony. Tessina snored softly from the adjoining room when she tiptoed back to bed. Her excursion a success, she thought of how blessed her life was and drifted into a contented sleep.

CHAPTER TEN

Tired from her late night, Biancabella slept in the next day. By mid-morning, an exasperated Tessina stormed into the room and flung open the shutters. Sunlight poured across the bed where the young girl laid. Begrudgingly, she sat up and rubbed her eyes. Remembering the night before, she examined her hands to see if they appeared altered in any manner, but she noticed no discernible change. If any magic existed in her, she did not feel it, the tingling and warmth from the garden forgotten.

"You can't just go on sleeping the whole day away, miss. Your mother is waiting for you in her . . ." the words froze on Tessina's lips when she looked at Biancabella.

What did she see? Dirt? A stray leaf? The panicked girl, convinced her secret visit would be discovered, tried to think of how to explain any oddity away. But the maid's face widened into a broad smile. "My, you look very lovely today."

"Er, thank you."

Confused, Biancabella climbed out of bed and rinsed her face in the bowl on the nightstand. Tessina stood behind her, a dress of soft blue in her hands. Once Biancabella slipped it on, she sat at the vanity to have her hair done. The reflection in the mirror might have shown her skin with a fairer glow than ever before, but otherwise, she disappointingly felt like the same ordinary girl. The magical sensation from the night before seemed only a dream.

Although the cuts and scratches from her first trip to the garden had vanished without a trace.

Tessina fished a blue ribbon from a drawer, which burst with a multitude of colorful bands and beaded combs. Pulling the child's hair back over her shoulders, the maid picked up a brush and swept a long stroke down the length of Biancabella's fair tresses.

Clink

They both looked to the floor where a grape-sized sapphire now lay.

"Huh, now where could that have come from?" the maid wondered.

She scooped it up and placed it on the table. Biancabella did not recognize the jewel. Perhaps it fell off one of the decorated combs, though she should remember a gem of that size on any of her hair ornaments. Tessina performed another pass of the brush.

Clink

Again, they both look down. This time to where a fat ruby tumbled to the floor. Biancabella stared in wonder, a realization forming in her mind—the gifts Samaritana spoke of. In the mirror, the girl's eyes locked with the maid, who had a strange glint of awareness on her face. Without a word, Tessina ran from the room, leaving the door open behind her. For a moment, Biancabella did not move. She eyed the brush left on the vanity as if poison coated it. Hesitantly, she grasped it and ran it down the full length of her hair.

Clink

Clink

Two more jewels winked up at her from the stone floor. Biancabella dropped the brush as though it scalded her. Before she could think any further, clipped voices sounded from the hallway.

Her mother burst into the room with Tessina at her heels. One look at her daughter and Adeleta's face broke into a smile.

"My, you look very lovely today." Her words echoed Tessina who uttered that exact phrase moments ago.

"Thank you, Mother," Biancabella managed through a throat tight with nerves.

"What is all this nonsense you are babbling about," the marchioness demanded of the maid.

"When I brushed her hair, jewels fell out of it," Tessina stated, wringing her hands.

"Now I don't see how . . ."

"It's true, Mother," Biancabella interrupted. "Brush it yourself and see."

Defiantly, Adeleta grabbed the brush, ready to prove the others wrong. She smoothly ran the bristles down the length of her daughter's golden locks.

Clink

Clink

Clink

The marchioness stared at the brush a moment and then at the ever-growing pile of gems on the ground. She repeated her actions.

Clink

Clink

"Oh my," Adeleta backed away, her face as white as a sheet. "How is this possible?"

She faltered and sat on the edge of the bed to compose herself. Meanwhile, Tessina, on her hands and knees, collected all the jewels. Biancabella chewed on her lip while she assessed the situation. If producing gems was her power, then it did not seem an evil one. Surely, she could put a positive spin on the occurrence.

"Perhaps it's magic," the girl proposed with all the innocence she could muster, "like a gift."

Thoughts of Imelda bombarded the marchioness. The warning, the potion, the cloying taste of the green liquid in the back of her mouth. "Has anyone come to you? Bothered you in any way, Child?"

"No," Biancabella asserted, keeping her promise to protect her sister. But then, she doubted herself. If Samaritana was indeed her sister, that gave her mother another daughter, of sorts. Did she not deserve to know about the situation? Her mother's reaction quelled any further wish to share the truth.

"Whatever shall we do?" Adeleta wailed, though the question did not seem directed at either her daughter or the maid.

Distressed by her mother's anguish, Biancabella jumped from her chair. She ran to the bedside, compassion flowing through her. "Do not worry, Mother. All will be well. Please calm down."

When she went to hug her mother, her hands tingled. Tiny violets sprung from her palms and cascaded to the floor. Once more, all three of them froze until Adeleta's weeping broke the silence. The more Biancabella tried to comfort her, the more flowers fell from her hands. "Don't cry, Mama. These are my gifts."

The marchioness stopped mid-sob. "Gifts? Who told you such things?"

"No one, Mother," the girl hedged, resolute in her vow to Samaritana. "You always said I was special and see, I am."

"Yes, I suppose that is true." Adeleta wiped her tears with a handkerchief.

"And jewels and flowers are good things, aren't they?" Tessina added as if to convince herself as well as the others.

"Yes, of course," her mother agreed. She thought of
Imelda's words that magic would come out for good or evil.
Clearly, her daughter had been blessed and not cursed. Pure
gratefulness sprung in her heart, all worries evaporating. "You are
a lucky girl indeed, Biancabella. Let me brush your hair again."

This time they all laughed in amazement at the gems which
issued from her fair curls. Tessina gathered them up with a wide
smile, any worries about ominous ramifications for the girl
forgotten. In fact, both women were quite charmed by her every
move and with each profession of love Biancabella uttered, more
flowers sprung from her hands.

"We must show the marquis," Adeleta insisted.

With brush in hand, they marched to his receiving room.
He looked up from his desk, quill hovering over parchment,
surprised by the interruption. While the marchioness ordered his
assistant from the room, Marquis Lamberico looked from his wife
to Tessina.

"What is this all about?' he demanded. His eyes fell on his
daughter and he uttered the now familiar phrase. "My, you look
very lovely today."

"Nardo, I have wonderful news. Our daughter has been
blessed—her hair produces jewels and her hands flowers."

"Are you feeling all right, my dear wife?" he asked, the
crease between his brows deepening with his concern.

"Just watch," his wife ordered in a firm tone she rarely used
with her husband.

Tessina brushed the girl's long hair and tiny jewels
sprinkled the floor, sparkling like rainbows in the sunlight. The
marquis rose from behind his desk and bent to pick up a handful,
which he eyed with amazement. "These are gems of the finest
quality I've ever seen."

"And watch," Adeleta ordered. "Biancabella, give your father a hug."

No sooner had the girl outstretched her arms to the man, tiny pink roses emanated from her palms, their scent infusing the room. Astonished, he stepped back at first. Then, he wrapped his arms around her and lifted her off the ground and spun her in a circle. She squealed in delight along with the other ladies.

"How incredible! What wonderful gifts our daughter has been granted. She will be known throughout the land for her beauty, charm, and magic," he pronounced.

He placed her down and embraced his wife. Biancabella beamed at them, the tingling sensation from the night before returning full force. Samaritana was right, she possessed magnificent gifts. Her sister helped her awaken them and she would treasure her newfound sibling forever.

CHAPTER ELEVEN

Word of Biancabella's amazing gifts was heralded throughout the land. Far from being considered a bearer of witchcraft, people deemed the girl to have been touched by divine grace. Travelers arrived from far and wide to witness the spectacle, many asking for Biancabella's blessing as well. The wealth and renown of the marquis and his blessed daughter grew and with it the prosperity of his march, now the destination of many pilgrims. Every citizen down to the lowliest peasant benefited from the girl's gifts due to this influx of tourists and commerce. Her status rose from beloved to near goddess-like, a responsibility she bore with her trademark goodness.

Biancabella made herself available nearly every morning to bestow blessings upon those who journeyed to see her. Though flattered by the attention, she wondered how much good a blessing from her truly amounted to, yet every time flowers fell from her hands, the visitors cried with thankfulness. At the tender age of twelve, wishing to be of more concrete help to those who sought her out, she directed a fund be made from some of her hair jewels. A newly established committee oversaw the endeavor, distributing food, clothing, and medicine, adding even further to the glorification of her name.

Despite her busy schedule, Biancabella snuck back into the garden whenever possible to see Samaritana. The gates, still hidden from all view, opened easily for her. She had cleared an area near the fountain for them to work on honing her gifts, so Biancabella could garner more control over them. Samaritana patiently instructed her sister on how to control the energy within to influence the flow of the flowers and gems.

"What a relief it is to have some power over them," Biancabella said, "and not have to worry about being buried alive in petals. Twice now, Father had to pull me out of a giant pile."

"Yes, manipulating your gifts is important. This helps strengthen your magic. Someday when we are grown, we will each be able to transform from human to snake at will."

"Oh, won't that be wonderful," Biancabella exclaimed, joyful at the thought of Samaritana as a girl like herself. "I cannot wait!'

"We both still have much to learn from my teachers," her sister stated, sliding up to the edge of the cracked fountain, in the shadow of the mossy pitcher.

"The other snakes you told me of?" Biancabella asked, sitting down on the ledge. "What else have they told you?"

"They have assisted me with my gift of healing and are preparing me for my main purpose in life," Samaritana replied and wound herself up in Biancabella's lap.

"Your main purpose?" She brushed an errant stem from her shoulder. It rose from the neglected fountain, the cherub now all but covered from sight.

"That I am to protect you from the evils of the world. That we must remain together and love only each other. Do you swear to it?"

Biancabella, too young to understand anything of romantic passion, swore it with all her heart. She could not imagine ever being parted from her newfound sister, whose life she vowed to make as perfect as possible.

"Then all will be well," her sister murmured, coiling into the folds of Biancabella's neck.

～◇◇～

One afternoon, after an exhausting number of pilgrims filed through the throne room for a blessing, Biancabella took her mother aside to discuss an idea which brewed in her mind.

"Mother, I was walking the grounds the other day, when I came upon your old, abandoned garden," she began, sinking onto a blue, tufted couch in her mother's personal receiving room.

The briefest glint of panic passed across Adeleta's face, but she snuffed it out. "Yes, my garden from long ago, before you were born."

"Can we restore it? I would love to spend time there." In truth, she wanted to fix it up for Samaritana, who deserved a well-cared for place to live, not a place overrun with weeds and mold.

"I don't know if that is such a good idea," the marchioness replied, thinking of the snakes that had chased her away from her beloved garden. "It's been forsaken for so long, it may be better to just knock it down."

"Please? It will mean ever so much to me to have a private place to relax and rejuvenate myself after a long morning of comforting pilgrims and greeting well-wishers."

Since the awakening of her gifts, the pull of the girl's wishes was too much for anyone to counter. Her mother could not help but agree and flowers poured forth from Biancabella's hand with the ensuing hug. Adeleta ordered the gardeners to restore the neglected space. Biancabella raced to tell Samaritana the news.

The snake was moved by her sister's kind gesture. Within days, thanks to exemplary pruning and weeding, it resembled its former glory. Biancabella peeked in to check the progress. The head gardener noticed her and beckoned her inside.

"It's coming along nicely, my lady. Even a sandalwood tree, imagine that! Only thing is, the fountain is too broken to fix. We will have to commission a new one. Any ideas what you would like?" Dirt made the creases in his face look deeper when he smiled at her.

After a moment's thought, Biancabella replied, "I would like two snakes intertwined, the water falling from their mouths coming together on the way down. Like this."

She bent and drew a rudimentary rendering in the dirt.

"Snakes, huh? A powerful choice. I like it," he commended. "I will let the mason know."

With a pat on her golden head, he returned to his work, feeling as though sunshine itself had visited him.

Biancabella continued to visit each day after the workers left to see how Samaritana and the other snakes, who she never saw, were managing. Though they were anxious for the restoration to be done, the project did not interfere with their life in the nest. The sisters circled the space to see what new discovery they could find. Biancabella listened to all Samaritana's suggestions and passed them on to the head gardener.

One month later, the project was finally complete. Biancabella burst with excitement as she dragged her mother to see the transformation. Newly polished brass gates pushed open before them, and the marchioness gasped, feeling as though she stepped back in time. The wisteria, the lavender, and the roses bloomed just like she remembered, the same meandering path, set with new stones, under her feet. Benches overhung with bowers sat in their usual places, rife with memories of past days. The tinkling of water filled the air with its same sense of calm. For a moment, Adeleta was too overcome to move.

"Isn't it wonderful?" Biancabella gushed, darting from one area to the next. "And look, the fountain has been redesigned!"

The marchioness gaped at the sight of two white marble snakes coiled together, their heads lifted almost touching where water fell from their mouths into the pool below. Unlike the beloved cherub, who comforted her in her youth, these serpents unsettled her. For the first time, the marchioness worried her daughter knew the secret she kept all these years, but she was too frightened to ask. If Biancabella had somehow learned of her unusual birth, it had only brought the family good fortune. Better to leave the matter unspoken.

"You don't like it!" Biancabella cried, noticing how her mother blanched.

"It was just . . . unexpected, that is all." Seeing the joy fade from her daughter's eyes made it impossible to disparage the snakes. "My cherub was so different. Yet now that I look at this new fountain, I think it is perfect. As lovely as the rest of the garden. What a magnificent idea this whole venture was."

Biancabella hugged her mother's waist, flowers showering from her hands to the path below. Adeleta smiled and continued to fuss over the new space. However, once they left, she never returned to the garden again.

The restoration pleased Samaritana, who particularly admired the fountain.

"It so nicely represents our bond," she would tell her sister.

Biancabella visited the garden daily if her schedule and the weather allowed it, except in the winter months when the snakes hibernated. No one ever accompanied Biancabella on her visits.

Like her mother, Tessina had no desire to be there. Piero thought a secret garden sounded too girly and passed most of his free time in the stables learning to ride. The two sisters grew ever closer over time. Once at Samaritana's request, Biancabella brought a mirror. The snake wrapped herself across the golden lines of the girl's neck where she still fit precisely, much to her sibling's delight. They were sisters in every sense but the form, yet neither's feelings were subdued by their differences. As Samaritana so often said, they completed one another.

Biancabella often reflected on how lucky she was in life—the darling of her parents and the entire march, her every whim was accounted for. Happily, her spirit was one of compassion and generosity, so a situation that would have spoiled many a child rotten, only increased her kindness. Never did she make unreasonable or selfish demands but strove to make the lives of those around her better. She took her obligation to the pilgrims and any unfortunate being seriously and believed in the goodness of the world, which only enhanced her preciousness to all. Only Piero dared to tease her, as playmates do, secretly wanting to be jealous of his cousin but unable to conjure any ill-will toward her until one fateful summer afternoon.

CHAPTER TWELVE

Shafts of sunlight streamed across Biancabella where she sat on a garden bench. Samaritana, wrapped around her arm, guided her sister who attempted to control the flower magic. Violet petals poured from the girl's palm, now a vibrant purple mound at her feet.

"You have the power to curb their flow if you want. Just concentrate on closing the link," the serpent instructed.

Biancabella tried to stem the tide of blossoms, which slowed to a trickle before stopping. Samaritana looked up at her proudly, the scent of the flowers strong on the air. Biancabella rose and picked up a handful of the petals. She walked to the fountain and tossed them onto the water, where they floated like tiny fragrant boats.

"Honestly," she joked, "sometimes I feel like I can't make enough. The pilgrims love them so. They take the flowers home with them as though they were sacred. Lately, I'm exhausted from producing them along with all the gems."

"There are blessings in them, imbued with your kindness and compassion. If nothing else, they bring comfort to those who need it," Samaritana asserted. She coiled up her sibling's arm to encircle her neck and nestled along the golden marks. "Let me try to transfer you some of my energy. It will make you stronger."

"That makes me feel so much better," Biancabella sighed in contentment, a surge of vitality filling her.

"This is why we must never be parted," Samaritan remarked. "Stay with me and all will be well."

Biancabella settled down on the ledge of the fountain and a gentle mist showered them, a respite from the summer sun. She craned her head to its warm glow, her eyes closed. The warmth of the sun coupled with her sister's treatment revitalized her and she happily thought of all those she could help with her fresh energy.

A crash brought their attention to the path, where Piero stood, mouth agape, a shattered pitcher scattered at his feet. Before Biancabella could utter a word, he turned to run, but his foot caught on one of the pitcher's shards. He tripped and crumpled to the ground. Blood gushed from his ankle where a sharp piece of the pottery protruded.

The girl rushed to his side. "Oh my goodness, Piero, you're hurt!" Biancabella wailed, distressed at the sight of her injured cousin.

The boy grasped at his lower leg, crying when his hand came away bloodied. Biancabella took out a handkerchief and attempted to staunch the bleeding. Her efforts failed against the deep wound. Blood pooled around them, a dark ruby stain streaming across the paving and sinking into the ground.

"Remove the shard," Samaritana ordered. She slithered down to the ground.

"But won't he bleed more?" Biancabella asked, eyes brimming with tears.

"Just do as I say," the snake commanded, her tone firm but calm.

"Who are you talking to, Biancabella?" Piero quavered, looking around. He shrieked when his cousin pulled out the fragment of ceramic.

No sooner was it out when Samaritana entwined herself around his ankle. At first, he panicked, trying to push the creature off him, until he realized how much the pain had subsided. The cousins watched in awe as blood stopped spouting and skin fused back together. When the snake uncoiled, only a faint pink line remained. Samaritana slithered back to Biancabella and wrapped around her wrist. Piero sat momentarily dumbfounded until fright filled his eyes.

"You have nothing to fear," Biancabella assured, worried the shock of Samaritana was too much for the fragile boy.

"I don't know what magic this is, Cousin," he sputtered, rising to his feet, "but it is not of this world! We must tell your parents at once."

"No, please!" she pled, worried what would become of her sister if word of her existence got out. "They may not understand. She is my sister, you see. We must remain together."

A strange awareness flashed across Piero's face. "Pomma spoke once of something unnatural happening at your birth. But your parents are accepting of your magic, why would they feel differently about . . . her?"

"I don't know, Piero. All I know is people fear witchcraft. A girl who makes flowers and gems is one thing, but a snake who can perform magic? It may frighten people, and I cannot let anything happen to her."

"I'm not sure . . ." her cousin hedged, worrying his bottom lip. He loved his cousin, but knew nothing of this snake. He hoped that keeping this secret would not put Biancabella in danger.

Samaritana, as if sensing his reluctance, rose her head high from Biancabella's wrist and stared at the boy, who heard a voice quite clearly in his mind. "Say nothing about this. You are right, my abilities are magical. Be thankful I used them for good purpose with you. If you tell anyone, I will be sent away and your cousin will be broken-hearted, and then who is to say what magic I will unleash upon you? We don't want that, do we?"

Piero shook his head and glanced at Biancabella. He knew she had heard the snake's message to him. Samaritana coiled up her sibling's arm to encircle her neck and nestled along the golden mark, her eyes never leaving the boy.

"Please, Piero," his cousin pled, "let this stay between us. You can come to the garden anytime you want. It will be our little secret."

Such were Biancabella's gifts that one look in his cousin's eyes filled Piero with the desire to do whatever she requested. Samaritana breathed a sigh of relief. The boy would tell no one. His unwavering dedication to his cousin coupled with her magical ability for others to want to satisfy her wishes left no room for argument.

"Of course, this will remain in my confidence, dear cousin, though I must be honest, I want nothing further to do with this," Piero said.

He turned on his heel and hurried out of the garden. And though he never returned to the place or mentioned it again to his cousin, he was true to his word throughout the years.

Biancabella stooped to pick up the broken pieces of the pitcher, her cousin's blood still wet on some. She put them in a corner where the gardeners could dispose of them. Samaritana uncoiled and went back to the fountain ledge.

"You were right to tell him to keep our secret, but you should not have made it seem as though you would use your magic to hurt him if he did not obey."

"My dear sister, you only choose to see the good in people. If he did not feel there would be dire consequences, he would be unable to keep our secret, the pull to expose it would be too much to overcome, despite his strong loyalty to you. You overlook this tendency of human nature."

"I suppose you are right. That is why we are perfect for each other. One balances out the other."

"Exactly, my dear. As I told you, when we are together, all will be well."

The years passed and Biancabella, with her sister's secret, remained intact. The marquis and marchioness showered their daughter with affection as did Tessina and even Piero, though he kept more of a distance. People came from far and wide for her blessing, which she bestowed with grace. Her bond with Samaritana grew and filled her with such an abundance of love, she felt her heart overflow. So complete was her surety in this happiness, she never realized the true enemy that lurked in the shadows, growing in strength with each passing second—time.

CHAPTER THIRTEEN

Biancabella grew to maidenhood, her beauty and kindness renowned in all corners of the earth. At the age of thirteen, suitors began asking for her hand, but the marquis insisted she was too young. Now three more years had passed in which her loveliness only multiplied. Requests for betrothals increased in turn, but in truth, Marquis Lamberico remained loath to let his daughter go. Still, he needed to keep up pretenses and allowed the petitions to continue before finding a reason against each new applicant.

Kings and princes from Genova, Sardinia, and Sicilia presented themselves for a chance to land such a gifted wife. None ever asked for a dowry, the jewels which fell from her hair alone considered payment enough. While her father hosted these guests, Biancabella snuck looks, through a slatted screen on the side of the marquis' receiving room, at the wide range of men who offered their proposals. Some were gray-haired, older than her father, while others barely had the down of a beard on their face. Their different styles of dress, distinctive accents, and various mannerisms fascinated the girl, but she never seriously considered marrying one of them. And while she saw them, her father never brought her out for them to regard her.

In the safety of her garden, she regaled Samaritana with stories each time a new suitor arrived. There were now six of them staying at the castle, hoping to sway the marquis' choice in their favor. The sisters delighted in discussing each one as if it were a game, neither truly believing anything would change in their futures. Indeed, the snake visited the castle herself under cover of darkness to assess the men who vied for her sister. In shadowed recesses, she listened to them in their private chambers, where tongues flowed more freely than in front of the marquis. She never heard anything malicious or worrying from any, yet she did not consider any of them worthy of Biancabella, not that she disclosed her spying to her innocent sister.

"King Bashir came all the way across the sea from some land called Tunis," Biancabella explained, perched on the fountain ledge next to her sister. "He wore clothing, the likes of which I have never seen, a long shirt that came down to his calves over baggy pants and shoes with curled toes."

"The shirt is called a jebba," her sister informed her. Browned leaves skittered around the garden of flowerless plants.

The girl, who never questioned Samaritana's boundless knowledge, continued, "It was made of the brightest blue silk, a color I've only seen in paintings of peacocks, and there were jewels sewn all over it. Oh, how it glinted in the sunlight!"

"But you, my sweet sister, have jewels of your own. They fall from your hair at your very command, even this king could never compete with that."

"True," Biancabella readily agreed, "and despite his great efforts at etiquette, he came across as quite stubborn, as though he is used to always getting his way. I didn't like that. Besides, what more could I want from life than I already have?"

She wrinkled her nose in displeasure at the thought of the arrogant king. Samaritana coiled up her arm to rest a head on the girl's shoulder. The evening air, tinged with the chill of fall, breezed across the garden, wafting the empty stalks into a gentle dance. Biancabella leaned her cheek down onto Samaritana's head and sighed. In this moment of contentment, marrying anyone and leaving her home remained an unfathomable thought. After all, who could be truer to her than her sister.

"Enough meaningless talk," Samaritana said. "Let's try working on changing. We don't have much time until I need to hibernate."

For months now, the sisters tried to garner the magic to transform into each other's forms. Samaritana came close once, conjuring the shadowy outline of a girl for the briefest of seconds. Biancabella failed at any attempt to change into a snake. Still, they pressed on, hoping one day, they could be twins in every sense of the word.

This evening, Samaritan tried first. She focused all her energy on the thought of a human body. Slowly, she felt her body stretch, limbs appear, and hair fall down her shoulders. It took every ounce of strength to hold the form before, sapped of power, she coiled back to the ground.

"You were so close, Samaritana," Biancabella exclaimed. "I could see you as a woman with long dark hair. It won't be long now until you can transform entirely."

"Yes," the snake agreed. "Now you try."

Biancabella concentrated on her body, willing it to shrink to a graceful sheath of scales. Her fingers and toes tingled, and she fixated on the desire to become like her sister. Heat burst through her in a rapid flash and the next thing she knew, she fell to the grass, but found herself still very much a girl.

"I swear, I felt something more that time. It just must happen soon. I am trying so hard!" She pounded the ground in frustration.

"Relax, dear sister," Samaritana comforted. "This is difficult magic to harness. We will get there eventually."

"Of course, you are right," Biancabella said with a smile. "After all, we have years to practice with each other and you always have much greater power in the spring after you sleep."

"Yes," her sister agreed

They shared a wistful touch, knowing winter meant enduring each other's absence for a few months, the longest months of the year in Biancabella's opinion. She wished they could skip the season entirely and go right to spring rather than enduring the drudgery of wintertime.

Two weeks later, another grand procession appeared with King Ferrandino of Naples, who had sent word of his arrival. Biancabella heard the commotion out her window while she dressed for breakfast. She ran for a peek, but only saw the last two horsemen pass, the tails of the steeds swishing in time before disappearing into the courtyard.

"How many kings and princes need wives, anyway?" she asked Tessina. "There seems no end to them."

Tessina smiled. The girl was too naïve to realize what a prize she was. Certainly, some marriages were dissolved simply to make a man eligible to ask for her hand. But Biancabella need not be told any of that. "Your gifts are well-known, my dear, it is the source of much interest."

"Unfortunately, I have no interest in any of them," she proclaimed

Indeed, she told as much to her father, who was more than happy to hear it. He assured her that he entertained petitioners merely to show good faith to surrounding kingdoms, but he had no intention of parting with his daughter. In the end, he planned to tell everyone there was no fair way to choose among them and it was better to keep her here with him rather than cause any hard feelings among his allies. Father and daughter kept this bit of knowledge to themselves.

"Let's see if we can get a glimpse of this one. Do you know anything about him?" Biancabella asked on her way to the door.

"The gossip is he is newly crowned after the untimely passing of his father," Tessina confided, hurrying to keep pace with her charge, "so at least that eliminates old from your list of worries. Not much else was said of him."

The ladies ducked through a hidden door and came out behind the screen in the receiving room. There they peered between the narrow slats at today's contestant in an unwinnable game. The marquis stood to welcome his guest, who knelt to bestow his host with a sword sheathed in a scabbard of intricate leatherwork. Marquis Lamberico admired it with words of praise. He sank into his chair and ordered the man to rise. The downturned head of dark curls lifted upward as he stood and Biancabella gasped, her hand flying to her mouth. After a parade of old men and scrawny boys, this one stood out. He was the most handsome man she had ever seen. Tessina nudged her to be quiet, and she slowly lowered her hand to her side.

"I thank you, King Ferrandino, for the splendid gift. What brings you to my humble march?" Knowing the answer full well, the marquis settled back with a look of attentive interest.

"As you may have heard, I am newly crowned, my honorable marquis, and in need of starting a family to secure my legacy. I seek your daughter's hand in marriage if she will have me."

"Ah, I thank you for your interest in my daughter. But you have traveled far. Please take time to refresh and rest. We can speak of this matter at dinner." Marquis Lamberico motioned for two servants who escorted the King of Naples from the room.

The maid took Biancabella's arm to lead her out, but the girl stared at the retreating king, the words *"if she will have me"* playing in her head. None of the other suitors ever expressed such a sentiment, one which indicated her thoughts on the issue mattered. A strange sensation filled her, one she had never felt, but with it came the certainty that she wanted to speak to King Ferrandino herself.

CHAPTER FOURTEEN

The afternoon air felt like winter. Leaves blew from the trees, colorful confetti floating to the ground. Biancabella hurried to the garden, her footsteps a burst of staccato on the flagstones. She pushed open the gate to find the space awash with fallen foliage. A forlorn silence filled the enclosure, heavy on the air.

"Samaritana?" she called, making her way to the fountain ledge. A gust of wind blew droplets of cold water across her and she wiped them off her face.

"I thought you were not coming. It is late." The snake slithered up next to the girl and took refuge on her lap.

"My father asked to talk to me and it took longer than I expected," Biancabella explained, though her words were untrue. She had asked to speak to her father, not the other way around.

"The weather grows harsh," Samaritana said, twining around her sister's arm. "I must join my fellow snakes underground and hibernate."

"Are you sure you can't live in the castle somewhere during the winter?" the girl pleaded.

Though Biancabella asked every year for the snake to move to the warmth of the castle, she refused to do so.

"You know I don't want to be seen by anyone. I belong here. It is safer for us both. Besides, I told you, if you are in trouble come here and call my name and I will appear."

"But the long months alone are so hard to endure," Biancabella cried, who had not had a need to seek out her sister in the winter yet. "I miss you dearly."

"All will be well, Sister. We have made it work all these years. Spring will be here before you know it. Hopefully, by then, I can transform into a woman and then we can be together always."

This thought cheered the girl somewhat. They spent a few moments together before the clock chimed four times, the echo reverberating across the garden. The sound reminded Biancabella of a funeral dirge as the long winter months stretched out before her.

"I must go, the sun will set soon. I will see you in the spring," Biancabella promised, kissing her softly on the head. "I love you."

"I love you too. Do not despair, my sister. Remember—as long as we are together, all will be well."

"I know." The girl stroked Samaritana's head fondly and placed her back on the ledge.

With a last longing look, she left. For a moment, she stared at the snow-covered peaks of the Alps, the stalwart mountains a source of constancy in her world, along with her sister. On her way back to the castle, Tessina intercepted her.

"I've been looking for you, Miss," she said, exasperated in the cold. "Time to get ready for dinner."

In fact, the earlier meeting between Biancabella and her father had been about this meal. After spying on his meeting with King Ferrandino, the girl was determined to meet the young monarch. Before visiting the garden that afternoon, she visited her father's study.

"Biancabella, what a wonderful surprise," he said and stood for an embrace, which she reveled in.

"I came to speak with you, Father, about all the suitors. Perhaps it's time I meet some of them." She settled into the chair across from his desk. Fond memories of playing underneath it when she was little rose to mind, her father always indulgent with her games.

"I don't know if that is necessary," the marquis balked, a territorial urge rising in him.

"I think they need to see my face. If you keep me hidden, they will wonder if I am truly available and some may lose interest. I know our plan is for me to stay here, but I would like to see what all the fuss is about instead of hiding in my room like a criminal. Please, Father, it would mean so much to me." She looked up through her lashes, a beguiling smile on her lips, the expression all daughters know will take no refusal, as if anyone could refuse her magical pull, anyway.

"All right," he chuckled. "I see your mind is made up. Tonight, I will entertain a few of them at dinner. You may join us."

"Thank you, Father!" She jumped from her chair clapping with excitement.

"But, you will sit next to me and I will guide all conversation. Agreed?"

"Of course," she vowed and hurried out before he could change his mind.

He smiled in the wake of her exit, to his eyes, she was still the little girl who used to climb about at his feet. Once her curiosity was addressed, she would forget all about the suitors. He sighed wistfully and returned to his work.

Now, Tessina laced up the back of a vibrant purple gown. Biancabella ran her hands over the soft silk bodice, careful not to disturb the intricate gems sewn into it. Threading of gold accentuated the sleeves and the skirt. Next, the maid styled her hair, always a tedious process. Biancabella tried to stem the flow of jewels from her hair, but her excitement made it hard to concentrate. Tessina caught every small gem which fell and placed them in a chest on the vanity for this specific purpose. After a touch of makeup was applied, Biancabella admired herself in the mirror. For the first time, she imagined herself as a potential husband may see her and was pleased with the outcome of Tessina's fussing.

When she entered the dining room, all the men rose. Her father held out a hand to guide her to the seat at his side. She smiled at her mother, who would sit on her other side, an approving look in her eyes. Once everyone returned to their seat, the staff served the first of many courses. Biancabella picked at some cheese placed in front of her and waited for the conversations to start without gawking too obviously at the King of Naples.

On the other side of her mother sat the King of Tunis, his garb of bright orange was trimmed with enough gold and diamonds to fill a large coffer. King Ferrandino sat on the other side of her father in a black velvet tunic with a red sash; the girl preferred the simple elegance of it. Clearly these two men were the upper hierarchy of the suitors. Biancabella smiled at a few more men seated further down each end of the table. One lifted his glass in salute.

"So how was your journey here, King Ferrandino?" the marquis asked his newest guest.

"Long, but not full of hardship," he replied. "And well worth the effort."

He smiled brightly at Biancabella, who felt her cheeks flush. Warmth tingled inside her, yet it was different from the usual magical feelings; her heart felt both light and constrained at the same time. Whatever the sensation was, she drank it in eagerly.

"Well worth the effort indeed," agreed the King of Tunis. "She shines more brilliantly than any jewel in the world. Stories of her great beauty were not exaggerated."

Biancabella smiled at him but saw only greed in his eyes as he assessed her. Quickly, she looked back to her plate, which now held a pile of steaming meat. *What an awful man.*

"We were sorry to hear about your father's passing. How are things down in Naples?" her father said, turning back to King Ferrandino.

"Thank you for your condolences. It's been a challenge to get things in order. My father's death was sudden, so there were many loose ends to address. And then, the summer was unusually hot causing a bit of a drought, but the rains have thankfully returned."

"I've heard the weather in the south is much warmer than here, that you do not even have snow in the winter," Biancabella ventured, eager to exchange some words with this handsome man.

Before he could reply, King Bashir broke in, "Not only is there no snow in my country but the southern half of it is all desert. Sand as far as the eyes can see."

Once he started, the King of Tunis did not stop regaling them all with stories of his homeland. Biancabella tried to be polite and listen, hoping the conversation would turn back to the King of Naples, but her father peppered Bashir with questions, leaving no opening.

While she pushed her pie and custard around her plate, she stole a look at the young king, who had graciously ceded the floor to the older royal. For the briefest of seconds, their eyes met and in them she read the same disappointment she felt about their interrupted dialogue.

CHAPTER FIFTEEN

Weeks passed without any opportunity to speak to the young king at any length, King Bashir always there to dominate any conversations. Stolen glances served as the only means of exchange between the two. One morning, an icy air greeted Biancabella when she stepped out of bed. Throwing open the shutters, she let out a squeal of delight. Fat snowflakes fell, dappling the fallen leaves in pure white, the Alps remained hidden in the low-lying clouds. It was the first snow of the season, the kind which usually melted off by afternoon, yet still beautiful to behold in the stillness of the new day.

Once dressed, she left her room and wandered down an outer hallway to further watch the snowfall. Tessina, hesitant to let her go alone, insisted she come straight back as she stuck a fur-lined cap on her head and tucked her hands in a muff. This outer corridor was one of four which ringed an inner courtyard, its paths and benches bright with the newly fallen flakes. While she admired the beauty, a movement caught her eye. King Ferrandino stepped from the opposite hallway into the courtyard, his face lit with amazement.

Without thought of propriety, she stepped out to join him. "You've never seen snow before, have you?"

Startled by her words, he dropped into a low bow. "Forgive me, my lady. I did not see you there. Yes, this is the first time."

"It's beautiful, isn't it?" she asked, her arm sweeping across the frosty courtyard.

"Yes, my lady, but, if I may be so bold, not nearly as beautiful as you."

What might have sounded like a practiced court compliment rang genuine with the nervous tremor in his voice and eyes too bashful to meet hers. A strange sensation of warmth sprang up in Biancabella's chest—the mixture of curiosity and queasiness that blooms with the awakening of attraction. She stood before the handsome king, scared and thrilled at the same time.

"Thank you." She found herself too timid to look at him as well. "I'm sorry we did not get to speak more at dinner last night."

"As am I, my lady." Their gazes met, his shy smile matching her own.

Neither looked away. Biancabella felt entranced by his warm brown eyes, wishing she could read his thoughts to see if he was touched with the same exhilaration. The courtyard and the snowflakes melted away, leaving only the two of them in a world of their own. Her cheeks reddened, not with embarrassment, but with the prospect of knowing him on the deepest levels.

"Biancabella!" Tessina's voice broke the spell. "Your parents await your presence."

King Ferrandino bowed once more before leaping away like a startled deer. The girl trudged over to the maid, disappointment coursing through her at levels previously unimagined. *Would she ever have a chance to talk to the king without someone interfering?* Her toes throbbed, wet and cold in her silk slippers, but she barely noticed, all thoughts on Ferrandino's beseeching eyes.

"You should know better than to talk with a man alone," Tessina scolded. "For goodness' sake, what would people say if they saw you! I can only imagine the gossip. Please behave appropriately."

The girl did not reply, eyes downcast as she followed behind to the breakfast room. In fact, her head was so full of thoughts of the king, she hardly noticed the reprimand. Biancabella greeted her parents, distractedly bumping into a servant who spilled juice on the table. She took her seat, mind still a swirl, laying aside her muff and cloak. A maid jumped in to hang them up while another blotted up the splattered liquid.

"Are you all right, Biancabella?" her mother asked. A gentle touch on the girl's arm seemed to focus her.

"She must be tired from dinner last night," the marquis stated. "That King of Tunis could talk the ears off a statue."

Biancabella smiled at the quip. She selected an orange from a fruit bowl held out in front of her. Already peeled, she pulled the sections apart, enjoying the sweet bursts on her tongue. Adeleta scrutinized Biancabella's wet feet, which the girl tucked further under the table, avoiding her mother's puzzled expression.

"Listening to men talk of kingdoms all night must have bored you dreadfully," the marquis continued and he patted her hand. "Don't worry you need not join us again."

"How am I to get to know them if I do not attend?" Panic rose in her at the thought of not seeing Ferrandino and she dropped the orange unceremoniously on her plate.

"Why on earth would you want to get to know them?" her father blustered, crumbs of toast falling from his mouth.

"Just in case you ever decide I should marry someday." She grasped at straws and she knew it; their pact to keep her unattached made years ago.

The marquis' face clouded at the mention of marriage. Instead of answering, he viciously broke his boiled egg, shards of shell hurtled across the table, which a servant rushed to clean.

Silence followed. The marchioness studied her daughter intently. A mother's instinct seldom fails her and Adeleta was no different.

"Is there a suitor in particular who has caught your attention?" she asked, guessing the answer already.

Blushing, Biancabella stared at her hands. Although the bluntness of the question distressed her, the girl realized she could not lose the opportunity to speak, or else she may lose any chance to ever see the young monarch again. Her heart pounded against her chest and sweat beaded on the back of her neck.

"King Ferrandino." The words came out as a whisper.

"That boy king?" her father erupted. "The crown is barely on his head, his reign not yet stable. He will not do at all for my precious daughter."

Tears welled in the girl's eyes despite a mighty effort to stop them. There was a connection between her and Ferrandino, a strong one, of this she was certain. Her every thought bent on seeing him again, the urge beyond her control, but her confounded father was unlikely to care about this.

"Biancabella, why don't you leave us to talk," her mother ordered, a calming press on the girl's arm when she rose to leave.

They watched her plod to the door, shoulders drooped. A servant shut it behind her. Once alone, the marchioness turned to her husband. "Really, Nardo, we will have to let her go at some point. It is inevitable. Piero will inherit the march with whoever he marries. I'm sure he will be good to her when we are gone, but don't you think she deserves more? To be queen in her own right?"

The marquis heaved a sigh at the truth before him. Though his mind understood the circumstances, his heart wanted to hold on to denial for dear life, but he knew deep down, she was not his little girl anymore.

"I'd always hoped to avoid it," he admitted. "She and I agreed when she was younger that she would never marry, but I suppose feelings change with age. I don't think anyone worthy of her, but a match with a strong southern ally would not be such a bad thing."

"Let's have them get to know each other under our supervision," Adeleta suggested. "This way, we can get to know his character as well."

"As long as we agree that I will only sanction their betrothal if he makes Biancabella genuinely happy. I will not parcel my daughter out like some prized farm animal. She is dearer to me than life itself." Now it was the marquis' turn to hold back tears.

"I think this a wise approach, dear husband," the marchioness said and stood to embrace the shaken man.

When news reached Biancabella, elation filled her—followed swiftly by nausea. She longed to see Ferrandino more than anything, but she also dreaded it. *What if he did not find her attractive enough? Or smart enough? Or the kind of woman he wanted as a wife?* Conflicting emotions whirled through her and she barely sat still while Tessina did her hair. The maid smiled to herself, remembering the trials of budding infatuation. She hoped the relationship could measure up to whatever Biancabella imagined once the two got more acquainted with each other.

"Remember, it is only for one hour and there will be chaperones. Try to keep your composure as every word will be brought back to your father," the maid advised, catching one of many small gems that fell. By the time the Biancabella's hair was done, the bucket overflowed with a rainbow of colors, the girl too emotionally wrought to control them.

Biancabella and Ferrandino met in a small salon where they sat on couches facing one another. Tessina and two other staff members stood against the far wall with King Ferrandino's valet. For all her excitement to talk to him again, words failed her entirely once they were seated.

"You look lovely, as always, my lady," he admired, the words loud in the quiet room.

"Please, sire, call me Biancabella," she requested.

"Only if you call me Jaco, my given name," he replied, with a sly glance into her eyes.

"Tell me about yourself and Naples, Jaco."

Over the course of the hour, the dialogue never ceased, a comfortable rhythm between them. They discovered mutual interests in music and art. An accomplished horseman, he promised to help her become more confident in the saddle. But it was not so much the content of the conversation as the ease of it, as if two souls once well acquainted found each other once more. They parted with the promise to visit again tomorrow.

Back in her room, Biancabella could not concentrate on any task, not needlework, books, or even dinner were enough to take her mind off her new beau. She floated through the evening, her head in the clouds. Tessina shook her head after she left her charge in bed. There was nothing like the elixir of new love discovered by the young. With a smile, the maid sat in her chamber to work on some stitching before bed.

Biancabella settled under her blankets, Jaco's face and voice playing in her mind. For the first time since she found

Samaritana, she had not spared her sister a single thought the entire day.

CHAPTER SIXTEEN

The courtship was double pronged, one point easier than the other. Biancabella reveled in the idea of a betrothal, little else filled her mind beyond thoughts of Ferrandino; their time together passing with ease. Marquis Lamberico was another matter. His daughter possessed special gifts, ones which only the worthiest of men deserved. The young monarch spent many unnerving hours under the scrutiny of the marquis, yet try as he might, Lamberico could find no obvious fault in the engaging young man.

Biancabella's feelings for Jaco grew with each meeting, but inside a small pull of doubt plagued her. *What would he think of her gifts? Did he love her or the thought of the riches she would bring?* So far, he never once mentioned anything about her special abilities, but surely, they were enough to tempt even the most unassuming man. Every day when Tessina did her hair, she looked at the bucket of newly fallen gems and wondered.

"What is wrong?" the maid asked one day, concerned by the forlorn expression brought on by the coffer.

"I'm worried that King Ferrandino will only love me because of these." She kicked the bucket with her toe and a splash of color sprinkled to the floor.

"Well now, your parents and I love you and it has nothing to do with these jewels. We love your heart and kind spirit. I'm sure it is the same with the King of Naples." Tessina continued to brush the long golden locks.

"I suppose," she mumbled, less than convinced.

"Let me ask you, Biancabella, what if the situation was reversed, and he was the one with the special gift? Would you love him only for that?"

"No! Of course not! He is smart, thoughtful, and handsome, a bunch of gems would make no difference."

"Exactly." The maid smiled as light returned to her young charge's face, any misgivings put to rest.

Over the next few weeks, the couple spent more and more time together, their chaperones ceding more space each time. By now, they were both so besotted with each other, they hardly noticed the constant watchers, who blended like blurry images in the background of their vibrant romance. The other suitors, King Bashir of Tunis most notably, bristled at the amount of time afforded to the King of Naples, but Biancabella barely remembered other men had come to seek her hand and scarcely gave them any attention at all.

One chilly afternoon, they walked hand in hand around the grounds, the chaperones behind like a cluster of goslings. Ferrandino marveled at the magnificent Alps with their snow-covered peaks. He told her of Naples with ardent words for his beloved home and its beauty, so different from the colder north.

"I wish I could see it right now," she exclaimed as he spoke of the towering Vesuvius which stood guardian over his city. "Wait! Maybe there is something in the library."

Snatching his hand, they ran across hallways, Tessina and half a dozen others on their heels. The head librarian jumped to his feet in alarm when they burst through the door. After recovering from his shock, he retrieved some large books full of drawings.

The twosome took them to a table and spread open the first one. Inside were detailed sketches of Naples—her coastline, her cathedrals, and Vesuvius. Biancabella admired each page while Ferrandino explained and extolled every picture. At the sight of an outdoor amphitheater, he stopped, a wistful look filling his face.

"Where is that?" she asked.

"That is the Campanian Theater. My father and I enjoyed going there together . . . before he died." The end of the sentence came softly and fraught with grief.

"I was so sorry to hear of his untimely passing. It must be hard for you," Biancabella consoled.

"Yes, but one must get on with the business of living, right? I only hope to be half the king he was." His voice broke with emotion.

Instinctively, Biancabella put her arms around him to comfort the man she loved. White flowers fell from her hands, dusting the open book like snowflakes.

Ferrandino watched them flutter down in amazement. In wonder, he whispered, "It is true then."

Biancabella's cheeks flushed. She worked for so long to keep the flowers under control, but her passion for Jaco unwittingly brought them out in her. "I'm sorry. I didn't mean to . . ."

He grabbed her hands, kissing them delicately in turn. "Never apologize, my dear. Rumor is love produces these flowers. I am honored."

For so long, Biancabella worried he would react greedily to her gifts. She grew teary, the burden lifted from her shoulders. She bid Tessina to fetch a comb so he could watch the jewels spring from her hair. He laughed in delight at the sight.

"Yet know, my darling, not one gems compares to your beauty," he assured, "and your love is more precious to me than all of them put together."

One other characteristic of Biancabella interested Ferrandino. Tessina had left with the bucket of gems and the remaining chaperones stood at the far end of the room out of earshot, so he used the opportunity to quietly ask, "I would like to know about those golden circles around your neck. Are they special as well?"

She paused, deliberations at war in her head over what to say. In the end, she decided if they were to be wed, Jaco would need to know the truth. Softly she replied, "I was born with a snake around my neck. Her name is Samaritana, and she is my twin sister. She helped me enhance my gifts and in time she will take human form so we can be together always."

For a moment, the young king said nothing, a quizzical expression on his face, until he burst into laughter so loud, it echoed off the walls and down the aisles of books. The head librarian gave the couple a withering look before turning his attention back to the manuscript he pored over. On the far wall, their guardians appeared shocked by the outburst. Ferrandino, chastened, composed himself.

"My dear Biancabella, you do not need to make up fanciful stories about the origin of your gifts. You have been blessed by God and you should never be ashamed. I love you with all my heart and that will never change."

Bewildered, and a bit hurt, Biancabella decided not to discuss the matter further. In truth, it did sound like a fairy tale and she understood that the story may be hard to accept at first. She would get Samaritana to come Naples with them and, when the time was right, they could show him the truth of her words together. For now, the fact that he embraced her gifts so graciously would be enough.

"I feel for you as I have never felt for another," Ferrandino continued softly, "when we are together, I feel complete. Please tell me you feel the same and that you will be my wife."

"Of course, I will," she exclaimed, drawing another disdainful glance from the librarian. Neither cared, and he kissed her hands while any doubts he would eventually accept Samaritana flew from her mind.

As the days passed, their love grew. Biancabella knew without question she made the right decision when she agreed to marry him. Ferrandino expressed concern about the marquis' acceptance, but the girl worried little, her father never refused her anything. She did what she could to foster a relationship between the two men, arranging special dinners and hunting excursions. King Ferrandino, skilled with a bow, impressed the host with his prowess. Envoys filled the marquis' ears with stories of the wealth and grandeur of Naples, a lustrous city on a sparkling bay. In the end, her father conceded the match to be a worthy one.

One snowy evening in December, he stood from his chair at dinner, the entire room falling silent. He walked behind the chairs where Ferrandino sat next to Biancabella.

"King Ferrandino of Naples, it has been my pleasure to get to know you these past months. You are an honorable and admirable man." He directed his attention to the dining hall. "To all my fellow citizens and guests, I would like to announce the betrothal of this man to my precious daughter, Biancabella."

Applause rang across the room, no one who had been paying any attention surprised by the declaration. None smiled wider than the newly engaged couple as well-wishes and congratulations were offered.

Only the King of Tunis did not celebrate. He approached the dais and glared into the young king's eyes. Ferrandino looked down in unease. King Bashir turned to the marquis, "Sir, I don't know what I have done to offend you. Not only was I here first, but this little Naples by the sea pales in comparison to the splendor and majesty of my kingdom."

"I am sorry if you feel aggrieved," Lamberico replied. "There were a number of suitors to consider, but in the end, only one man won my daughter's heart."

Bashir only gave him a cold stare before turning to future groom. "You come in here like a strutting peacock and take what is rightfully mine. Today you have victory in this battle, but remember my friend, the war is far from over."

With these words, he strode from the room to prepare his caravan to sail at the first light of dawn.

Stunned by the encounter, the marquis and every head in the room stared in silence at the door which slammed behind the King of Tunis. Before the scene could grow, the marchioness ordered the musicians to play a lively tarantella, and soon dancers filled the floor. More courtiers came forward to wish the couple well, the festive mood returning.

While dancing with Ferrandino, Biancabella noticed the distraction in his eyes. "Do not worry about King Bashir. He will find another court soon with a princess more suited to become his queen."

"I hope you are right. He is a man who is known to hold a grudge." Stories of King Bashir's spite were legend.

"So let him," she exclaimed. "Look around. Everyone is happy, happy to plan a wedding, happy for us."

Relief filled the young man's face. "You are right. I am foolish to let worry ruin the happiest night of my life. I am so lucky to have found my true love."

"And I have found mine," she affirmed. "There is nothing ahead of us but happy days."

She kissed him, and they danced amid the adoring crowd. Cheers and smiles flooded the room everywhere—except for one small spot. On the floor in a crack between stones. Samaritana watched the couple, tears in her eyes. Unable to watch any further, she curled back around and slithered to the garden.

Samaritana woke with a start. Biancabella was in danger. Her sister needed her. She uncoiled herself from the enlaced pile of her elders, who all slept soundly. Perhaps she only had a nightmare. On occasion, she dreamt of her sister in need of rescue and not reaching her in time. A worry which plagued her during their winter months of separation. In the gloom of the den, she worked to focus her energy for guidance, yet as the minutes passed her disquiet for Biancabella did not abate. After a brief contemplation, she decided to check on her sister. If she discovered any threat, she would return to tell Ulani and the others.

At the opening of the cavern, icy air filtered down from the garden. She pushed her way up from under the sandalwood tree and glided across the snow. The grounds were a lush white blanket, twinkling in the pale moonlight. Her underside turned frigid against it, but she admired the beauty, nonetheless. When she reached the castle, the stone floor's touch felt no warmer, and she longed for the den and its comfort. But Biancabella's safety mattered more than her coldness.

She traversed the inner recesses of the walls toward the hum of voices which led her to the dining hall. A grand party unfolded before her, diners and dancers reveling in a festive atmosphere. Through this gap in the wall, she saw feet underneath tables but little else so she searched for a better vantage point. Another crevice further down the wall brought her a view of the marquis and his family on a dais at the head of the room. Biancabella sat at the table, a wide smile on her face, and relief flooded Samaritana. Her sister remained safe and well.

Warm now, she decided to stay a bit longer, the mere sight of her sister a pleasure to watch. Contentment filled her until a young man sitting next to Biancabella touched her arm and was rewarded with a smile Samaritana believed only belonged to her—one filled with love. *Who was this strange man?*

She did not wonder long because the marquis rose to address the guests. To Samaritana's astonishment, he announced the betrothal of the man to Biancabella. The ground spun underneath her, the dizzying sensation of total shock. All the conversations about her sister never taking a husband played in Samaritana's mind. *How could this be? This man had usurped her place in only a matter of months?* What she did know was he brought danger with him and she intended to warn her sister as soon as possible.

A loud commotion in the room brought her back to reality. One of the other suitors, angered by the pronouncement, stormed out of the dining hall. Biancabella appeared upset, but the marchioness commanded the musicians to play and in no time, her sister danced with the man, smiling at him as if he were the only creature on the face of the earth. Tears filled Samaritana's eyes, and she took a deep breath to calm herself before heading back to the den. The elders would know how to help.

She returned to find them awake and waiting after they sensed her disappearance. The frigid journey back did nothing to squelch the burning rage inside her. After all these years, all their promises, she had remained true to Biancabella only to have her sister toss aside all there was between them. The others stayed quiet, forming a circle around her while she gathered the composure to speak. An icy draft blew down from above and the others huddled closer, but Samaritana did not notice.

"I woke because I perceived Biancabella was in danger. I went to the castle to find her worried for the worst. But instead, she was happy and well," Samaritana cried, "and she is to be married to some strange man I never saw before and he will take her to Naples."

"Married?" Elke repeated in surprise. "I thought she wished to remain here with you."

"As did I," Samaritana ranted. "How am I to protect her there? Why should I when she betrays me like this!"

"Did she betray you?" Ulani countered.

"Of course, she did," Oda answered. "She was to stay with Samaritana, who has done so much for her. And now she's forgotten her promises and put herself in danger. I say we let Samaritana bite him in his sleep tonight so he never wakes. That will solve the problem."

"But Biancabella must love him, she would be heartbroken," Adriel interjected. "How could Samaritana cause her sister such pain?"

"That is enough from all of you," Ulani rebuked. "Samaritana and I will speak alone."

The others slunk back to the slumbering pit to form a cluster of enlaced scales. Their glows faded, and though they said no more, Samaritana was certain they listened. In the dim light cast by her and Ulani, she waited to hear what the leader would say. Instead, Ulani stayed silent, her eyes fixed on the young snake, who felt tears well again in her eyes.

"How could she do this to me?" she wept.

"She fell in love, an emotion quite beyond the power of any human to control," Ulani said, gently wrapping her tail around Samaritana's.

"But she promised to stay with me always. She promised we would never be separated." The distress in her voice echoed in the hollow cavern.

"Then you must go with her," the elder stated, her tone calm despite the other's obvious misery.

Samaritana bristled at this thought. "I have been with her, helped her hone her gifts, vowed my lifelong love to her and she chooses another? I will not go and be second choice in her eyes. I will remind her that she must obey me or fate will turn against her."

"It is true the stars foretold you must be together, yet not necessarily here," Ulani reminded. "Be careful you don't confuse protecting with imprisoning."

The truth of the words stung but not as much as seeing her sister with that man. The idea that Biancabella had so much room in her heart for another wounded Samaritana to the core. Never once in all their time together had she questioned her sister's love for her, but now, she felt discarded, cast aside for a better option. She would never put someone above Biancabella and would not accept losing even a portion of her sister's affection.

"No, I cannot take it," Samaritana sobbed. "I cannot share her with anyone."

"Even if he accepts you as part of her life?"

"But I sensed danger around him," the young snake insisted, stubbornly clinging to her resentment of the man.

"All the more reason for you to be with her, don't you think?" Ulani advised, truly moved by the snake's despair.

"No! I must go warn her. She needs to listen to reason. She needs to stay with me so all will be well."

"She needs to stay with you? Or you need to stay with her?" Ulani questioned but received no response. "There is no need to warn her. She will seek you out. That conversation has also been foretold. For now, be patient and reflect on what is truly important in your heart. You will know what to do when the time comes."

"How?" Samaritana demanded, unable to relinquish any of the anger coursing through her.

"This is your duty, your life's undertaking, Samaritana. Only you can decide what path to take."

With these words, Ulani slid back onto the pile of serpents and shut her eyes. Her green glow diminished, leaving Samaritana in the darkness.

CHAPTER SEVENTEEN

The next several weeks were dedicated to wedding preparations. Every citizen looked to contribute. Farmers brought their fattest cattle and pigs to be slaughtered, vineyards sent their best barrels of wine, aged for a special occasion such as this. Dress shops overflowed with customers seeking the perfect outfit. People bustled about the winter streets, blowing on their cold hands, but always with a smile for Biancabella, so beloved by all, who was finally being united in marriage.

In the castle, the bride-to-be was pulled in all directions, the chefs, florists, and musicians all with a myriad of choices for her. Adeleta spent countless hours with her daughter to choose the detail of every dish, table arrangement, and song. And of course, there was the dress. A famous stylist summoned from Venice created the masterpiece. Biancabella stood on a stool for days, a human pincushion, multiple seamstresses toiling to attach gemstones and seed pearls to all manner of silk, satin, and tulle.

A week out, ambassadors and envoys arrived from far and wide, all bearing gifts for the couple. The city burst at the seams, every available building utilized for guests. A large flow of pilgrims also made the journey, hoping for a special nuptial blessing from the bride. With no room left inside the city walls, they camped in the open fields outside the gate, a situation that distressed Biancabella given the cold weather until her father assured her they would be quite fine. If she had her way, she and Ferrandino would marry quietly, without such fuss, but her father made it clear that was not an option.

"Important people must have important weddings," he proclaimed. "You are marrying a king after all."

Yes, he was the king of a prominent territory, but to Biancabella, Jaco was simply the man she loved, the man she wanted to spend her life with. The more time they spent together, the drunker they became on each other's presence. She had read about love, but never gave any credence to its blissful description, until now. Jaco made her feel as though she walked on air, his very presence an intoxicant.

"The delegation from Naples arrives tomorrow," he said one evening. They sat next to a roaring fire enjoying some private time at the end of another busy day.

"I hope the journey was not too stressful," she replied, the winter wind whipping against the palace walls. "It is a difficult time of year to travel."

"You will not have to deal with such weather in Naples." He pulled her closer to his body on the settee they shared. Tessina, who sat in a chair across the room, looked up from her needlework but decided all was proper.

"I'm sure I will love it there. I only hope the people will love me." She leaned into him with a shiver from both cold and doubt. She had never been away from home and the veneration of the citizens of the march.

"They will adore you, Biancabella. Of that, I am sure. How could they not? Your beauty and spirit will win them over immediately." He stroked her back with his hand, and she felt comforted. "I must warn you though, my stepmother can come across as quite stern, do not let her manner offend you."

"She must still be grieving the loss of your father," Biancabella said, heart filled with sympathy for the recent widow. She could not imagine the depth to which she would mourn the loss of Jaco.

"She was always a cold woman, not one for affectionate gestures," he explained. "Even to her own daughters she seems more domineering than motherly. Still, she helped my father overcome his great bereavement of my late mother. Both he and the kingdom languished until her arrival, and he truly cared for her, so I must do my best to take care of her going forward."

"I will do my best to make her happy just as I will do my best to help you rule," she promised, even more love for him welling in her heart.

"Indeed, you are learned in the ways of politics, and you have a natural affinity for people. Together we will see the glory of Naples rise."

A log split on the fire sending a sudden hailstorm of sparks through the grate. Biancabella stole closer to Jaco, holding his hands. From her seat in the corner, Tessina could not help but smile at the pair, heads resting against each other's. *Such sweet naïveté they both possess*, she thought, *I hope fate is kind to them.*

After breakfast the next morning, the Neapolitan group wound their way up the hill to the castle gates. Marquis Lamberico greeted them at the king's side with the marchioness and Biancabella standing nearby. With Ferrandino leading the way, three women peeled apart from the others and walked over to where his future bride and Adeleta awaited.

"Ladies, may I present to you my stepmother, Dowager Finola, and her daughters, Lady Lisabetta and Lady Renata. This is Marchioness Lamberico and my betrothed, Lady Biancabella."

The dowager, a tall woman, looked down a long nose at her hosts. Still dressed in mourning black, she resembled a wrought iron post, her tight salt and pepper bun like the decorative finial at its top. Lisabetta, the elder daughter, had rich ebony hair which complemented her smooth olive skin. She wore the same disinterested expression as her mother. Renata appeared small and mousy next to them both. Her fair complexion and dirty blond hair paled against the beauty of her sister and she held an air of jumpiness one sees in an unbroken colt.

Formal greetings were exchanged with the marchioness, who welcomed them warmly. The ladies presented the marchioness with an exquisite cameo pendant crafted from special shells found in the Bay of Naples. Biancabella had never seen such a unique piece of jewelry. Adeleta thanked them before gesturing for her daughter to step forward.

"It is my pleasure to meet you." Biancabella smiled kindly at each of them. "I look forward to making your further acquaintance after you have had a chance to rest and refresh."

The dowager merely looked at Biancabella and nodded. With bows of their heads, she and her daughters hurried off in the wake of the page who escorted them to their rooms. She watched them walk away, dismayed by their complete lack of manners. Her mother stroked her shoulder on the way back inside and told her not to worry, but a sense of uneasiness filled her. Though no word was spoken, Biancabella noticed a gleam in Dowager Finola's eyes, one she had seen before in King Bashir's gaze—the glint of greed.

CHAPTER EIGHTEEN

Two days later, the wedding took place, a spectacle talked about for years to come as the marquis had spared no expense. After the ceremony, the bride, encased in a white cloud of fabric and jewels, danced with her husband, broad smiles on their faces. Food and wine flowed freely from the castle down to the streets, where even the smallest children romped with excitement. Marquis Lamberico and his wife heaped praise on the young king, now their son-in-law, a circumstance that elevated both the cities and their leaders in status.

At the end of the evening, Biancabella stood alone for a moment, Ferrandino entertaining a few diplomats at a nearby table. Dowager Finola and her daughters made their way over to the new bride. They had not spoken to her at all over the course of their visit so far, a circumstance that made Biancabella more uncomfortable by the moment.

"Congratulations, Biancabella, we are delighted to welcome you to the family," the dowager said. The kind words did not match the cool tone in which they were spoken.

"Thank you," Biancabella replied and embraced the woman, the contrast of her white dress stark against the dowager's stiff black wool. Even at this festive occasion, Finola chose her mourning clothes.

Next, the daughters hugged Biancabella. Where their mother's outfit was somber, Lisabetta's was brightly colored with ostentatious jewels around her wrists, a feathered headband crowned her ebony tresses. Her beauty attracted much attention at the event. Renata wore a dress of bright blue, but with far less showy trimmings than her elder sister. She appeared happy to draw as little notice to herself as possible, her eyes darting around like a scared fawn.

"We look forward to you joining us in Naples," Lisabetta declared. Renata nodded in agreement. "You must be looking forward to having sisters, especially as you have been an only child all these years."

As the trio departed, Biancabella stood frozen, the word *sister* sent a pang of grief to her heart. Her infatuation with Ferrandino these last months, led her to neglect Samaritana. How could she have been so selfish? She meant to go see her many times but did not find a chance in the end. She must speak with her immediately to explain her absence and ask her sister to join her in Naples. Overcome with regret, she excused herself from the room on the pretense of preparing for the wedding night.

While Tessina went ahead to ready the room, Biancabella ducked out a doorway, the cold air punishing on her lightly covered skin. The long train of fabric at her feet grew soggy, dragging a path in the snow behind her. The garden gate loomed ahead. Fear pitted in her stomach, perhaps her sister bewitched the door against her. A surge of relief washed over her when the entry opened at her touch, though the comfort was short-lived at the thought of facing her sister.

"Samaritana?" she called.

Silence filled the garden, more forlorn than usual on this dark winter's night. Biancabella walked to the fountain. Frost coated the entwined snakes, a deep V of snow between the two heads, seemingly pushing them apart.

"Please come out, Samaritana. I know I have been remiss and I am so sorry if my absence has hurt you." Tears streamed down her cheeks in icy tracks. "I have news to share with you."

Still there was silence. Biancabella rose to search for the snake, but found no sign of her, not even a hint of a trail in the snow. Green grass grew under the sandalwood tree, but there was no sign of a snake. Panic rose in her as she remembered all the times she promised her sister they would never be parted. If she could not find her, how could she tell her that she was leaving for Naples?

"Sister, I am so sorry to spring this on you so suddenly. I am married to a wonderful man and set to leave Monferrato." Silence hung in the air. "I know this must come as a shock. I did not mean to fall in love, but it happened. If you met Jaco, you would understand. Please be happy for me. Come with me to Naples so we can be together."

More silence.

"Please, Samaritana, you are my sister and I love you dearly, but I love him too."

From a small crack in the fountain, Samaritana appeared. Biancabella gasped and scooped up her sister, overjoyed to see her. But the snake, coiled around her arm and sternly said, "Do you remember your promise to me? To love me above all others?"

"Yes. But that was before I knew Jaco." Surely, her sister realized you could love two people at once.

"He is dangerous, Biancabella, I can sense it," the snake warned.

"Dangerous? Jaco is the furthest thing from dangerous. He loves me and I love him, I will not live without him," she insisted.

For the first time, she felt frustration with her sister's inability to understand.

"I sense the danger in him. It is your gifts he is after, your gifts that his greedy heart loves," Samaritana hissed.

"You are wrong about him. He is good and kind and he loves me truly. I must go with him to his home," the girl maintained, crossing her arms across her chest.

"Do you remember the rest of what was foretold? That all will be well if we stay together, but fate will turn on us if you leave me?"

"But if you come to Naples, we will be together," Biancabella insisted, exasperated her sister refused to listen to reason, to give her husband a chance.

"And you will tell this Jaco all about me? About us?" The snake wound higher to look the girl in the eyes.

Now Biancabella was silent.

"So, you would have me come with you but continue to deny my existence to all?" Samaritana snapped. "We are one, you and me. You need to understand that as does he."

"It's not that simple," Biancabella defended, not wanting to tell her Jaco's original reaction. "My gifts are one thing, but he needs more time to accept that my twin is a snake. When our marriage is strengthened, I can tell him, we can tell him."

"Biancabella, don't you see? If you leave me and break our bond, we will both suffer. I do not say this to be punitive, Sister, it is written in our destinies."

"You have not seen the love between me and Jaco. There is no way something that perfect could lead to suffering. Please, come with me. I beg you. In time, I will be ready to tell him about you. When we can both transform from maiden to snake, he will see what we say is true."

"You cannot leave me, Biancabella, it will be your undoing."

Angry at her sister's unyielding stance, the girl snapped, "You are just jealous that I love someone other than you. You don't want to see me happy so you refuse to come with me. The fault lies with you."

She regretted the words as soon as they left her mouth. Samaritana uncoiled from her sister's arm and slithered down onto the fountain ledge.

Long moments passed, Biancabella stood frozen to the bone before she finally realized there was no hope of convincing her sister to join her. With leaden legs, she returned to the gate. At the threshold, she turned. "I love you and will miss you, Sister, always."

With a choked sob, she shut the gate behind her and staggered back to the castle.

Samaritana curled around herself. Biancabella did not understand how her choice would cause them both to suffer by breaking their bond. She knew her sister was too blinded by love to listen, could not perceive the truth of her words. They would both pay for her sister's choice and Samaritana's heart shattered at the thought.

CHAPTER NINETEEN

Tessina was beside herself when the bride showed up to the room bedraggled and half frozen. She could extract no explanation for her state, so the maid set about drawing a hot bath and rubbed perfumed oils into the girl's hair and skin. Biancabella mourned the loss of her sister, but revived by the warm bath, she remembered what the night held for her and her new husband. When the maid helped her change into an exquisite nightgown, color and a smile had returned to the girl's face. Tessina wrote off the incident as a bout of nerves about the wedding night. By the time Ferrandino arrived, Biancabella was so caught up in nervous excitement, all thoughts of Samaritana were displaced.

In the morning, she woke euphoric with the satisfaction of being a true woman and enthusiasm of being a wife to her beloved Jaco. After a celebratory breakfast with the court, the newlyweds and their entourage prepared to leave on the long journey to Naples. The goodbyes were bittersweet. Her parents cried with her and promised to see her soon. Piero, now a handsome, though scholarly young man, hugged her. "I will miss you, Cousin. Don't worry. I will look after your parents in your absence."

"Thank you," she replied, grateful he would be with them. "I will miss you too and all the mischief of our youth."

At length, the caravan was ready to depart. Biancabella settled into her carriage, its plush cushioned seats designed to protect her from all bumps and jolts. Tessina joined her after a tearful farewell with Adeleta. There was no one the marchioness trusted more with her daughter, so she insisted the maid go to Naples with her. The carriage lurched forward following the king, who rode in front on his horse, the walls of the castle drifting further away. Biancabella gave one wistful look back.

"It's hard to say goodbye," Tessina stated, stroking the girl's hand.

"Yes," Biancabella agreed, especially when the most important parting had gone so badly. She knew a Samaritana-sized hole would forever be in her heart.

～⌇⌇～

The journey took a little over a week, the weather milder with each passing mile. Warming temperature and the loving glances from her husband created a balm for the sting of leaving Samaritana. The caravan stopped at many palaces and estates along the way, powerful people happy to host the rising young couple, who were well received at every stop. By the time they were a day from home, a fervor grew throughout the city, the citizens anxious to welcome their king and new queen.

Biancabella was awed by her first sight of Naples, a splendid treasure on an azure bay. Such color it boasted—the jewel-box painted houses a rainbow tumbling to the shore, the swarthy inhabitants with tanned skin and ebony hair, the ornate cathedral, its white façade gleaming in the sun, the stunning domed palace, its piazza a jumble of vibrant vendor stalls, and all of this magnificence at the feet of Vesuvius, its cratered pinnacle more daunting than the snow-capped Alps. Captivated at once, Biancabella reveled in the city's beauty and the enthusiastic welcome of its people, her people now. Ferrandino watched his wife's eyes dart from one place to another, delighted to see her so happy.

A large contingent awaited the party at the palace entrance. Ferrandino stepped down to embrace a few before he called his wife over for introductions. With so many new faces in the household, Biancabella knew it would take time to learn all the names but was touched by how friendly and caring their greetings were. Her husband insisted on escorting her to her new chambers himself.

"I hope you find them befitting of your status, my queen," Ferrandino said as they stepped inside.

Biancabella gasped at the grand room, bright and airy with doors open to a balcony on the far wall. The first room held a large desk, carved of mahogany and inlaid with marble. A large table stood parallel to the balcony, six tufted chairs around it. Vivid murals covered the ceiling, filled with foliage and angels. Fresh flowers stood in vases on every surface, all unfamiliar and exotic. She wandered into the sleeping chamber where a glorious, canopied bed anchored the room, its mattress overflowing with pillows of velvet and silk. An elegant marble vanity sat in the corner near a large closet. Against the back wall a door led to the king's chambers next door. A well-appointed bathroom and a simple but tasteful room for Tessina completed the space.

Returning to the main room, a sound caught her ear, a soothing rumble. She ran onto the balcony where the grand gulf spread out below, the tide ebbing and flowing on the sand. Tiny sails of white bobbed on the pristine surface with gulls swooping down around them. Warm air tinged with a scent of salt filled her lungs. Ferrandino joined her, their arms touching as they rested on the railing.

"The rooms and this view . . . they are more beautiful than I could ever imagine," she said.

"All eclipsed by your beauty, I assure you." He brought her palm to his lips where they lingered a moment. "Now, settle in. I have some business to attend to. We will dine together at the feast."

He took his leave at the same time Tessina came in from her adjoining room, her head still turning in every direction to take it all in.

"Lovely, isn't it?" the maid remarked.

"To say the very least," Biancabella replied, and they laughed at the idea these remarkable rooms belonged them.

"You are lucky in your match, my lady. That is for sure. Now, let's get you ready for your first official dinner as queen. I want you to outshine all others in the room," she vowed.

Tessina made good on her promise. Biancabella mesmerized all the guests in a dress of raw silk threaded with gold. Her fair hair and complexion, a stark but stunning complement to darker characteristics of the Neapolitans. After the meal, a dizzying procession of nobles, ambassadors, and military leaders presented themselves to the young queen, all consistent in their wishes of good will. Biancabella charmed them with her kindness and genuineness. Smiles graced all corners of the room apart from one, which Dowager Finola occupied with her daughters. The mother whispered behind her hands with Lisabetta while an ignored Renata looked uncomfortable, their black attire like an ink splotch on the colorful painting of the ballroom. Cold gazes from the two gossipers never left an unknowing Biancabella. Tessina alone took note from her place among the servants.

The maid had her own set of people to meet in the large palace staff with whom she would now work. They were friendly and accepting, some taking extra pains to make her feel welcome. She stood with Aurelia, a girl assigned to assist her with the queen. Her young eyes glowed with excitement while she pointed out different guests to the newcomer, adding bits of information about each. Tessina listened carefully to the girl's loose tongue, eager to learn anything useful for the sake of the queen.

"Such a wonderful night," Aurelia exclaimed, finally pausing for a breath.

"The dowager and her daughters do not seem to be enjoying themselves," Tessina commented, annoyed at how they glared at Biancabella.

The girl's face grew dark, and she leaned closer to speak softly, "No, they rarely enjoy anything. Like a flock of ravens, they are."

"But, they are in mourning for her husband, I suppose that could account for it," the maid replied, with little compassion in her tone.

"I suppose. Except . . ." Aurelia stopped, but at a pointed stare from Tessina she continued in a whisper, "except, there are rumors that the dowager poisoned the late king."

"Who says that?" Tessina uttered dumbfounded.

"The doctor's assistant is married to another servant girl who I am friends with. He expressed his concern it was poison when the body was examined, but the doctor would hear nothing of it, and what could he do about it being just an assistant with no proof?"

"Does King Ferrandino know of this?" Tessina asked, wondering how the topic never came up while he was in Monferrato.

"I don't know, to be honest. Please don't tell your mistress. It could cost me my job," Aurelia cried, worried she had shared too much.

Tessina nodded in consent, but her blood ran cold. She looked again at the dowager and her eldest daughter, their frosty stares fixed on Biancabella who danced gaily with her husband to the delight of the crowd. If her mistress had walked into a viper pit, Tessina must be ready to guard her back.

CHAPTER TWENTY

The first few months in Naples were a sheer joy for Biancabella. King Ferrandino showed off his new bride on tours of the city where he described to her its rich history and explained his plans to modernize certain aspects. Everywhere they went, citizens threw flowers in their path. The new queen, overcome with gratitude, sent out a shower of petals from her palms, eliciting a frenzied response from the crowd.

Her husband had asked for no dowry, the jewels from her hair payment enough. Though in truth, he loved her so much, he would have married her for nothing. Even so, each gem she produced was recorded and taken to the treasury which now burst at the seams. Merchants and traders received loans to improve business and drive more commerce into the city, with profits floating down to even the lowliest servants which further elevated the city's love for its queen.

Nobles sent gifts of every kind to Biancabella, the finest dresses, the most delectable sweets, beautiful paintings, even a peacock to adorn her garden. She made time every week to bless the pilgrims who now trekked far to the south to receive her blessings. Her days busy with learning her new kingdom and her evenings filled with her loving husband left her little time to miss the life she left behind in Monferrato. Yet, on some nights, when sleep did not come quickly, her heart ached for Samaritana. While she stroked the gold markings on her neck she wondered, if perhaps she had been more insistent that Jaco listen to her story, her sister would be here now. But it was too late. Her sister had stayed behind and Biancabella must move forward in life without her.

Unlike the rest of the Neapolitans who were besotted with their new queen, Ferrandino's stepfamily remained cold toward her, despite every effort on her part to win them over. Dowager Finola and her Lisabetta loomed like sinister shadows in her sunny life. Renata, who seemed less hostile, drew icy glares from the others at any kind comment. After the first few weeks, the girl ceased attempting to befriend them, and instead, settled for a forced cordiality among them when they had to be together.

"Truly, Jaco, I have tried everything I can think of, but they are still so unfriendly," she complained one day after the three women scurried from a sitting room at the sight of the royal couple's entrance.

"I will speak to them," Ferrandino stated, leading Biancabella to sit on a tufted couch. "They need to accept you as both queen and family."

Biancabella sighed and leaned into him, her compassion overcoming her annoyance as it usually did. "It must be hard for them. Finola lost her husband, and the girls must have looked up to him as a father figure. Their grief is still new. I should be more patient with them. If you ever died, I would grieve forever."

"Oh, my beautiful and thoughtful wife, you are too kind for your own good," the king exclaimed, wiping a tear from her cheek, "but that is why I love you so much and I am sure they will love you the same in time."

Later that day, King Ferrandino visited his stepmother in her chambers. He had been a small boy when his mother had passed from a summer fever. A few years after, Finola had won his father's heart but never his. Though she fawned over him in the king's presence, he never warmed to her. Lisabetta and Renata, near to his age, did not become the playmates he hoped for and kept mostly to themselves under the watchful eye of their mother. When his father died, Finola mourned, flagrantly so, though how authentically, Ferrandino could not tell. She promised to be the person he could come to for any parental advice now that he was bereft of his own and in truth, prior to his trip to Monferrato, she had been a sound counselor to him.

"To what do I owe this honor?" Finola crooned when he entered. After a slight curtsey, she offered him a seat. The room, though well-furnished, held the inhospitable air Ferrandino always encountered with this woman.

"I just wanted to see how you and my sisters are doing," he replied, trying to adopt a regal stance in his chair. For some reason, the dowager had always intimidated him especially since she took to wearing black all the time.

"We are well, my son, thank you for your concern. It is kind of you to visit me. Your schedule must be busy now with a new wife to amuse you." Though her lips pursed into a tight smile, her eyes were as sharp as a hawk circling prey.

"That is another reason I have come," he acknowledged. "Biancabella is family now and I hope to see a relationship develop between you, one which befits her status as queen."

"Have I or one of my daughters offended Her Highness? If so, I assure you it was unintentional." She spread her hands wide in innocence, the cloying scent of her perfume wafting with the movement.

"No, there was no offense," he said, his shirt felt uncomfortably tight at his neck, and he tugged at it, second-guessing his decision to come. "I would merely like to see more familial interaction between you. She very much wants to be close with you."

"But of course, my son, I will speak to the girls about how we can make Biancabella feel more welcome here. After all, she is our queen."

"Thank you, Stepmother." Though the words were what he wanted to hear, he could not wait to be out of the room and away from her penetrating stare. He rose to leave.

"Anything for you, my king," she responded, walking him to the door.

At the threshold, Ferrandino smiled at her and she smiled back until the door closed and a dark scowl filled her face.

Good to her word, the dowager saw to the three women befriending Biancabella; dining nightly with the royal couple, introducing her to courtiers, teaching her the popular parlor games of the city. The young queen, pleased by their efforts, made every attempt to be as warm and engaging as possible. While Lisabetta's manners always seemed a bit contrived, Renata had a warm smile for her every day. Never had Biancabella had any female friends her age, only Samaritana, who promised to love and protect her only to abandon her. Biancabella thought of the snake's warnings of an evil fate and shook her head. Things could not be any better for her in Naples. With the acceptance of her new family, she felt happier than ever. If only Samaritana were here, all would be perfect.

One afternoon, after a round of card games, the courtiers cleared the parlor to prepare for dinner. After everyone else left,

Lisabetta and Renata huddled in one corner giggling with each other. Biancabella walked over and they made space for her to join them.

"Did you see how he looked at me?" Lisabetta exclaimed, her face flushed.

"He could barely keep his eyes from you," Renata squealed, evoking another fit of laughter.

"Who?" Biancabella asked, caught up in their excitement.

"Viscount Tedesco," the older sister gushed, the rings on her fingers tinkling as she clasped her hands together.

Biancabella pictured the striking young man with his bright smile and quick wit. He was most popular with the ladies of the court. "Oh, he is very handsome. You think he is interested in you?"

"Of course," the younger sister chimed in, with animation unusual for her timid character. "He is entirely smitten with her."

The young queen smiled, happy to be included in their camaraderie. Lisabetta wrapped one a long black curl around her finger, her captivating green eyes aglow with delight. She outshone the mousy Renata, and all the other ladies at court. It came as no surprise she caught the attention of Tedesco.

"What a lovely couple you would make," Biancabella declared, and the girls shared an exhilarated sigh.

"A lovely couple?" boomed a harsh voice. The dowager swooped down on the group, her black dress as menacing as her tone. "Certainly, *my* daughter can marry better than a viscount. A duke preferably, but if not, a marquis at the very least."

The smiles faded from the girls' faces, the ecstatic mood deflated. Renata looked down to smooth her skirt, not wishing to meet her mother's eyes. Lisabetta turned her head to try and fight back tears.

Angered, Biancabella snapped, "The viscount is a handsome and kind man. He would make your daughter happy, which is all that should matter."

Dowager Finola stared icily down at her. "I must use marriage to elevate the status of my daughters. We are not all so fortunate to have jewels fall from our hair to attract a king. Come, girls."

They leapt at the order and followed her out of the room. Renata looked back sadly at a shaken Biancabella.

"Can you believe she said that to me?" Biancabella cried while recounting the incident to Tessina.

"Actually, yes I can," the maid said, braiding the girl's golden hair for bed. "There is something I should tell you."

After learning the rumor of the former king's poisoning from Aurelia, Tessina spent the last few weeks gleaning information from the household staff and some of the merchants she saw regularly at the market. Though no one spoke of it in anything but whispers, the notion expressed by Aurelia, that Finola may have poisoned the late king, turned out to be a common opinion among all. The maid grappled with whether to share this knowledge with the new queen, but so far, seeing Biancabella's blissful state, she had not had the heart to upset her.

"So, tell me," the queen insisted when the maid hesitated.

"There is a rumor, a rumor mind you, with no proof whatsoever, that Dowager Finola poisoned the late king."

"What? Who would say such a terrible thing?" Biancabella jumped from her chair.

Tessina took her by the shoulders. "Many on the palace staff, and even merchants in the marketplace."

"But why would she kill her husband? And how did she get away with it?"

The maid led the shaken girl to the bed and lowered her on the edge. Kneeling in front of her, Tessina took the queen's hands and looked her directly in the eye. "I don't know how she got away with it but I do know a reason why. Before we got here, she wanted Lisabetta to marry Jaco. She wanted her daughter to be queen. That was her plan—until you came along. Be very careful, Biancabella, the dowager and her daughters are not to be trusted."

CHAPTER TWENTY-ONE

The shocking news of the dowager's rumored deed did little to dampen Biancabella's spirit, still enjoying the euphoria only young love can produce. She was happy here, happier than she had ever been. Besides, King Ferrandino never mentioned an ill word against his stepmother, which the girl took as proof enough that the information was merely malicious gossip. Finola's dour attitude toward the world left her open to such talk. Biancabella forged ahead with befriending her new family. The stepsisters warmed to her, Renata more so. The fair-haired girl lurked forever in the shadow of the raven tressed Lisabetta. While her elder sister enchanted the male courtiers, Renata hung back, giving Biancabella more of a chance to bond with her in a genuine manner. Finola's attentions, though pleasant, seemed forced, which the girl dismissed as part of her grieving process.

Tessina watched from the sidelines, sizing up the dowager and all her movements. Still concerned about the validity of the rumor, she encouraged Biancabella to speak to her husband about it. The girl agreed, more to put the maid's mind at ease than from any actual worry.

The new queen broached the subject one morning as they breakfasted in the garden where birds sang in the warm sunlight. "You never told me how your father died."

"He died in his sleep. One night, he went to bed and never woke up."

"That must have been so difficult for you," she consoled, placing her fork down to take his hand. A few violet petals fell from her palm.

"Yes, it came as quite a shock. He appeared to be so healthy. That very morning, we hunted, and he chased a boar with great vigor. We dined that evening and all seemed fine," the king replied, a wistful look on his face.

"Did the royal physician tell you what happened?" She inched toward her point slowly but surely.

"He said it was a failure of the heart. Though rare, it can happen to a seemingly healthy man without warning." Ferrandino's answer, though mournful, held no trace of doubt.

A servant refilled their glasses with juice and Biancabella waited for him to return to the kitchen before softly asking, "Did anyone suspect foul play?"

"If they did, I never heard of it. The doctor was certain the death was from natural causes. Sometimes I wonder if the boar hunt was too much for him. I mean, he was not a young man after all," he replied with a sorrowful sigh. "Now, let us leave this sad subject behind and speak of more cheerful topics."

Convinced her maid was misinformed, Biancabella gladly spoke of the happy times which lay ahead for her and the king.

∽ᘜᘑᖰ

Spring turned to summer and Biancabella experienced heat and humidity as she never had in the north. She tried many tricks to counteract the heat each day yet still felt drained by evening. By

Midsummer's Day, exhaustion overtook her. Besides constant tiredness, her stomach acted up only adding to her discomfort.

"Perhaps I have a summer fever," she ventured one day to Tessina, too tired to rise from her bed despite the mid-morning sun pouring into the room.

"Try to sit up," the maid encouraged.

Biancabella rose her head off the pillow and sat on the bed's edge, her nightgown stuck to her sweaty skin. She brushed her unkempt hair out of her eyes and tried to force nausea away, to no avail. Once more, she grabbed the small pot at the side of her bed and heaved.

"I don't think it's a summer fever," Tessina stated. She sat next to the girl to stroke her back. "When were your last monthly courses?"

"I'm not sure. Let me think," the young queen mumbled, clutching the pot closer. She searched her disorganized mind, the queasiness made it hard to focus. "Was it when they dedicated the new altar at the cathedral? Yes, I remember starting them that morning."

Tessina set down the pot and took Biancabella's hands firmly in her own. "That was two months ago and now you are sick in the morning? That can only mean one thing."

The maid waited for the realization to dawn on the girl. It took a moment for the pieces to fall into place, but when they did, a broad smile filled her face. Her hands flew to her stomach.

"I must tell Jaco at once!"

She threw on a robe and dashed through the connecting doorway into the king's chambers. He sat at his desk reading over the morning's correspondence. Her sudden entrance startled him, his elbow knocking a teacup onto the floor. A servant quickly went to work cleaning it up.

"Biancabella, my love, is everything all right?" he asked, concerned at the state of his wife.

"Yes, more than all right, dear husband. I think I am with child."

After a pause of stunned disbelief, Ferrandino sprang to his feet. He scooped her into a giant hug.

"You there," he shouted to the servant, still on her hands and knees wiping tea, "go fetch the royal physician."

Upon examination in the privacy of her chambers, the physician summoned the king to join them.

"She is with child, Your Highness," he proclaimed, his short, white beard framing his lips. "She will deliver at the beginning of the year."

The young couple was delirious with happiness, a sentiment that spread throughout the kingdom. Though still suffering from morning sickness for the next month, Biancabella delighted at the idea of the baby growing inside her. Ferrandino left the planning of the nursery for her. The stepsisters, caught up in the excitement, assisted her. Even Dowager Finola shared a congratulatory remark to the couple yet stayed clear of any baby planning.

"A baby due at the start of the year, what a wonderful time as light returns to the world," Renata gushed.

The three girls sat in the shade of a tree in the garden, though it did little to counter the oppressive grip of the sun, even the breeze off the bay was heavy. An unusually hot summer plagued the citizens with drought. Food spoiled quickly; the ice storages unable to accommodate the sheer quantity. Thoughts of this new baby was one of the few things that buoyed the Neapolitans spirits.

"And so much easier than laboring in weather like this," Lisabetta groaned. "Our poor mother had us each in August, two years apart. She thought the humidity alone would kill her during birth."

"I was born in a driving snowstorm," Biancabella said, her fan only distributing hot air around her face, "like this little one may be. And I agree, any weather would be better than this."

"We will all be blessed when the child arrives," Renata insisted. "It is absolutely a good omen. Just what the city needs to get us through these long days."

The day stretched on in the blazing heat. From her balcony that evening, Biancabella watched the haze of heat ripple just above the azure water as the late sun set. Night brought little relief; even with all the doors open to the outside, her chamber still felt like an oven. She tossed and turned in a fitful sleep. She dreamed of giving birth, but instead of a baby, a giant snake emerged from her womb. It wrapped its long body around Ferrandino squeezing him to death while she watched helplessly. She woke with a racing heart, her breath coming in short pants.

Haunting the recesses of her mind was the story of her own birth, one Jaco thought merely a figment of her imagination. Her hand stroked the golden lines around her neck, the place her sister occupied in the womb. Her husband was convinced it was merely a mark of her gifts, not the true cause. What would happen if she delivered a snake with her child as well? She shuddered at the thought. So preoccupied with the baby, she had not thought of Samaritana in a long time. Sometimes, she wondered if she only imagined the snake. But the hole in her heart told her otherwise. She loved and missed her sister greatly, and wished more than anything to speak to her again. Stroking her stomach, she thought of Renata's words which calmed her. The baby was a good omen. She was sure of it.

Alarm bells woke her in the early dawn after only a few agitated hours of sleep. Groggily, she sat up and tried to gain her senses. Loud voices rang out from the Ferrandino's chambers. She ran in, not even bothering to grab a robe, worried he was ill. Relief flooded her when she saw him up, well, and fully dressed. Men scurried in and out following the orders of the master-at-arms who stood by the king's side.

"Jaco, what is it? What's wrong?"

He turned to face her; concern lined every inch of his face. "It's King Bashir of Tunis. His fleet sails to attack us. I must prepare the navy and leave immediately."

Ulani's words proved correct. Biancabella sought out her sister in the garden the night of her wedding. The previous two weeks had done little to quell the Samaritana's anger. In the frosty garden, she sat under the sandalwood tree each day where the grass remained forever green. She ruminated on how to make her sister listen to reason, to understand the danger Samaritana felt in connection with this man. The other snakes kept any opinions to themselves, the problem Samaritana's to solve. In the end, she concluded Biancabella needed to be reminded of their foretold destiny and how Samaritana must protect her from evils she did not perceive. That should be enough to sway her sister to stay.

Unfortunately, the evening of their encounter, Biancabella would hear none of what she had to say. Her misguided idea of being in love blinded the girl to the truth. When Samaritana reminded her sister what destiny foretold, she asked the snake to accompany her to Naples so they could remain together. The idea rankled Samaritana and then Biancabella revealed yet another betrayal. They must wait until this King Ferrandino was ready before they told him about their bond. Her twin sister would deny her existence to this greedy man, who only wanted to exploit her gifts. Fury filled her as her tearful sister left. Even knowing fate would turn on them, Biancabella still chose this man over her.

Liquid hot rage surged through every inch of her. She barreled into the den prepared to tell the elders the injustice perpetrated against her. They would counsel her now that Biancabella refused to see wisdom. Her anger quickly turned to panic at a what she discovered—the den was empty. The elders were gone. She searched the full lair and the entire garden, but they were nowhere to be found. Distressed even further, she returned to the cavern and coiled around herself in despair. In one night, she lost everyone she had ever loved.

Ulani's words rang in her head, *"This is your task, only you can decide."*

A realization hit her full force. The elders had finished training her; the choice on how to proceed lay in her hands. All night she lay awake, her feeble glow barely able to cast a shadow in the vast hibernacula. The bite of her resentment endured, yet remorse tempered her emotions. Her sister still needed her protection from whatever danger she failed to grasp in this delusional stupor she confused for love. Perhaps Samaritana had been too swift to refuse accompanying her to Naples, after all, nothing remained for her here now. Safeguarding Biancabella was her life's purpose.

When dawn's first light broke in the sky outside, she was satisfied she chose the best course of action. She would accompany the party, but stay hidden to watch over her sister, whose unflinching sense in the goodness of the world led her astray. Once the king showed himself as the treacherous person he truly was, Samaritana would leap in and save Biancabella, who would shower her with eternal affection and gratefulness. If traveling to Naples opened her sister's eyes to the truth and restored their bond, it was well worth the journey.

On the day the caravan left Monferrato, Samaritana slithered in between two wooden trunks stored on a wagon, settling into a dark, dusty corner. Her heart ached at leaving the nest, the only home she had ever know, but the space would never be the same without the elders. The days passed slowly; her hiding spot cool but dry. In the evenings, she came out to feed while the convoy of vehicles stood in a line devoid of all occupants. A few of these nights, she slithered into whatever estate hosted the royal couple. Each time, Biancabella glowed with happiness on the arm of her new husband and each time Samaritana detected danger.

Foolish girl, she thought, *she does not understand her peril.*

Ferrandino's face shone with the same affection as his wife's. Samaritana watched him carefully for any sign of his diabolical nature but saw only kindness in his actions. She concluded he must be a consummate actor while here in the public eye because the sense of danger Samaritana felt only intensified as they traveled south. This man was a threat and his true colors would be exposed in the end. He would lead Biancabella to a tragic end unless Samaritana put a stop to it—and she intended to.

When the party arrived in Naples, Samaritana scouted out the castle and its grounds. Far warmer weather produced a new array of colorful plants and unfamiliar animals which captivated her attention as she traveled far and wide off the property. After barely escaping a fox on her second exploration, she decided to say closer to the castle. Luckily, the stone edifice offered plenty of space between its ancient walls for her to navigate. An endless quantity of mice and bugs provided easy food. She nested in the wall by the corner of Biancabella's room where she could keep a close watch on her sister.

Biancabella, beautiful before, bloomed fully in Naples, her happiness evident in every expression and movement. Try as she might, Samaritana never saw any hint of evil from Ferrandino, who treated his wife as a most precious gift. The palace staff, courtiers, and citizens were besotted with the new queen, who enthralled all who met her. Only the dowager and her two daughters failed to fall under her spell at first, but soon the two young ladies made an effort to include Biancabella.

Weeks passed, and even though the sense of danger stayed with Samaritana, Biancabella confronted no discernible threat. Doubt crept into Samaritana's heart. Biancabella did not seem to miss her at all. Perhaps following her to Naples had been a bad idea. She was alone with no one to train with or even talk to. Each day, resentment built a bit more. The destiny foretold in the stars must be incorrect. Samaritana suffered from their separation, not Biancabella. The beloved queen did not need her sister to protect her.

One morning, the snake heard Tessina and Biancabella. The maid uttered words that crushed Samaritana's already fragile spirit—Biancabella was with child. A loving husband and a baby rendered Samaritana inconsequential in her sister's life. Instead of one heart to share, there would now be two. Devastated, she left the castle, where her sister celebrated the news, with no intent to return.

CHAPTER TWENTY-TWO

The day passed in disarray, both soldiers and servants hurriedly preparing for the departure of the ships. King Ferrandino spent most of his time huddled in meetings with admirals and advisors. Biancabella paced her balcony either wringing her hands or cradling her belly. All Tessina could do was watch as the girl worked herself into a panic.

"Don't worry," the king assured his wife in the moments before he left. "Victory will be swift, and I will be back before you even have a chance to miss me."

"Please, just come back to me soon," Biancabella wept, her tears wet against Jaco's neck while they embraced a final time.

Citizens crowded the pier to see the fleet off, their queen at the front. Cheers of encouragement rose as the ships pulled out into the bay. They would sail south into the open Mediterranean to meet Bashir's fleet head on. The sun dipped low, an orange orb against the horizon outlining the black silhouettes of the ships which grew smaller with each passing moment. Biancabella stood on the dock long after the crowd dispersed, her heart sinking as the sky darkened. King Bashir bragged about the fierceness of his soldiers. A man used to getting what he wanted would not give up easily, and the King of Tunis wanted Biancabella. For a long while, she stood gazing into the night, the lap of the tide and the salt-tinged breeze her only companions.

A somber mood hung over the kingdom the next day. With no appetite, Biancabella wandered the gardens all morning, her mind a jumble of thoughts. The garden reminded her of the days spent with Samaritana, whose warning of ill-fate crept into the queen's thoughts. Her maid followed behind, dress heavy with sweat, concerned by the heat which the girl took no notice of.

By mid-day, Tessina approached her. "Please, my lady, get off your feet and into the shade. Eat something too, for the sake of the baby."

Biancabella relented and sat for lunch under a veranda, which though shady, felt only mildly cooler. Lisabetta and Renata joined her, the former distressed over the departure of Viscount Tedesco with the fleet. She still harbored ideas of a match between them despite her mother's adamant forbiddance. Renata perceived the sadness of her two dining mates and tried to console them.

"I am sure the fleet will be back soon with stories of a decisive success." She smiled, but neither woman returned it. "In the meantime, we should plan a trip to the lake in the hills. It will be a cooler way to pass some time."

Biancabella pushed chicken and vegetables around her plate, very little reached her mouth. She and Ferrandino enjoyed the lake when his busy schedule allowed a visit. On their last trip up there, they soaked their feet in the shallows and discussed baby names. The thought brought tears to her eyes which fell in large drops on her uneaten food.

"Please don't cry," Renata pled. "All will be well in the end. You will see."

These words, the exact echo of Samaritana's phrase, startled Biancabella, but what came next stunned her even further.

Dowager Finola who, until this moment, sat quietly on a bench embroidering, harshly replied, "All will not be well, Renata.

The king will likely be killed in this battle and it is all Biancabella's fault."

"My fault?" the queen exclaimed, tears still flowing down her cheeks. In her whole life, no one ever blamed her for anything.

"It's your gifts Bashir wants. He never made a secret of that. Unlimited jewels from your hair could fund Tunis for decades to come and that man spends gold like water. Now we must fight against those barbarians. Your marriage to King Ferrandino put his life in this jeopardy. Naples would have been better off without you."

It was less the cruelty of the words than the matter-of-fact tone which offended Biancabella the most. She rose and spoke with an authority she never realized she had. "How dare you speak to me in such a way. Remove yourself from my presence at once and keep to your chambers until the king returns. Then you will be dealt with accordingly."

Finola stood, clutching her handiwork, and strode to the exit. At the threshold, she turned back to the queen. "I think you will find things will turn out quite differently than you imagine in the end."

With these words, she left, her daughters scurrying after her, their heads down. Renata snuck one quick look back at Biancabella's crestfallen face.

Tessina, who witnessed the scene from the edge of the veranda, ran to the queen. "Sit down. There now, breathe deeply, try to calm yourself."

"Can you believe how horrible that woman is?" Biancabella managed to growl through clenched teeth.

"Yes, I can. Stories about her are disturbing to say the least and I'm happy to see you finally take notice. But you must look to yourself, all this agitation is not good for someone in your condition." The maid stroked the girl's shoulders. "King Ferrandino will return soon, and she will learn her place."

Back in her chambers, the dowager fumed, her anger mostly directed at herself for not biting her tongue. Ever since the king decided to wed Biancabella, Finola had schemed. She had intended to put Lisabetta on the throne. Indeed, she thought the idea a safe bet, slowly sowing seeds of the idea in Ferrandino's mind, even before the death of the king. Now with her plans completely upended, she tried to plot a new course, yet no ideas came to her so far on how to rid the kingdom of Biancabella. But she could not afford to show her hand. If life taught her anything, it was patience. She need only wait and a moment would present itself, she was sure of it.

Unbeknownst to Finola, in her fury that evening, the tide was about to turn in her favor.

⁓⁓⁓

Later in the week, a fever struck the city; the extreme heat of August a perfect host, first afflicting citizens outside the walls, before creeping inside. Servants were the first to go down, weak and bedridden. The castle operated with a skeleton crew, only the bare minimum of tasks completed. Tessina confined Biancabella to her chambers where they waited out the tense days, sweat-soaked and anxious. The maid allowed no entry by anyone. One of the remaining servants left a cart at the door at mealtimes with food and came by later to collect it, and Aurelia dropped off fresh linens and took soiled laundry every morning. Other than that, the queen had no contact with anyone.

One hot afternoon, a sharp rap on the door startled both the occupants who lounged on the balcony. A white piece of paper appeared from the crack under the door. Tessina fetched it, her face paling at its words.

"What is it?" Biancabella cried. "Is Jaco all right?"

"Yes. Please stay calm. The message is not about the king," Tessina began. "Lisabetta and Renata have both contracted the fever. They are quite ill and the royal physician warns we should prepare for the worst."

"Oh, how horrible!" the queen cried.

Tessina placed the paper on the desk and returned to sit with Biancabella in the shade of an awning. The bay spread before them, a mirror of blue, the city spilling down to its beaches. Only a few white sails dotted its surface, a testament to the toll of the illness. Usually, boats crowded the water at this time of day, sailors jockeying for position, but no longer. Every day, the queen watched the horizon for the sails of the king's ships, and every day she was disappointed.

A long sigh escaped her lips. "Poor Lisabetta and Renata. I wish there was some way I could help them."

"There is nothing anyone can do, Biancabella," Tessina stated, wiping sweat from her brow. "This illness must run its course. Let's concentrate on keeping you well."

"I just feel so badly for them. I even feel bad for Dowager Finola. Mean as she is, I feel sorry her children are sick." She absently stroked the tiny bump forming in her belly, her child safe inside.

"God forgive me for saying this," Tessina whispered, even though they were alone, "but in a way, I'm relieved. Rumor is the dowager always wanted one of her daughters on the throne. With them gone, I feel you are safer."

Though Biancabella saw the logic in the remark, her kind heart was still saddened. Lisabetta and Renata were like family now. She did not want them to die, nor could she wish this kind of suffering on anyone, not even the dowager. Her thoughts drifted to Samaritana. Wherever she was, Biancabella hoped her sister was safe.

Across the castle, Finola sat between the beds of her daughters' wiping their feverish brows with damp cloths. The hint of a smile graced her lips. For where Biancabella saw tragedy, the dowager saw opportunity.

CHAPTER TWENTY-THREE

He waited in the dark recesses of the castle, by a dank tunnel that led to a sewer. Even at night, the heat magnified the stench, making it an unpopular place to linger. He needed all the help he could get to conceal his enormous frame. The tiny crescent of a moon, still low in the sky, was the only way to judge time. He cracked his thick knuckles impatiently. With the barest whisper of footsteps, she was at his side.

"My lady," he said with a short bow. "How may I be of service?"

"I have another job for you, Tuccio," the woman murmured, her face hidden in the shadow of her cloak.

"You need only name it; I've proven my loyalty. I am yours to command." Silently, he wondered how the reek and the heavy cape did not cause the lady to pass out. His body was slick with a sheen of sweat in half the garments.

"There is much danger in what I ask now," Dowager Finola stated, lowering her hood.

"More dangerous than sneaking poison into the goblet of the king? I am not easily cowered, my lady," the giant of a man countered.

"I know, Tuccio, only this job involves some contact with the fever." She waited for his reaction but all he did was shrug.

"This sickness does not frighten me. I am strong. Too strong to catch such an illness." A life of evil crimes and murderous deeds with no punishment had left the man feeling rather invincible.

The dowager stepped closer, her voice even lower. "It also involves murder but will pay handsomely."

"That's fine. I'm sure we can come to an agreement beneficial to us both. Tell me the particulars."

Once she explained the details of the mission, he added his thoughts. After some deliberation and agreement on price, they settled on a plan. Tuccio was no stranger to dealing out death. The occupation paid well, so well, that this time he could take some much-needed time off to see his mother in Sicily. Thoughts of her tiny yellow cottage in the rustic hills filled his mind, his childhood days spent exploring the rugged island.

"So tomorrow at eight," the dowager confirmed, evaporating thoughts of his youth.

"Yes, and you are sure you have the correct people bribed inside the castle?" A gust of wind blew the unbearable stink down on them and he longed to be gone.

"Really, Tuccio, after all our jobs together, you doubt me?" He could sense the malicious smile on her face, invisible in the darkness.

With a wry smile and a shake of his head, he vanished into the night. Finola returned to her chambers, the only witness a black cat slinking down the hall, its green eyes illuminated in the darkness. She briefly checked on her daughters, who still burned hot as ever. Satisfied her scheme would be successful, she settled down to a contented sleep.

The next morning found Tessina and Biancabella still in the queen's chambers. Food was delivered and the monotonous routine of the quarantine continued without end. They played dice and cards, but grew bored, the novelty of the games long since passed. At mid-day, there was a knock at the door. Tessina cracked it to find Aurelia, her arms full of bed sheets, on top of which sat some paper and charcoal.

"I thought Her Highness may like a new way to pass the time," the young servant explained.

"This should cheer her greatly. She loves to draw," the maid said, relieving Aurelia of the bundle. "Be safe."

"You both as well," she replied with a smile.

Biancabella was elated when Tessina turned to hand her the thoughtful gift. "Thank you, Aurelia."

"You're welcome, Your Highness." The girl dropped into a curtsey before hurrying back down the hall.

While Tessina changed the sheets, Biancabella sat at the desk to sketch. As a child, drawing had been a favorite diversion in the long winter months. The maid, happy to see the pleasure of the queen, tidied up the room, a task they had neglected in the lethargy of their confinement.

"There," Biancabella declared after a few hours perfecting her work. "I think it's finished."

She held up her rendering, and Tessina smiled. In the picture's center stood a small castle on the top of a hill, with neatly ordered buildings cascading down the side against a background of majestic snow-capped mountains. So precise were the details, the maid envisioned the real place before her eyes.

"Home," she sighed.

"Our old home, yes," Biancabella agreed, a wistful look on her face.

"What a lovely job you did. I think you should sign and date it. After this wretched fever is gone, we can have it framed and hung."

Biancabella loved the idea, enthusiastically writing her name with a flourish in the bottom corner before adding the date. Just then, the dinner cart rumbled down the hall, its squeaky wheel always a herald of its arrival.

"I have worked up quite an appetite," the queen said, laying the drawing back on the desk.

Tessina admired it one last time, happy the gloom of the dreadful fever was lifted, if only for a moment. The pair dined on the balcony, the faintest hint of a breeze wafting up from the water. After, they stayed to watch the setting sun. *Soon*, Tessina thought, *soon the weather will turn colder and drive out the illness. We just need to hang on a little longer*. Night settled around them in an eerily quiet city.

Both women jumped at a loud pounding on the door. Biancabella watched with a quizzical expression when Tessina hopped up to answer. Outside stood a distressed page, so young his chin showed no sign of a forthcoming beard. He wrung his hands together, his large eyes wide and uncertain.

"Yes?" the maid demanded, but regretted her tone when he skittered like a new fawn.

"Dowager Finola sent me. You must come at once with the queen," he stammered. "The royal stepdaughters are near death, and the dowager overcome with grief. She calls out for the queen."

Biancabella, who now stood directly behind the maid, stepped forward. "We will go at once. Come, Tessina."

Before the maid could protest, Biancabella followed the page, who traveled as though fire bit at his heels. The bulk of the journey consisted of one long hallway which usually bustled with servants, yet they passed no one. Tessina chalked it up to the fever. The boy stopped abruptly before the dowager's door and nodded for them to enter before darting back down the corridor out of sight.

"Biancabella, thank goodness you are here," Dowager Finola said, the door clicking shut behind her.

The queen processed the scene inside. The dowager stood in the middle of the sitting room, completely composed. On the back wall leaned a large man, a sword hung at one hip, a mace on the other, a coil of rope encircled his shoulder. On the floor lay the body of an unfamiliar woman, her dead eye's staring at the ceiling. Confused, Biancabella looked for the physician and his assistants, but saw none.

Tessina realized the trap and tried to push the queen toward the door, but the man moved too fast.

"Get out . . ." the maid cried, her voice cut off by a wicked blow to her head.

Before Biancabella could scream, the man grabbed her, his thick hands forcing a gag into her mouth.

"I'm sure you are wondering what this is all about, Biancabella," the dowager purred. Coming to place a finger on the girl's chin, she raised her face up. "You ruined my plans to put my daughter on the throne. But I intend to remedy that now. Unfortunately, Lisabetta succumbed to the illness this evening, but I still have Renata. She will be put in your bed and all will think you suffer the fever. I will tell everyone my daughters died tonight. That," she nodded at the corpse on the floor, "will serve as Renata's body."

While the dowager spoke, Tuccio secured Biancabella's hands and legs with a rope. The girl struggled mightily, but to no avail.

"Sadly, your maid passed from the illness as well," Finola continued, her eyes on Tessina's still frame. "No one will check the bodies for fear of contracting the fever. So my word will be final. My friend here will take you far away and dispose of you where you cannot be found."

Tears filled Biancabella's eyes. Tessina tried to warn her about the dowager, but she never believed such evil could live in a person's heart. Now, her friend was dead because of it, and her life and the life of her baby were in danger. She saw the man retrieve a sack from a nearby chair.

"So, I suppose this is goodbye, Biancabella."

The last thing the queen saw was the smug smile on Dowager Finola's face before the world was covered in darkness.

CHAPTER TWENTY-FOUR

Dawn emerged in a haze of orange and pinks. Aurelia stood outside the laundry area where large fires dried the royal linens. Steam flowed out from the opening of the rudimentary building, all inside drenched in sweat. Aurelia, glad she was not assigned to that oven-like environment, waited while a soft breeze lifted her hair. Though the days were still beastly, cooler air lingered in the morning. A stout woman appeared in the doorway, a pile of sheets in her chubby arms.

"Here you go," she said, beads of perspiration dripping off her wrinkled face, her head cloth soaked through, damp gray curls sticking to her cheeks. "All ready for the queen."

Aurelia accepted the bundle, and the woman waddled back to her station. The young maid stopped in the kitchen on her way up, where her friend Livia, snuck her a sweet roll. In a forgotten corridor, Aurelia sat to enjoy her treat. Wiping the crumbs from her apron, she picked up the linens and walked to the royal tower.

To her surprise, the door to the queen's chambers stood open, loud voices spilling into the hallway. She stopped at the threshold to find a number of people scrambling around, a cacophonous disarray of motions. Sibona, the dowager's head maid, noticed the girl and yanked her inside.

"Good, clean sheets are here," she announced to no one in particular and left Aurelia standing alone to observe the scene.

The dowager leaned over the bed, mopping the brow of the figure in it. While the royal physician conferred with two of his assistants. Sibona stripped the bed of its canopy and curtains while two more maids rushed in and out of the bath area.

"What happened?" Aurelia asked a young servant she managed to grab.

"Oh, it's simply dreadful. First, both the dowager's daughters died of the fever last night, and now the queen suffers—near death herself."

"How terrible!" she exclaimed, surprised by the unfortunate turn of events.

She strained to catch a glimpse of the queen, who seemed so healthy only yesterday. When she finally managed a full view, she started. The woman in the bed, pale with fever, looked very different from the woman she saw the day before, much more wasted with sickness than one night could produce. A strange feeling crept into her stomach, one she instinctively knew to keep to herself.

"You there." Sibona pointed at her. "Put the clean sheets down and leave."

Aurelia did as ordered, placing the sheets on the nearby desk. The picture sketched by Biancabella the day before caught her eye. She looked around the room, but no one paid her any mind. For reasons she could not explain, she slid the drawing under her apron and left the room.

News of the queen's dire condition soon circulated the kingdom and prayers came from all directions. In the royal bedroom, the dowager mopped Renata's brow, though not a perfect decoy, she worked well enough, especially with hefty bribes to the royal physician and Sibona to perpetuate the untruth.

Lisabetta was prepared for burial along with the dead servant, whose corpse was obtained by Tuccio. This body was passed off as Renata. Tessina was put in the dead servant's clothes and her body taken to a mass grave for palace staff with word put out the fever had claimed her life.

Finola relaxed, a slight smile on her lips. So far, her plan was a success. If Renata managed to survive, one of her daughter's would be queen after all.

Biancabella wavered between consciousness and blackness. Tuccio easily carried her over his shoulder from the castle to the waiting horse where he bound her to the saddle in front of him. They began a long journey of dread. She lost track of time, jostled from her stupor whenever they hit a rough patch of terrain. They stopped only once, and she was thrown to the ground, her hood stayed in place. She was not even offered the water she heard him gulp She drifted back into unconsciousness, awoken later when she was flung back onto the horse. Her hands and feet were long numb from the bindings, but every other inch of her screamed in pain.

Their path climbed on an uneven trail up into the mountains. A long time later, the horse's pace slowed. When the animal came to a full stop, Biancabella's stomach lurched, knowing they reached their destination. Tuccio grabbed her from the saddle and pulled off the sack. She stumbled to the ground. Momentarily blinded by the sunlight, she tried to cover her eyes with her tied hands. A moist breeze filled her face, the sound of moving water in her ears. Lowering her hands, she found herself in a small glade by the banks of a rushing river. Tall trees stood around the edge of the clearing, thickening in every direction, a truly remote spot.

Her captor cut her hand bindings, but left the ones on her deadened feet, which would not hold her weight, anyway. He removed the gag from her dry mouth.

"Why are you doing this?" she rasped, her voice but a whisper.

"I am a mercenary. I do what I am paid to do and the dowager pays well," Tuccio stated in a matter-of -fact tone, removing a knife from his bag.

"You would kill your queen?" she asked, wide eyes on the blade.

"I have no queen, and no kingdom. I owe loyalty to no one but myself." He stood and walked toward her. "And you are not my first job for Dowager Finola. She already hired me to poison the late king, whose own son is too foolish to figure out. Now let's get this over with."

He grabbed her head, pulling it back. Her weakened body attempted to struggle but was no match for his strength. With a prayer, she waited for the knife to pierce her throat. Instead, Tuccio hacked off chunks of her hair and stuffed handfuls of it into the sack he took off her head.

"She wants my hair?" Biancabella choked in surprise.

"Yes, she intends to make some sort of magic wig from it," he answered, slight puzzlement in his voice.

To produce the jewels, Biancabella thought horror-stricken. *To help pass Renata off as me.*

"But don't worry," Tuccio continues, "it's not just your hair. She wants your hands and your heart too. The rest will be washed out to sea by this river."

Biancabella had witnessed little cruelty in her life. She never imagined it dished out with such calm apathy. Fighting was futile, there was no escape. The angry river roared behind and she had little doubt her body would ever be found. Her thoughts went to Jaco, his handsome face, full of love flashing before her. She lowered a hand to her stomach, unable to protect the innocent baby growing inside her. Tears filled her eyes and she remembered Samaritana's words of warning. She was wrong to disobey her sister who foresaw this disastrous fate.

Once finished hacking off her hair, Tuccio pried one of her hands to him. A great pain flooded her when he chopped it off followed quickly by the other. He tossed them into the sack like garbage. She fell to the ground, and he leaned over her, dagger raised high to strike her chest. Though her head spun, Biancabella saw a green snake coil up Tuccio's thigh where it bit down hard.

The mercenary shrieked in horror, flailing at the snake, which uncoiled in a flash and slithered out of reach. Tuccio staggered back, blood now pouring from not only his leg, but his mouth, nose, and eyes. Clawing at his face, he stumbled to the river where he collapsed backwards into the rough current. The water enfolded his corpse, his body pummeled by the white rapids.

Biancabella looked down to the stumps where her hands were. Blood poured from them unabated. She turned to the snake, who slithered toward her. She watched with increasingly heavy eyes while the creature encircled her wrist.

"Samaritana . . . " she croaked, with one last glance at her sister before her eyes darkened.

⟋⟍ SAMARITANA ⟍⟋

After leaving her nest near Biancabella's room, Samaritana took refuge from the blazing summer heat under a fountain at the far edge of the palace gardens; the irony not lost on her after the countless hours spent with her sister by their fountain. The moist stone kept her cool enough during the days that followed when she held a continual debate with herself on whether to remain in Naples or leave. *But where could she go?* The garden in Monferrato was the only home she knew, the elders the only other family she ever knew. Loneliness swallowed her in its gaping jaws. Protecting and nurturing Biancabella had been the entire focus of her life, one now bereft of any purpose.

A few times she thought to check on her sister, the sensation of danger ever-present in the back of her mind. Ferrandino had sailed away on some emergency, according to the kitchen staff she eavesdropped on while hunting in the herb garden each morning, but all seemed well otherwise, everyone excited about the pregnancy. With no imminent threat to Biancabella, Samaritan chose not to go, the jealousy of seeing her sister so happy too much to bear.

One morning, she emerged from under the fountain to see bodies lined up, wrapped like mummies in neat lines. Two servants came to carry them away one by one. Through their conversation, Samaritana learned of the deadly fever. Each day, her worry multiplied like the number of corpses outside her den. Perhaps this illness, and not Ferrandino, had been the threat to her sister all along. This notion frightened her. Though her elders taught her much about healing, she had not practiced channeling energy since she left Monferrato. Moreover, she primarily healed animals, her only human patient was Piero, whose leg wound was far less severe than a fatal fever. Yet, if Biancabella became ill, she must try to save her.

With a new sense of purpose, she practiced lessons of healing to the best of her ability with no instructor. Reconnecting with the healing arts stirred a passion in her, one she had forgotten, which gave her motivation for the future. If the fever left Biancabella untouched, Samaritana would leave Naples and search for more of her kind. Her gifts should not diminish even if her sister had no further need of her protection. This idea of finding a new objective for her life buoyed her and turned her mind to more productive thoughts than brooding on her anger. Weeks passed, the training taxing Samaritana to the brink of exhaustion by each nightfall where she collapsed in her nest.

An alarming awareness stung her from sleep one night, so powerful she reeled at the shock of it. Biancabella was in danger—greater danger than Samaritana ever sensed before. All feelings of weariness dissipated in the need to get to her sister and she bolted out into the humid darkness. She raced to the queen's chambers only to find them empty. A cold stake of fear hurtled down her body and the sensation of danger pierced her to the core.

Biancabella's scent led out of the room and down a long hall to another chamber. When Samaritana slithered in the shadows of the walls, she saw a body. Tessina, her neck at an odd angle. The vile dowager directed a pair of seedy looking men to wrap up the maid and dispose of her with two other bodies. Samaritana's blood ran cold, but she smelled that none of the corpses belonged to Biancabella whose scent she picked up by the door. She trailed the smell, mixed with that of an unfamiliar person, down a staircase and out a servant's exit at the back of the castle. Here, the odor mingled with the scent of a horse. Someone had taken Biancabella.

Samaritana used her perceptive tongue to guide her after the assailant. Down a hill and out of the city gate, she sped, the crescent moon a hook in the sky above, though night brought little relief to the oppressive heat. The scent led down a main road until it abruptly turned away from the bay into the open fields, where the trampled grass made for easy travel.

All night, she followed the track, losing all sense of time, but knowing they moved ever northwest of Naples. At one point, the odor became so faint, Samaritana feared she may lose them but soon the scent intensified again. She realized the horse must have stopped temporarily before moving on. She doubled her efforts to catch up. As dawn broke, the trail led to foothills lining the base of a long mountain range. Here the air felt cool and refreshing, which invigorated her for the chase. Still, the kidnapper set a brutal pace, and Samaritana focused every ounce of her will on the need to rescue her sister.

By mid-morning, she flagged, pulling to a stop for in a moment in the dense trees. A large, brown snake slunk out from under a pile of leaves. It regarded her for a long moment, but said nothing, before gliding away. Samaritana closed her eyes and drew what energy she could from the earth to fortify her. A gust of wind blew the strong smell of horse across her forked tongue. Biancabella was close.

With a renewed strength, Samaritana raced along the forest floor, emerging from the cover of the trees into a bright clearing where a horrific scene unfolded. A man stood over Biancabella, her hair shorn off, sticking out of a bag on the ground. He roughly grabbed each arm to cut off her hands, all the while taunting her about the dowager. Blinded by her jealousy, Samaritana had not recognized the true threat all along—not Ferrandino, but Dowager Finola. How could she have been so foolish? She had failed her sister and led her to this evil fate.

When the assailant raised his dagger to stab Biancabella's chest, Samaritana flew into action. She coiled around the man's leg and sank her teeth deep into his thigh releasing her poisonous venom. He bucked back and screamed in agony, scaring the horse, which took off at breakneck speed into the trees. She lunged toward him again, but saw it was unnecessary. Blood poured out of his leg, eyes, nose, and mouth, and he fell backwards into the river, dead before a drop of water ever touched him.

Samaritana hurried to Biancabella, who tried to mumble her sister's name before falling unconscious. Blood spurted from her wounded arms in thick pulses. With what little power she had left in her, she wrapped around one wrist to channel healing energy. Too weak to regenerate the girl's hands, she concentrated on stopping the bleeding. A green paste oozed from her body, covering the wound and sealing it closed. She performed the same act on the other wrist. Once certain the bleeding was staunched, she slid to the bindings on Biancabella's ankles, now swollen and bruised. As soon as the green paste touched the rope, it dissolved into a flash of smoke.

Samaritana wriggled over to the bag, where hair and hands jutted out gruesomely and disintegrated it as well. A check of her sister found a faint but steady heartbeat. She had done all she could for now. Coiling next to Biancabella, a stupor overtook her and the world went black.

CHAPTER TWENTY-FIVE

Light hovered at the edges of Biancabella's closed lids. She forced them shut tighter, willing herself back to sleep, consciousness complete agony next to the numbness of the dark. How long she laid there, she could not say. The brightness increased, shafts of sunlight warmed her body. Reluctantly, she opened her eyes to see the floor of the forest. Stones dug into her left cheek, the smell of earth heavy. A bird chirped nearby, its song not drowned out by the gurgling river, now farther away.

Biancabella rolled onto her back, the treetops above a web of branches. Leaves fluttered in the breeze, the sun peeking through the gaps. She raised an arm to block out the rays. Pain shot across her. With a gasp, she noticed the stump of her wrist, her hand no longer there. Bit by bit, the memories flowed back—the mercenary, the knife, the assault, his death, and the snake. Samaritana. Her sister saved her.

"Sa . . ." the word cut off in her dry throat. She tried again. "Samari . . ."

Her voice was so weak, it barely made a sound. No one would hear her and wherever Samaritana came from, she was not here now.

Tears filled her eyes. Her sister warned her all those years ago not to leave, foretold the misfortune that would follow. If only she listened. With all her strength, she attempted to sit, but collapsed back down after only a few inches. Thoughts flew to her baby, but the pain smothering her abdomen left her little hope it was spared. She had betrayed her sister, failed to protect her baby, and was now too disfigured for Ferrandino to want her. Broken and alone, she closed her eyes again, wishing for death.

Hours passed, maybe more. She had no awareness of time anymore, adrift between nightmares and blackness, and she began to lose any sense of who and where she was. A cool sensation on her forehead pulled her back to the world. Her eyelids fluttered open to a kindly face.

"There, there, my lady, stay still," the gray-haired man assured, wiping her brow with a wet cloth. His body cast a long shadow across hers in the late afternoon sun. He examined her wounds, concern deepening the wrinkles around his blue eyes. "Who would do something so evil to such a young girl?"

Biancabella opened her mouth, but no words came, whether from trauma or exhaustion, the ability to speak beyond her. The man continued his assessment of her injuries, blanching when he looked at her abdomen. He reached to his side and pulled an empty waterskin from his belt. He leaned down to the river to fill the sack. Cradling the back of the girl's neck, he placed it to her lips.

"There now, just a few sips," he coaxed.

Water ran in cool drops down her throat, the first tang of relief she felt. The man scooped her up to prop her against a tree. For a moment, the world spun, but like silt settling in a riverbed, everything around her came into focus. She inhaled and pain exploded in her stomach, her numb stumps unable to clutch it.

The man ripped fabric from the bottom of Biancabella's nightdress, which he used to bind up her wrists before tying a thin rope around each to act as a tourniquet. While he gathered up his belongings, she watched his bulky frame, hunched down, the axe strapped across his back glinting in a shaft of sunlight. He rose, wiping his hands on his pants.

"I'm Calvo," he introduced. "I think it would be best if you came with me. My wife will be more of a help to you."

Biancabella nodded, a movement that brought on more dizziness. Calvo bent to pick her up and her body sagged against his chest like a wilted flower. The whiskers of his beard tickled the top of her head. He cut a path through the quiet forest, the methodical rhythm off his steps lulling her to sleep as the sun dipped below the trees. She woke to voices, disoriented by light and sound.

"All I'm saying is you could be bringing a heap of trouble on us," an unfamiliar woman whispered.

"What was I supposed to do, Lucia? Leave her there to die?" Biancabella recognized the kind voice.

"It's just that it is not a normal attack," the woman countered, her voice fraught with fear. "Cutting off her hands and hair? What if she is a witch?"

"I cannot explain why someone assaulted her in this manner, but in good conscience, I could not abandon her alone and injured. I'd hoped as my wife, you would agree with that decision."

Biancabella listened. It took a moment for the memories to rush back. She had forgotten how Tuccio hacked off her hair and realized she could not even raise a hand to check. Her hands were gone. The brutal confrontation with the mercenary and his equally violent demise played again in her head. Thoughts of her sister and Jaco, of everything she lost. She prayed it was all just a nightmare and she would wake up in her bed with her loving husband, but her heavy heart told her otherwise.

"I don't know, Calvo." Skepticism still laced Lucia's tone. "We don't need any trouble."

"How could she be trouble? She was left for dead. Who would even know we took her? Let's just nurse her back to health and then we can ask for some answers."

A long silence was followed by a sigh of resignation. "All right. It is the right thing to do, after all."

Biancabella forced her eyes open and turned her head. The couple stood in the doorway of a small room where she lay on a bed under several woolen blankets. An oil lamp burned on a nightstand as moonlight shone through an eight-paned window and a rocking chair sat next to the bed.

The wife noticed her movements. "You are awake then?"

When their eyes locked, the woman nodded and disappeared. She returned a moment later with a steaming cup and a spoon.

"Let's try to get some broth into you, shall we?" She propped Biancabella up on the pillows followed by a spoonful of the hot liquid. The woman watched to make sure her patient swallowed. Biancabella felt warmth spread through her, awakening her senses. A feeling she did not welcome, numbness was better.

"My name is Lucia. Looks like I'll be taking care of you for now. Girls," she called over her shoulder, and three figures crept into the room. "These are my daughters—Alessandra, Ginevra, and Cecelia. We will make sure you are well tended."

They stood from tallest to shortest, like steps on a staircase, eyes wide with questions. Biancabella attempted to smile at the girls, who rushed out like a flock of frightened hens. How horrifying she must look, no longer the beautiful queen, now just a repugnant invalid.

"Not to worry, they just need time to adjust, my children will show you how friendly they are, mark my words. Alessandra, my eldest is very good with herbs. She will brew you some healing tea for tomorrow." Lucia continued to feed her the broth.

At the mention of children, Biancabella looked down at the plain muslin nightdress she now wore. Instinctively, her stump flew to her belly, no longer the small firm bump it had been. When she raised her head, Lucia's eyes watered, and she patted the girl's arm consolingly.

"I'm so sorry dear, but you lost the baby you were carrying. It looks to be a clean loss, so the possibility of other children still exists."

Biancabella ate the rest of the broth, Lucia murmuring words of encouragement. The girl hardly heard them, her mind in the grip of a thick fog of grief, too many sorrows to count. Not only had she been robbed of her hair and hands, but of her trust in the goodness of the world, in the hope she carried naturally in her soul, now a gaping void. When the cup was empty, the wife fussed around settling her patient back into bed and tucking the blankets around her.

"Now, get some rest. It's the best medicine," Lucia stated, picking up the oil lamp. At the door, she stopped. "You've been through a lot, you have, an awful ordeal. Take comfort in the fact you are safe here and we will see that you get well."

Lucia smiled before shutting the door. In the darkness, Biancabella wondered if she was safe anywhere or if, like Samaritana had warned, fate had turned against her. Thoughts of her sister and the baby she lost haunted her thoughts until she fell into a restless sleep.

CHAPTER TWENTY-SIX

Lucia and her daughters saw to the slow process of nursing Biancabella back to health. Besides her physical wounds, the girl's emotional state remained fragile. She barely spoke and hardly ate anything, much to the dismay of her nursemaids. Still, they pressed forward with their duties, hopeful one day the young woman would recover both body and spirit. Lucia worried the brutality of the attack scarred the stranger's mind more than her body and with good reason.

Biancabella appreciated their efforts which she noticed through a fog that refused to clear from her brain. Lost in this dense gloom, only a small part of her was present in the here and now. The rest wandered forlornly across a beclouded mental landscape. Never in her life had she witnessed true evil until Dowager Finola arranged her murder. This maleficence pierced her pure spirit, leaving her to question the goodness she always found so naturally in others. The trauma of the attack dominated her thoughts forever sucking her back into an inescapable abyss. Though she felt her body heal, her soul felt broken beyond repair.

"Here's some hot chicken soup and my special tea," Alessandra announced one afternoon.

The pretty maiden bolstered Biancabella's thin frame with some pillows from the other bed. Shortly after Biancabella's arrival, Calvo moved another bed into the room for Alessandra, which had previously been hers, so there was someone to tend to the patient at all hours.

The weather grew cold near the mountain cabin with the approach of autumn. Leaves blew outside the window, chasing each other in the wind. About eight weeks had passed since Biancabella arrived, one of the few things she could do for herself was count the days stack up on each other. For every other need, she remained entirely dependent on her caretakers, a former queen now humbled. The eldest daughter sat next to the bed and pushed her long black hair behind her shoulder with her free hand. With the other, she lifted a spoon to the patient's mouth. Gradually, Lucia added meat and vegetables to the broth in an effort to build the girl's strength.

"Such a chill in the air today," Alessandra declared. *She is likely about my age*, Biancabella thought with scant interest. "Though I am told up here it chills quicker than at the coast. I've never been, have you?"

Always they attempted to draw her out, to find some answers, to hear her speak. So far, two months in, these tries were unsuccessful. Besides *thank you*, the newcomer said nothing else. Her body recovered, the stumps of her wrists healing nicely, but her spirit remained shattered. Her mind ricocheted from Tessina, so savagely murdered, to Samaritana now lost to her, as were her baby and Jaco, the life she had known destroyed. The constraints of normal conversation were beyond her ability or desire. Lucia told her daughters that the girl needed time before she would open up and encouraged them to never give up the effort.

"I've never seen the Gulf of Naples, but I imagine it is more beautiful than words could describe. One day I'll get there. For now, we can both envision how lovely it is." She wiped

Biancabella's chin, the feeding finished, not realizing how her words of the city haunted the girl.

Alessandra straightened the blankets and saw tears in Biancabella's eyes. She had hope to fill her mind with pleasant images, but to no avail. With bowl in hand, she walked to the door.

"Thank you," whispered Biancabella.

"You are welcome. I wish there was more I could do," the other answered with pity in her eyes.

Days passed into months. Snow fell softly outside the window, the only view Biancabella had of the outside world. Somewhere in the recesses of her mind, she remembered her lost baby was due in the winter. A picture of the nursery flashed before her, followed by Jaco's handsome face. Had King Ferrandino returned from his battle with Tunis? Did he not see the dowager's deceit? Even if he did, it was doubtful he would find her here, and more doubtful he would want her if he did, invalid that she was. Who would want a wife with no hands? Even the simplest tasks were impossible. Her heavy lids drooped, and she slept, her only escape from the agony of life.

Then one evening, Cecelia, the youngest daughter, brought in her dinner balanced on a tray which looked as large as her. She placed it on the side table and spread a napkin across Biancabella's lap. The meal was a feast; pork with potatoes, carrots, and a slice of apple pie, all cut into bite-sized pieces.

"A special meal today," the young girl exclaimed. "It's Christmas. Mama worked hard all day on this meal, so I hope you enjoy it."

Biancabella had no response, any feeling of celebration unfathomable, but she ate when the girl raised a fork to her mouth. Cecelia glowed with the satisfaction of any happy child on this holiday, her green eyes filled with the wonder and innocence of youth. Biancabella tried to recall any Christmases from her past, but what little snatches of festivities echoed in the recesses of her mind felt as though they belonged to someone else—a person who did not exist anymore.

"I volunteered to feed you so Ali and Ginny could eat with Mama and Papa. I'm too excited to eat right now. Papa made me the most beautiful wood cutting as a present. Hold on, I'll get it."

Dropping the fork on the plate, she dashed out of the door. When she returned, she clutched a small square of wood in her hands, pleasure etched on her face.

"Here, look. Isn't it wonderful?"

She turned the crafted side to Biancabella. The carving showed tall snow-capped peaks with a small city below, houses marching orderly down the side of a hill. So extraordinary was the level of detail, Biancabella could almost picture herself there. It could have been any of a hundred mountain towns but Biancabella only saw one—Monferrato. The carving stirred something inside of her, memories from her happy childhood solidifying along with a bit of her spirit, which had lingered so long in a wasteland, lost and hopeless.

"These are some faraway mountains," Cecelia explained. "I want to see them someday. Papa said they are called . . ."

"The Alps," Biancabella muttered, her eyes glued to the engraving.

"Yes, the Alps," Cecelia squealed, too enthralled to notice the patient uttered something other than *thank you* for the first time. "Papa says there is snow on their tops all year round."

"He is right," Biancabella said, more memories of her childhood flooding back, a time when she was safe and fortunate, still believing in the goodness of the world. Surely that person was in her somewhere if she roused herself enough to search.

"You've seen them?" Cecelia could barely contain herself.

"Yes, I grew up in a city that looks just like that. They are very lovely. I hope you get to see them sometime."

A collective gasp caused both to turn to the doorway where the rest of the family looked in with astonishment.

CHAPTER TWENTY-SEVEN

"Papa, our new friend has seen the Alps!" the youngest daughter cried.

"Yes, I heard," Calvo stammered.

"Perhaps we can convince her to join us at the table for dinner," Lucia ventured, hope in her eyes.

After a moment's hesitation, Biancabella replied, "Yes, I would like that."

"Then you can tell us all about the Alps," Cecelia exclaimed. "This is the best Christmas ever! Isn't it . . . wait, we don't know your name?"

"It's Bella." If she was to build a new life for herself, she would change her name. Besides, she needed to protect this kind family from her true identity and the wickedness of the dowager.

"I love that name!" the girl cried.

Calvo led Biancabella on shaky legs out of her chamber for the first time. The girls bustled around to find another chair and helped her sit. Ginevra laid a blanket across her legs. A fire burned merrily in the hearth, stockings hung across the mantle decorated with holly next to a fir tree adorned with popcorn and berries. Cecelia ran to retrieve the dinner plate from the bedroom and slid in next to Biancabella at the table. The guest spoke a bit about her childhood in a city by the Alps, though she omitted the name. The family did not press, thrilled at her presence. That night, Biancabella slept more soundly than ever.

And so, the stupor finally passed, and Biancabella joined the world of the living again. In the confines of the small home, her spirits revived. With their help, she adjusted to the difficulties of being handless, both physically and emotionally. At first, her complete dependency on them for nearly every action of daily life left her depressed. Yet, they never made her feel less for her incapacities. When Lucia realized Biancabella could read, she asked if the girl would help her daughters learn. Biancabella threw herself whole-heartedly into teaching them, happy she could contribute something to the people who not only saved her life but welcomed her into their family. The Brizia's had little in the way of books, but Calvo managed to buy a few more in the village. The daughters were eager pupils and quick learners.

Biancabella grew stronger in both health and spirit. When questioned about her past, she remained vague and the family never pushed for more information. Her previous life faded to the edges of her mind; she could not allow herself to dwell on old memories or she would sink back into the chasm of despair. Instead, she concentrated on the present moment and getting to know her new family. If her lot was to live out her days with them, she needed to lock away all reflections of her old life forever, which she found easier on some days and harder on others, when the claws of the abyss reached out to grab her thoughts.

Calvo Brizia worked as a woodsman, chopping logs for the nearby village. In his spare time, he liked to woodcut, creating images or fancy designs on blocks of wood for decoration which he then sold to villagers or passing merchants. His talent was quite evident, though he brushed off any compliments or suggestions that he should make it an occupation.

"The farrier needs logs for the forge more than some pretty picture," he would say.

Lucia and her daughters worked hard to maintain the household. Besides tending to the animals and the garden, they mended garments and embroidered for the local villagers for extra money. Each girl worked from sunup to sundown without complaint. At night, the whole family sat around the fire in the main room where the girls took turns reading passages, and Calvo beamed while he whittled away on a new piece of art. A humble life, they were filled with more contentment than most courtiers in their splendid estates.

"Come stand here, Bella," Ginevra directed, holding up a new dress, a mid-morning sun of early February shining through the windows of the living room.

Biancabella did as instructed and Ginevra helped her out of an old dress of Alessandra's she had been wearing. The most accomplished with a needle and thread, the middle sister took it upon herself to make their guest some new outfits. Adjusting the garment around the girl, Ginevra took a step back.

"It's so pretty," Biancabella praised, admiring the rich navy fabric with her eyes.

"Yes, and warm for these cold months," Ginevra answered, pushing a stray lock of chestnut hair out of her eyes. "The length looks good too. It will be ready for you after our baths."

Bathing was a rare event in the cold months. In warmer weather, the family went to the closest stream, but today, Lucia boiled pots of water to pour into the wooden tub, a lengthy process which took most of the morning. Calvo had dragged the vat into the main bedroom before he left that morning. Lucia set up a clothesline around it, lined with blankets to help keep the heat in.

When it was full, she stepped out and said, "The water is ready. I think Bella should go first."

The others readily agreed. With their help, Biancabella slipped into the warm water. Lucia rubbed her with a soapy washcloth and gently washed her hair. Though she had bathed in opulent palaces, she took more pleasure in this bath than in any she could remember, the feeling of finally being clean leaving her refreshed in both body and mind. With assistance, she climbed from the tub and Alessandra hopped in with a sigh. Lucia helped her into the new dress. A brief look down at her stumps was all Biancabella could manage. The sight still horrified her. Lucia had made linen covers for them, but they were in the living room.

"There. You look lovely. Let me brush out your hair a bit," Lucia said, not seeming bothered by the girl's deformity at all.

Biancabella sat in a chair in front of the only mirror the Brizia's owned—one she had avoided until now. Since her attack, the girl had not looked at herself. With trepidation, she gazed at her reflection. The image looking back at her was thinner than she remembered, with hollows under her cheekbones and dark circles under her eyes. Her hair, so cruelly hacked off, stood in matted blonde tufts, longer in some places than others. A glint caught her eye where the gold bands ran around her neck. Lucia saw it too.

"Well, look at that," the woman said, stooping to take a better look.

"It's a birthmark," Biancabella whispered, wishing more than ever for hands to cover the marks.

Sensing her discomfort, Lucia stood and picked up a hairbrush. "Once I brush it out, I'll even it up a bit so it grows in nicer."

Carefully, she took a clump in her hands. After the first stroke, something dropped to the floor.

Clink

Biancabella stiffened, but Lucia ignored the noise, thinking one of the girl's dropped something. She brushed again, two more strokes.

Clink

Clink

Now a puzzled expression filled the mother's face as she noticed something fall out of the corner of her eye. She bent to retrieve whatever it was. When she rose, a look of wonder filled her eyes. Alessandra, now out of the bath, stopped drying her hair, a towel slipping out of her grip. They stared at Lucia's hand where three small rubies sparkled.

Cecelia, still waiting for her turn, rose from the bed and crept over to her mother. She looked from the jewels to Biancabella, who sat frozen with fear.

"Look, Mama, Bella can do magic!"

CHAPTER TWENTY-EIGHT

After a stunned silence, Alessandra took the brush from her mother, who moved to the edge of the bed where she wrung her hands. Cecelia ran from the room, the front door opening with a bang. The eldest daughter stroked the brush through Biancabella's hair.

Clink

Another gem bounced across the floor. Ginevra, who hopped out of the bath to see what all the fuss was about, picked it up, her eyes filled with wonder. By the time Alessandra finished brushing the rest of the girl's head, twelve jewels sat twinkling on the vanity. The daughters picked each up admiring them in turn. Lucia watched, her face pale. Biancabella kept her gaze focused on her lap, praying to disappear before the questions started.

Calvo burst into the house with Cecelia on his heels. In her excitement, she had run to the woods to find him.

"What is this girl talking about?" he boomed. "I think she's gone and lost her senses!"

"We discovered that when we brushed Bella's hair, gems come out," Alessandra explained.

Calvo took in the pile of jewels on the vanity, a guilty-faced Bella, and his ashen wife. Understanding filled his eyes.

"If she's a witch . . ." Lucia whispered, but stopped when her husband held up his hand.

"She's no witch," he stated. "She is Biancabella, Queen of Naples. Isn't that right?"

The newly revealed monarch nodded her head slowly, not daring to look at anyone, too afraid to speak. What would become of her now? Would the Brizia's tell her secret? Or turn her out to fend for herself? Her lungs felt squeezed of any air.

"A queen?" Cecelia cried, not at a loss for words like the rest of her family. "An actual queen?"

Ginevra rushed to take her little sister hands and motioned for her to be quiet.

"I've heard snatches of stories in the village about your gifts over the years. Never gave much credence to jewels falling from hair and flowers from hands. And never bothered to tell my family any of it. But, by God, here you are." The woodsman eased down next to his wife, cap in hand. "I guess there is more to your story than you have let on."

Silence resumed, all focus on Biancabella who felt obligated to say something.

"I was attacked. Someone wanted me dead. And they may as well have succeeded. I am queen no more, only an invalid. But you took me in without any expectation of repayment. You have nursed me to health and adopted me into your family, and all I have done in return is be dishonest with you. I understand if you don't want me here now that you know my true identity, but please, keep my secret even if you make me leave." Tears streamed down her face with this earnest plea.

Lucia sprung to her feet and embraced Biancabella. "Of course we don't want you to leave. You are part of our family now. And family looks out for each other."

The three daughters joined their mother, all wrapping the girl in a bigger hug. Calvo came to add his giant arms.

"Family does look out for each other," he declared. "Your secret is safe with us. We all love you."

"I love you all, too," Biancabella managed through her tears and to the wonder of all, rose petals issued from the stumps of her wrists.

~∾⟆⟆∾~

The winter passed, the bite in the air lessening each day. Eventually, the girls sat outside in the afternoons where small green shoots emerged from the dark earth. Alessandra readied the garden bed for planting, leaving the more skilled Ginevra to the embroidery. One day, she brought over a slate and piece of chalk. She drew a big rectangle and divided it into sections.

"Here is where we plant the vegetables," she told Biancabella, who sat next to her on a bench. "The berries go here and the herbs go here. I like to experiment with new ones. Do you have any knowledge of herbs and healing? It's always been an interest of mine."

"I have a basic understanding from my education, but a book would be a much better source of information," Biancabella replied. "Perhaps a doctor or healer in the village has one we could borrow. I would like to learn more, too."

"I will ask Father tonight," Alessandra exclaimed, delight in her eyes at the idea of possessing such a book. "Who knows what useful thing we will learn."

That evening Calvo agreed to ask around. Biancabella wanted to offer to buy the book but felt awkward to say. The Brizia's had been true to their word and her presence in their home remained unnoted, a secret easier to keep in the secluded cabin. No mention was made of her past life as a queen and no further questions about how she ended up assaulted and alone were asked. When Lucia brushed her hair, the woman gathered the jewels and placed them in a chest that Calvo kept buried under a floorboard in the kitchen. Never once did the family ask to keep even a cent for themselves.

So, she sat quietly, afraid any offer to pay for the book would give offense. A bittersweet contentment filled her heart, part of her felt empty, grieving for her lost life, yet to live with kind people she could trust was enough for the new person she had to become. It would have to be.

One day, she sat in the garden, Alessandra by her side. Yellow blossoms filled the tomato plants, flat basil leaves reached for the sky and ivy twined up the trellis against the side of the house. Scents of flowers wafted on the breeze and one stood out. Wisteria. For a moment, Biancabella was back in her childhood garden. She could almost hear the water splash into the fountain from the mouths of the intertwined snakes. Days spent with her sister . . .

"Once the ginger grows fully, we can mix it with the dandelion and calendula." Alessandra's voice startled Biancabella from her thoughts. "I want to try to make the healing paste we read about in the book Father bought me."

The eldest daughter's face had lit up like the sun when Calvo presented her with the book. Biancabella read a little with her each night finding Alessandra's aptitude for both reading and herbs impressive.

"Maybe it's like the salve that was on your wrists the night Papa brought you home," she commented from the ground where she collected some dandelion leaves in a basket.

"What salve?"

"There was a bright green salve on the stumps where your hands had been. Papa said you may have bled to death were it not applied, but he had no idea who put it on you."

Samaritana. Biancabella's eyes filled with tears. She recalled Tuccio's leg wrapped with the snake, the bite, his flailing arms before he fell in the river. Her sister had saved her not once, but twice that night. How she longed to see her again.

"Oh dear me," Alessandra exclaimed at the sight of her weeping. "Now I've gone and upset you with awful memories. Please forgive me."

After dabbing away her tears, she led Biancabella back into the house where Lucia and the girls calmed her with cake and tea. Their doting drew out a smile and Biancabella boxed up all thoughts of her old life tightly.

CHAPTER TWENTY-NINE

At dinner that evening, Calvo remained unusually silent, his wife's attempts to draw him into conversation unsuccessful. The older girls noticed and exchanged concerned glances, but Cecelia kept talking unaware of any difference in mood. Calvo nodded absently at her chatter. While the daughters cleared the table, he sat in his rocking chair, eyes fixed on the fire. An uneasy quiet filled the house.

"Bella." Calvo's voice broke the hush. He took his pipe from the mantle. "Come here. I have some things to tell you."

She sat in the chair across from him. The rest of the family gathered behind her except Cecelia who sat on the rug between her father and the fire. Biancabella's heart thumped against her ribcage, its dull beat echoing in her head. Though he never said as much, she sensed Calvo held misgivings about her true identity remaining a secret. Perhaps he decided the risk to family was too great.

"When I delivered some cords of wood to The Brass Boar today, Petrus insisted I stay for a drink. He's a talkative one, that Petrus, and never one to turn a deaf ear. He hears a great deal from travelers and such, running the inn and all."

Every head nodded at this assessment of the innkeeper. Even though Biancabella never met the man, Calvo related many stories he heard at The Brass Boar, courtesy of its proprietor. His propensity to gossip well-known.

"So, I asked if he has heard about Naples lately to see if he knew any rumors about the queen. I thought we should be aware of what information was out there for Bella's sake."

Biancabella stiffened but said nothing. Calvo filled his pipe with some tobacco leaves.

"Petrus had a lot to say on the subject. According to him, the city took quite a hit from the summer fever. Lots of folks died but King Ferrandino was spared as he was off fighting in Tunis. When he returned, the king found the queen nearly dead of the sickness. She has since recovered, though not fully."

"The queen?" Cecelia cried. She jumped to her feet. "But Bella is the queen. She can prove it too with the jewels from her hair."

"Surely whoever is masquerading as the queen does not possess Bella's gifts," Alessandra added. She went to her Cecelia and put an arm around her. They sat back down together on the rug.

"Rumor is the queen lost her gifts as a result of the fever," Calvo said, tamping down the contents of the pipe. "Now she is merely a shell of who she once was and the people mourn, at least this is the way Petrus heard it. We know the true queen is here, which makes the other woman an imposter. Do you know who it may be, Bella?"

"It is Renata, the daughter of Dowager Finola, the king's stepmother. She arranged my murder in order to place her child on the throne next to Jaco." A shudder ran through Biancabella at the memories of Finola, her evil brought back full force.

"Well now, that makes sense," Calvo replied, lighting his pipe. He took a long drag and exhaled a puff of smoke. "The story goes that after both of Dowager Finola's daughters died of the fever, she personally took charge of the queen's care to save her from certain death. She claims to have done this for the good of the realm, and even now, she stays ever at the queen's side. People speak of her sacrifice and benevolence."

"Humph," snorted Ginevra, "so benevolent she tried to murder Bella."

"And what of the king? He believes these lies?" Biancabella asked, wounded to the core at the thought.

"It seems so, though people say he is a changed man, stoic now, not the carefree, young king of old. Some think the rigors of battle matured him, others think he mourns the loss of his wife's gifts. Either way, he does not sound to be a happy man." Calvo paused to inhale his pipe.

"Someone should tell him the truth," Cecelia exclaimed, her head wreathed in the smoke of her father's exhale.

"Quiet, Celie," Lucia demanded. "This is not our secret to tell. Bella must decide for herself. Isn't that right, Calvo."

"Yes." He looked at Biancabella. "I told you this so you would know where things stand now in Naples. Only you can decide what to do. Just know you are welcome here if you wish to stay. Your secret is safe with us. However, if you choose to return to Naples to reclaim what is rightfully yours, we will help you in any way we can. Isn't that right?"

Lucia and her girls nodded in unison before the family left Biancabella to her thoughts. She sat in contemplation until bedtime. Her mind jangled with ideas and memories she tried to separate into a decision, but no clear one presented itself.

"To think, murdering a queen to pass off her own daughter," Alessandra grumbled after tucking Biancabella into bed. She blew out the candle in the bedroom they now shared. "I am sorry for all you have been through, Bella."

"Thank you," the ex-queen whispered in the dark. She hoped dawn brought clarity with it.

Morning came and went. The Brizia's went about their tasks while Biancabella sat in the garden. Birds sang in the trees, flowers bloomed in vibrant colors and soft wind blew warm spring air across her cheeks, but she noticed none of it, instead dwelling on all the choices she made in life and how wrong she had been. Pain and regret ripped a giant hole in her soul, a hole so deep it was beyond repair.

She betrayed her sister and for what? A husband who loved her so little he didn't even protest when she was replaced. Surely, he knew Renata was not her. Why had he not come looking for her? She cursed herself for believing their love was real. Her thoughts spiraled down even further. Even if Jaco did find her, how could he love her now? An invalid with no hands, she could not even feed herself, let alone be queen. There was no life left for her in Naples.

And Samaritana. Her sister warned her to stay in Monferrato, warned her of the dire consequences which Biancabella ignored. Samaritana loved her completely, had awakened her gifts only to be abandoned by a selfish girl who claimed to know what love was. And even after all that, Samaritana had stayed with her hidden until she bravely saved Biancabella's life.

A glimmer of hope filled her. Perhaps Samaritana lingered nearby as she had when Tuccio attacked her.

"Samaritana?" she called quietly, lest the others think she went mad. "Samaritana? Are you here? Please come out. I miss you. Please forgive me."

A long unanswered silence followed. In her broken heart, Biancabella knew she had lost her sister forever. The realization she would never be whole again without her sibling hammered down on her. Despair followed. Calvo and his family were kind, but her debilitation caused them hardship. Yes, they had her jewels, but if they spent them, it would draw unnecessary attention to both them and her. What if Finola suspected she lived and came after her again? That would put the Brizia's in danger. It was too much to ask of them. Just as there was no life for her in Naples, there was nothing for her here but an existence entirely dependent on the kindness of others, lives which could be imperiled by her very presence. By the time dinner finished that evening, she had made up her mind.

"What are you working on?" She sat by Calvo's side at the fire where he whittled away at a block of wood.

"Just a scene with a couple of rabbits for Mr. Santo's daughter. It's her birthday next week." He held up the woodcutting where the shape of the animals came into form.

"I'm sure it will be lovely," Biancabella complimented before turning to her real interest. "Do you remember where you found me in the forest?"

"Yes, I recall the spot well enough. It's not the sort of encounter one forgets," the woodsman stated, a long shaving of wood dropping to the floor.

"Could you please take me there? I was hoping it might bring back some memories."

"All right," he replied in a hesitant tone. "If you're sure you won't be troubled by bad memories."

"I'm sure," she assured. "In fact, I think it will be helpful."

"We can go first thing in the morning, if that sounds good."

"It sounds perfect. Thank you, Calvo, for everything." She kissed the top of his head. "Now I will retire."

He smiled while he whittled, pleased to make her happy. She watched him for a moment from the doorway of the bedroom. Alessandra helped her into her nightgown and tucked her into bed. A sense of calm filled Biancabella. She looked forward to returning to the last place she saw her sister, the one who had loved her above all others.

It was the perfect place to die.

CHAPTER THIRTY

They set out early; Calvo rose with the dawn most days. A perfect mid-spring morning greeted them. The rising sun sent warm rays diagonally across the trees. Puffy clouds blotted an azure sky. Bird songs filled the air and small creatures rustled amongst the undergrowth. The woodsman set a brisk pace but Biancabella soon lagged. Even with her months of recovery, she lacked the endurance to keep up and Calvo slowed to her side.

"Are you sure you want to go back there?" he pressed, sidestepping a downed trunk. "Not a place with any good memories I would think."

"I'm sure," she replied. "I think being there will bring me some closure."

Calvo nodded, and despite a quizzical expression, said no more. A small herd of deer grazed in the clearing just ahead of them. They leapt away at the sight of the pair, their white tails flickering in unison. More by instinct than by any clear path, the woodsman navigated the forest with the ease of one familiar with the terrain. Biancabella did not recognize anything and would have been quite lost without Calvo. The sound of water grew louder with each step an element she did associate with the attack.

"It's farther than I thought," she murmured.

"Is it too much for you?" he asked, his expression drawn with concern. "Should we rest for a bit?"

"No, I'm fine. I just can't believe how far you had to carry me the day you found me," she marveled. The fact that he discovered her at all in the forsaken spot a miracle in itself but to bear her back to the cabin was a testament to his fortitude.

"Oh, it was nothing." He brushed the words aside, a blush on his cheek. "Anyone could have done it."

Biancabella doubted that, but before she could say so, the trees parted. They stepped into a clearing along the riverbank. Bright flowers bloomed on the soft grass that ran down to the banks of the river, which streamed by in a noisy flow. Had she not known what transpired her, she would have found it a place of peaceful seclusion.

"Here we are," Calvo announced, pity etched on his face.

Though her recollection of that fateful night were not entirely lucid, the sound of the rapids and the smell of the earth brought snatches of memories to mind—Tuccio's attack, Samaritana's appearance, Tuccio's cry and fall. The stumps of her wrists ached at the thought. She stood frozen, the episode playing out over and over in her mind.

"How about we go home now," Calvo suggested after a few minutes passed.

"I know you have work to do. Go and cut wood. Let me spend a few hours here by myself," she instructed, the decision to end it all even more resolute now.

"Are you sure that's a good idea?" Though eager to start his day, uneasiness filled him at the thought of leaving the handless girl alone.

"I'm sure. I will be fine," she confirmed, a determined look in her eyes he could not argue with.

"All right, I'll be back soon." He walked to the tree line and called over his shoulder, "Be careful now."

"I will. And Calvo," she said, and he turned to face her, "thank you . . . for everything."

With one last glance of uncertainty, he disappeared into the forest. Biancabella strode to the river's edge. On that ill-fated night, she had only heard it, now she wondered at its size. The wide current flowed among jagged rocks, their tips protruding like beastly fangs. She followed the bank for a few yards, the roar of the rapids growing louder until they spilled over the edge of a waterfall. White mist spewed up to her face from where water collided with even larger rocks at the bottom. An image of Tuccio's body smashing against them played in her mind. What had Finola thought when her assassin did not return? It didn't matter; she had gone ahead with her plan in any case. Her daughter now sat in Biancabella's place on the throne. And Jaco either did not know or did not care enough to notice.

Biancabella's heart broke knowing the life she shared with her husband had ended so cruelly by the wicked woman's scheme. Emptiness filled her laced with self-pity. If only she could go back and heed her sister's warning and never have left her side. They would be in her garden in Monferrato right now if Biancabella had not betrayed her. But how could she have stopped herself from falling in love with Jaco? Her heart made the choice with no input from her judgement or reason. If only Samaritana had understood her helplessness against the force of love. And yet, her sister had secretly followed her to Naples and protected her from certain death that night. Perhaps she never left this particular place. The thought gave her a grain of hope.

"Samaritana?" she called. "Are you here?"

The rustle of leaves and the roar of the river were the only reply. She walked back to the spot where the attack occurred.

"Samaritana? Are you here? I miss you."

Silence enveloped the clearing. Biancabella sat down on an old stump, its sides covered in moss. Her sister was gone. Pain squeezed the last bits of faith from her heart in an unyielding grip. Regrets built up inside her at everything left unsaid and she felt compelled to utter them aloud, even if her sister could not hear.

"Samaritana, I want you to know how sorry I am for disobeying you. I see now you were right; fortune favored me while we were at each other's side. My memories of you are of happy days, days I should not have ended. Please know my disobedience was out of ignorance and not wickedness. I never meant to hurt you. I was blinded by my love for Jaco. I thought our love was true, but I was wrong. Yours is the truest love I have ever had." Tears streamed down her face.

"I would give anything to go back to our days in the garden, just you and me. Now I am useless, an invalid and a burden to others. Yes, I still have the jewels from my hair, but what good are they to me? Not only is my body broken but my soul, and gems cannot mend that. I pray wherever you are, you know how much you meant to me and how hurting you has been the deepest wound I have to carry."

With her head in her lap, she sobbed, yet a weight lifted from her with the verbalized confession. Her tears dried and an empty calmness filled her. Her life in Naples was over and her life with her sister as well. Nothing remained for her, a person who would never be whole again, either physically or emotionally. Biancabella was at peace with her decision.

She rose and walked down the riverbank to the waterfall's edge. She peered over the precipice at the rocks below, which seemed to beckon her. It would only be a moment of pain, and then she would be free. Stretching her arms out, Biancabella prepared to throw herself over. She leaned her weight back for the jump.

A second before she pushed off, a familiar voice called, "Wait!"

After the ruthless attack on her sister, a day passed before Samaritana found the wherewithal to open her eyes. Biancabella still next to her, handless, did not stir. Mist from the river blew on them in fitful bursts. Birds sung in the trees, flitting across the sky overhead. Samaritana faced a harsh truth. Her energy was too depleted to heal Biancabella and here, in the middle of nowhere, she did not know how to help her sister, who would die without food, water, and treatment. How could she have let this happen? How could she have missed the wicked designs of the dowager? A pit of despair formed in her stomach, her anger, her envy led to this. Fate had not turned on Biancabella—she had.

She wallowed in self-pity for a moment until she heard several thuds in succession. Focusing her attention, she concluded a human was nearby. This may be her one chance to bring aid to Biancabella. She slithered toward the noise to find man splitting logs on a stump. He paused for a moment to wipe his brow. Pulling a waterskin from his belt, he took a long gulp.

Samaritana had seen the evil humans could perpetrate, but she sensed no danger from this man. Her only option to save Biancabella was to trust this instinct. She closed her eyes and bent her thought on him, willing him to hear the river, to crave the feel of fresh, cold water on his parched throat. The man put the skin to his lips and drained it. A look of discontent passed over his face and he lifted his head in the direction of the river. Samaritana used her influence to pull his mind in that direction, and he walked toward the clearing. All hope now rested in the man's reaction to discovering the wounded Biancabella.

To Samaritana's relief, he immediately tended to her. He settled in the shade of the trees and filled his waterskin from the river. She stirred, and he comforted her. When he scooped her up, the snake followed him through the woods to a small cabin where he took Biancabella inside. Satisfied her sister was safe for the moment. Samaritana searched the area near the home and found the deserted den of some long-gone creature. Here she collapsed into a deep sleep.

Over the next few weeks, Samaritana built up her strength feeding on mice and birds. She watched the house where the kind family helped her sister recuperate. Besides the woodsman, his wife and three daughters lived in the home, none of whom brought any threatening vibes to her. Once she became certain they were decent people, she worked on regaining her energy, practicing all the lessons Ulani and the other elders taught her. She vowed to return to her full ability so she could heal her sister. Guilt dogged her; the notion her selfishness led to the near death of Biancabella ate at her heart. Ulani's wise words about protection versus imprisonment rang in her mind, their meaning now clear. Her efforts to keep Biancabella safe were based on the faulty notion that she must keep Biancabella all to herself. A mistake they each paid the price for.

Winter set in and Samaritana knew hibernation would be the key to reclaim her full power. In her small den, she settled down in a bed of leaves, alone and missing her elders but determined to return to the role of Biancabella's protector. The months of inactivity enriched her body, mind, and spirit, and in early spring she woke, her glow casting a bright, green light in the small nest. She slithered out into the daylight ready to get to work.

Over the next few weeks, she saw her sister only a handful of times, in the garden with one or two young ladies, never alone.

Biancabella seemed recovered in body, except for her missing hands, but her eyes were sad and pensive. Samaritana kept herself concealed lest she frighten one of the family members. She decided the best course of action would be to turn herself into a human and present herself as a person searching for Biancabella. Every day, she went deep into the woods to practice, and within weeks could transform herself in the blink of an eye. Her concern now was how her sister would receive her. *Would Biancabella ever forgive her or would she demand Samaritana leave her alone forever?* Given the horrific attack her sister endured, Samaritana would not be surprised with the latter. This uncertainty caused her to procrastinate the inevitable reunion. One afternoon in the forest, she resolved to reveal herself the next day and face whatever the consequences turned out to be.

The morning dawned bright and fair. To Samaritana's surprise, Biancabella left the house with the man in the early morning hours. She shadowed them into the woods where they walked for a long way. Calvo checked on Biancabella numerous times, concerned with the effort the trek required, but her sister continued, waving off his worries. Samaritana wondered where the journey would lead until a faint sense of recognition swept across her mind and she understood. They made for the clearing where Biancabella was attacked, though she could not comprehend a reason why her sister would want to return to that place. Once they arrived, Biancabella told Calvo to leave. When he was gone, she paced the riverbank then sat on a stump and called for her sister.

Samaritana froze. Shame filled her. *How could she face her sister? Would her sister accept her apology?* When she heard Biancabella's words asking for her forgiveness instead, tears filled her eyes. All this time, Biancabella felt like the betrayer, not the betrayed. This thought gutted Samaritana. The fate foretold of their bond held true, separation had led to tragedy caused by their anger and unwillingness to listen to each other. Each one bore a burden of blame, one that would never relent until they were together again. Biancabella needed to know Samaritana loved her and did not hold an ounce of resentment toward her.

Before she could reveal herself, her sister rose, a blank look on her face. Biancabella walked as though in a trance down the riverbank toward a waterfall. Her intentions suddenly became clear to Samaritan who rushed from the trees.

"Wait!" she screamed, as her sister crouched to leap over the edge.

CHAPTER THIRTY-ONE

Biancabella froze, and the shout came again, "Wait, please!"

She wanted to believe it was who she thought she heard, but doubt filled her. She turned around and there on the ground at her feet sat a long, green snake, which wound its way up her leg, across her waist, and onto her shoulder. Biancabella stared into the familiar golden eyes. She fell to her knees.

"Samaritana," she wept, "you're here."

"Yes. I never left you, not for long anyway. I followed you to Naples, followed you that dreadful night, and have watched your stay at the cabin in the woods."

"It is more than I deserved. I should have listened to your warnings. Now look at me." She held up the stumps at the end of her arms. "I have lost my husband, my hands, and my independence because I would not heed your words. Please forgive me."

"I am sorry for all of your suffering. I suffered too, a self-inflicted anguish on my part. I let anger and jealousy rule my actions. It took me a long time to realize that punishing you meant I would punish myself as well. But I have spent time working on my gifts for both of us. And now I can free us both from our misery," Samaritana professed. "If you will forgive me, too."

"There is nothing to forgive, dear sister," Biancabella swore, her heart full of love.

Samaritana slithered higher up to her sister's neck and coiled around the faint golden lines. Once she fit into them exactly, Biancabella felt a click. Bright light surged outward, knocking them to the ground. A white-hot flash radiated across Biancabella's entire body. Amid the intense light and searing pain, she imagined death must be near, before the world turned black.

Time passed. Pain and peace warred inside Biancabella, her mind not in the realm of consciousness. Thoughts of Samaritana fluttered around her. *Was her sister harmed?* She tried to will herself awake, but a dreamless sleep overcame her. Sunlight warmed her face when her eyes finally fluttered open. Although the sun had barely moved in the sky, Biancabella felt as though she woke from a long slumber. She sat up, rubbed her eyes, and froze, staring in wonder at her hands fully restored. Her fingers flexed and bent at her command. Tears came which she could now brush away herself. She was healed.

"Samaritana, how did you do this?" she asked in wonder.

"I, too, have gifts."

The voice issued not from a snake, but a young woman who stood over her, a mirror image of Biancabella, except for the hair and eyes. Where her tresses were fair as day, the newcomer's were dark as night, and amber eyes stared at her blue ones. Biancabella rose to the level of her twin. After a stunned moment of silence, she threw her arms around her sister, happy to find a solid form and not a conjured image. Flowers burst forth from her hands like a tidal wave.

"Samaritana, this is better than anything I ever imagined. To be healed and to have you here like this is a blessing beyond words." Tears poured from her eyes onto her sister's shoulder.

"We will never be parted again," Samaritana assured.

The girls sat in the grass next to the waterfall's crest and discussed all that passed since Biancabella left Monferrato—Naples, the dowager, and of course, Jaco.

"He must not have loved me, Sister. How else could he accept an imposter as his wife?" Biancabella declared, anger mixing with her sorrow.

"I'm sure he is terribly confused and heartbroken. Do not give up on him yet. Your love for each other was strong, as strong as our love for each other is. I should have understood that sooner."

Surprised by the words of support for her husband, Biancabella thanked her sister, and would have questioned her more but Calvo walked into the clearing.

"Are you ready to . . ." His voice trailed off at the sight of the two women.

Biancabella jumped to her feet. "This is my sister, Samaritana. She is a healer. Look."

She held up her hands, and the woodsman's eyes widened in astonishment. He looked from one girl to the other too flabbergasted to speak, knowing that a healer of even the greatest skill could not have restored missing hands. Moreover, he never heard of the Queen of Naples having a twin but could not deny the certainty of the fact as they stood next to one another. He bowed his head in reverence at the phenomenon before him, one certainly not of the ordinary world.

"I am happy to meet you," Samaritana broke the silence. "Thank you for taking care of my sister when she needed it most. You and your family are forever in our debt."

"Of course," Calvo asserted when he rediscovered his voice. "Bella is a part of our family now, and we welcome you equally."

Both ladies embraced the woodsman before he led them home. He kept a few paces ahead, glancing back at the sisters, who walked hand in hand, and his wide smile mirrored their happy faces. He had grown to think of Bella as another daughter and the sight of her healed, both physically and emotionally, filled him with contentment. What Calvo lacked in questions and suspicion for the sisters, his wife and daughters made up for once they returned to the cabin.

"How did you know where to find Bella?" Lucia asked, an accusatory tone laced the question.

The Brizia women encircled Biancabella protectively, while they interrogated the newfound sibling. Though delighted the girl was healed, they worried about the intentions of this strange woman toward the person they so lovingly cared for.

"I followed her from Naples to where she was attacked. After that, I followed her here."

"And how have you managed to care for yourself all alone in the woods?" Ginevra asked with genuine curiosity.

Samaritana looked at her sister who saw the unasked question for permission.

"Yes, show them. They need to know everything," Biancabella instructed.

Samaritana took a deep breath. Green light poured from her as she shrank down to her snake form. She coiled her way up Biancabella's frame until she came to rest in the golden rings around her throat.

"I knew that mark meant something special," Cecelia exclaimed, delighted by what she witnessed.

The others stood quietly while the snake coiled back to the floor and with another green flash transformed back into the dark-haired young woman.

"We are unusual twins," Samaritana explained. "She was born a human and I, a snake, yet we both have the power to change from one to the other, though that is a skill Biancabella still must learn. We each also have unique gifts."

"They know about the gems and the flowers I can produce," Biancabella informed her sister.

"And what unique gifts do you possess?" Alessandra asked Samaritana, on whom she still cast a wary eye.

"One of my gifts is the ability to heal."

"I cut my finger today when chopping carrots," Cecelia proclaimed, holding up her index finger to show a jagged red line. "Can you heal me?"

"Cecelia, that is not polite," Lucia admonished.

Samaritana merely laughed, a mesmerizing, soft sound. "No need to scold. Come here, young lady."

Cecelia skipped over and offered her finger. Samaritana wrapped her hand around the digit. For a brief second, a bright light glowed around it. When Samaritana released her grip, the child gasped at her unmarked finger, fully healed.

"Thank you. I must show Father!" Cecelia squealed and ran outside.

In the silence that followed, Biancabella looked from one Brizia to the next. She noted their expressions which held not only awe, but a touch of fear. Guilt crept into her heart. This family had given her so much. She did not want them to suffer any misgivings with her and Samaritana's presence.

"You have been kinder to me than I could ever possibly deserve," she said to them. "If my sister and I make you uncomfortable with our gifts, we will find somewhere else to go. You will have my eternal gratitude for all you did for me."

"Nonsense," Lucia stated, surprising Biancabella with her assuredness. "You two are part of this family and are welcome here as long as you want. Isn't that right, girls?"

Alessandra and Ginevra readily agreed. They all embraced, laughing when rose petals showered the floor. Cecelia scampered back in with Calvo, who joined in the celebratory mood. Relief flooded Biancabella's heart. At the start of the day, she did not plan to live to see the end, but now, she was healed and had not only the Brizia's but her sister as well.

Lucia decided to prepare a special dinner. While Cecelia swept up the flower petals with Samaritana, the two older girls helped their mother with the food. Biancabella set the table, happy her healed hands were able to contribute in some way. During the meal, Alessandra offered to move into the room with her sisters, so Bella could share a room with her Samaritana. The newfound sisters accepted the arrangement with thanks.

That night, while they sat in their room together, Cecelia knocked on the door and peeked in.

"Can I still brush your hair?" she asked, eager to continue the nightly ritual.

"Of course, I wouldn't have it any other way."

Biancabella sat at the vanity. The girl brushed with even strokes, giggling every time a gem dropped to the floor. When she finished, Cecelia scooped up the handful of gems and left the room.

"At least they had the jewels to help pay for the cost of caring for you all those months," Samaritana commented once the child left.

"Actually, they have not spent a single one. Calvo keeps them in a chest hidden under the floorboards for me to have whenever I decide I need them."

"Then they truly are wonderful and deserving people," her sister replied. "Soon, we will make sure they are rewarded for their kindness."

CHAPTER THIRTY-TWO

Over the next few weeks, Samaritana settled into life with the woodsman's family. She helped the daughters tend the garden, which gave her a chance to teach an eager Alessandra much about herbs and their medicinal uses. With her hands restored, Biancabella embroidered again, passing her knowledge of the skill onto a grateful Ginevra. Cecelia bounced between them all, a million questions on her lips, while Lucia smiled every day at the bustle that filled the house.

Samaritana resumed training Biancabella to transform into a snake. For an hour each day, the sisters practiced in the woods away from the cabin not wishing to cause the family any unease. At first, Biancabella found the task impossible, but with persistence managed to convert into a snake for a few moments one day. Samaritana glowed with pride at her sister, who though exhausted by the process, could not wait to try again. Biancabella seemed content with her new life in the quiet forest, but Samaritana knew they could not hide from the queen's old life forever. Without answers, there could be no true closure.

One warm evening, Biancabella sat in the garden. Her sister sank onto the bench beside her. The summer sun lounged in the sky, in no hurry to meet the horizon. Its warm glow cast rays around the yard, where a cat hid in the bushes ready to pounce on some birds splashing in a puddle. A light breeze fluttered the grass near their feet, the scent of flowers in its wake. Cecelia's laugh rang from somewhere inside the cabin.

"It's beautiful here, isn't it?" Biancabella sighed.

"Yes, it is," Samaritana agreed, "but I don't think this is where you belong."

"What makes you say that? The Brizia's have been nothing but kind to me . . . to us."

"They have." Samaritana took her sister's hand. "But your place is in Naples, by your husband's side."

"My husband! The man who does not even notice his wife is a different person?" Biancabella's cry scared the birds who flew off in a scatter to the dismay of the cat. She yanked her hand out of her sister's grasp.

"You don't know what King Ferrandino thinks or why he acts the way he does," Samaritana pointed out.

"I don't care what he thinks." She leapt from the bench, her hands balled into fists. "He accepted what that wicked woman told him. He never even questioned it."

Her anger gave way to a flood of grief. She fell to her knees and wept. Samaritana sank to her side, stroking her hair. The cat walked over and gingerly rubbed against them both. All the sadness Biancabella tried to lock away flowed out in a torrent.

"I don't understand," the ex-queen sobbed. "We loved each other. I know we did. How could he have relented so easily?"

"There is only one way to find out. We must go to Naples."

"You don't know the kind of evil Dowager Finola is capable of. She already proved she is not above murder. She will not give up her position without a fight. Besides, Jaco must not have loved me to give into her explanation so easily. I would have gone to the ends of the earth to find him. Why would I leave here where I am finally happy?" She wiped her tears and propped her back against the seat of the bench, her finger twisting a blade of grass.

"Biancabella, this is not your destiny. You know that in your heart. We must return to Naples. I think the best plan is to go in disguise and assess the situation. It is the only way to find the answers to the questions which still torment you."

"What about the Brizia's? They have been so good to me. I can't just leave," Biancabella protested, absently stroking the cat who curled up by her legs.

"I've been thinking of that as well. After getting to know them, I want them to come with us. I think we could help them make a good life in the city. Calvo's carvings alone could support them," Samaritana said, clearly having given the matter lot of thought. "If they choose to stay here, we will leave them the chest of jewels as compensation for all they have done."

Biancabella tilted her head up to the sun as it slid below the treetops. She did need answers and they would only be found in Naples. Though not convinced what her destiny was anymore, she needed closure from her past life to move on. Samaritana's plan gave her that chance.

"All right, Sister, we will go back to Naples." She pressed her forehead against her sister's while a peaceful dusk filled the garden, wishing she could freeze this moment in time and remain in it forever.

The next morning, the girl's sat down with the Brizia family. Biancabella explained the plan to return to Naples. Though her audience did not look surprised, a sadness permeated the room until she added, "We were hoping you would join us there."

Five sets of stunned eyes looked back at her. Calvo took a long sip of coffee, the rest of the family turned to him awaiting his reply.

"Well now, I don't know. We are country folk and all. I'm not sure the big city has need of a woodsman, and we would not feel right living off your money."

"Perhaps there is no need of a woodsman," Samaritana agree, "however, your wood carvings are such fine quality they would sell easily. Alessandra, with her knowledge of herbs, could work for a healer, and surely there are seamstresses who would admire Ginevra's talent. Not to mention, the marriage prospects for all your daughters would increase a hundred-fold."

The three siblings, who could barely contain their excitement at this picture of life in the city, watched their father wide-eyed. Biancabella suppressed a smile. Like the foreign men who enticed snakes from a basket, Samaritana charmed with her very voice. After a long, pensive moment, Calvo turned to his wife. "What do you think, Lucia?"

The woman had not looked up from her lap since the discussion started. When her head lifted, her brows knit together in concern. She looked from one hopeful daughter to another before she met Samaritana's gaze.

"While I agree there may be fine prospects for us in Naples, I wonder if it is wise for Biancabella to return," Lucia commented. "The king's stepmother tried to murder her once already and will need to keep up her charade. Biancabella would walk into a dangerous situation."

"It may be dangerous," Biancabella said, touched by Lucia's concern, "but I need answers—answers I can only find there. I need to know the truth of why King Ferrandino accepts another in my place. I will have no peace in my heart until I know."

"And we have already considered this," Samaritana added. "We will be going in disguise."

"What kind of disguise?" Cecelia asked, excited at the prospect of intrigue.

"We will dress as they do in the East, in saris with our faces covered," Samaritana explained.

"A good plan," Alessandra commented, "but Biancabella's distinct blue eyes will surely not pass as Eastern-born."

"Fear not, I can place a charm on her to mask her true identity until the moment is right."

Everyone nodded in wonder at this statement, though none doubted its certainty. Unable to take the wait any longer, Cecelia jumped from her chair.

"Mama, Papa, can we please go to Naples?" she cried.

Calvo and Lucia shared a long look. The wife nodded her head ever so slightly.

"Yes," the woodsman replied, "we will go. Biancabella belongs there. The truth needs to be revealed to all."

CHAPTER THIRTY-THREE

Over the next few weeks, the family prepared for the move. Calvo finished his outstanding orders and prepared an apprentice to take over his customers. Lucia and her daughters decided what to take with them and what to leave behind in the cabin. The apprentice's young family planned to live there in the Brizia's absence. On the morning of the move, they packed up their wagon, hitched it to a team of horses, and headed for Naples. Lucia looked back wistfully at the home where so much of her life had unfolded. The daughters only looked ahead, excitement in their eyes. Biancabella looked at her restored hands in her lap and wondered what awaited them.

Samaritana had gone ahead of the family a few weeks earlier to find a suitable residence. After selling a few jewels for money, she procured a villa near the palace which had been vacated since last summer when the fever claimed its previous inhabitants. She then hired a staff, saw to the redecoration of the home, and acquired all necessary possession for a family of the stature the Brizia's would now hold. A few days before the family left for Naples, Calvo received a letter with the address and directions. Now, he navigated the crowded streets of the city in search of their destination.

Lucia and the girls marveled at the sights. Shops bustled with customers. Restaurants overflowed with diners. Horses and pedestrians clogged the streets. The aroma of fresh bread and spices blended with the reek of horse droppings and privy gutters. Clanging church bells merged with shouts of people and the bellow of animals. Cecelia gaped and gasped, fingers pointing in all directions while Lucia urged her to be more ladylike. Biancabella, hidden under a cape, gazed at her old city with new eyes.

Her previous stay in Naples had kept her well-guarded from its seamier parts. In the castle, high atop a hill, with the grandeur of Etna in the background, the city appeared quite different. From there, red-roofed buildings tumbled down to the deep blue bay, where clusters of colorful structures stood rooted like wildflowers. There was a beauty and serenity in this distant view. Up close, the jumble of people and cacophony of sounds overwhelmed Biancabella after her months of seclusion in the mountain cabin. As they wound their way up the hill, properties grew larger and the atmosphere quieted to the level typically afforded to the wealthier sections of urban life.

Calvo guided the wagon to their new home where servants opened the heavy iron gates. In a terrazzo-tiled courtyard, stable boys came to attend to the horses. Samaritana glided out the front door and down a grand staircase. A fountain, carved in the likeness of Neptune, spouted water from the mouths of marble fish in the middle of a circular courtyard. Rose covered trellises lined the cream stucco walls of the villa, heavy with pink blossoms. The entire cabin could have fit inside this outside area alone with room to spare. While the servants took the luggage and packages inside, the travelers stood dumbstruck by the beauty and stateliness of the residence.

"Lovely, isn't it?" Samaritana asked, sweeping an arm at the surroundings.

"It's so . . . big . . . " Alessandra managed while they climbed the stairs, all heads still spinning in different directions.

A tall, airy atrium sat inside the main entrance. Large rooms opened off each side down the length of the building. Directly in front of them rose an opulent marble staircase, which split in two directions when it reached the upper floor. As the newcomers wandered from room to room, Biancabella took note of the intricate tapestries, the ornate vases filled with fresh flowers, and the richness of the wood paneling. Samaritana had acquired lodgings fit for a princess.

"Let's go upstairs. There is a bedroom for each of you. See if you can guess whose is whose," Samaritana told the girls and led the family up the staircase to the second floor, which was just as elaborate in its décor.

"It's all so much," Lucia murmured when she saw her new bedroom. "So extravagant."

"Too extravagant for the likes of us," Calvo interjected.

Samaritana laughed at his skepticism. "You are wealthy patrons of Naples now. Your reputation precedes you as a consummate woodcarver who made a fortune in foreign lands and now returns to home."

Calvo nodded, too awestruck to speak. He joined his wife to admire the bedroom. Unlike their parents, the daughters, exhilarated by the splendor, raced between their respective chambers, each filled with a wardrobe of new clothes. Their squeals of delight echoed down the stone hallways. When they noticed the gardens below the bedroom windows, they dashed down the staircase to go explore the grounds, Lucia yelling at their unseemly behavior. Calvo only shook his head and wandered as a man lost in a labyrinth.

"I thought we might still share a room," Samaritana said from entrance of a large bedroom where her sister stood.

Sunlight streamed in from glass doors open to the balcony. The smell of the briny bay wafted in on the breeze. A large, canopied bed anchored the room with a burst of colorful pillows atop. Two doorways on either side led to a bathroom and a closet overflowing with saris and veils, their new disguises. A pair of vanities filled the wall opposite the bed, a plush settee between them. The gold silk-covered walls held a regal elegance, much like the rest of the villa.

"That would be wonderful," Biancabella agreed before asking the question which most pressed on her heart. "What have you learned about Jaco?"

Samaritana took her hand and led her onto the balcony. The azure bay spread out in front of them, its surface dotted with boats of all size, sails fluttering in the breeze. To their right, the palace rose high, the standard of the king flying atop the tallest tower. Memories flooded Biancabella's mind—her and Jaco together, their love and devotion, the evil Finola stealing her life, Jaco accepting another in her place. So much had happened. *Could things ever go back to how they were? Did she even want them to?* Unsure of her feelings, she steeled herself for her sister's reply.

"The story is as we heard it. King Ferrandino returned successful in his battle against the King of Tunis at the end of the summer. He found a city ravaged by fever. He was told his wife nearly succumbed to the illness but survived. Dowager Finola lost both her daughters but tended to the queen. According to servant gossip, some suspected the new queen was not actual you, but were too afraid of the dowager to say anything, even to the king. Those I spoke with here say he is a different man—not the outgoing, benevolent king he once was, but brooding and unhappy.”

Biancabella’s heart broke at the thought. Deep down, her love for Jaco never diminished.

“I have to know what happened. Does he know it’s Renata and not me? Does he even care? We must find a way to see him.”

“Do not fear, Sister,” Samaritana consoled. “I have planted stories around about Calvo’s family and the exotic guests he brought from the East. I’m sure this has made its way to the king. Now all we need to do is invite him for a visit to make our acquaintance. But you must be strong, Biancabella. You must maintain your disguise until we can ascertain the truth about what the king knows and about Dowager Finola’s standing at court. Can you do that?”

The ex-queen knew her sister was right. As hard as it would be to not run right up to Jaco and reveal herself, she must see how things stood first. Dowager Finola tried to kill her once and would no doubt try again if she suspected Biancabella lived. The woman would also use every trick at her disposal to discredit Biancabella when she came forward and perhaps, she had enough sway over the king to get away with it. Until she knew what Jaco thought, her identity must remain a secret.

“I will not give myself away until we know it is safe,” Biancabella assured. “And until we know the dowager will receive the punishment she deserves.”

CHAPTER THIRTY-FOUR

The Brizia family sent a messenger to the palace inviting the king to the villa for introductions. A reply stated he would visit in two weeks' time, so the waiting began.

The adjustment to city life was an easier task for the daughters than for Calvo and Lucia. Their simple life in the cabin left them unprepared for life with servants. Many times, in those first days, Samaritana shooed Lucia away when she tried to assist with cooking or cleaning, insisting the family must learn to act like nobility.

Samaritana had ordered a fine workroom built in the back of the house for Calvo. Here he had every tool for woodcarving at his disposal. She lined up orders for both religious works and landscapes. Before long, Calvo happily spent his days producing marvelous carvings, which garnered him the reputation as the fine artisan Samaritana purported he was.

The daughters loved to explore the city's nearby market district. Overwhelmed with their recent good fortune, they were content to merely browse the various shops and soak in the finery. Lucia usually accompanied them, out of sorts with her new role of lady, which entailed far less work than she was used to. Still, the happiness of her children bolstered her.

Biancabella hardly ate or slept in the days leading up to the king's visit. Samaritana tried to distract her with lessons on transformation and harnessing her gifts again. Since her hands healed, flowers fell from them with little control and Biancabella needed to keep this ability in check. The sisters spent most of their time inside so as not to draw any unnecessary attention before the time was right.

The morning of the king's visit found the villa in chaos. Lucia sought to supervise the kitchen staff on the light lunch menu. Never had so much detail gone into planning a meal. The daughters raced in and out of each other's rooms, selecting the perfect gowns. Servants hurried about ensuring every corner of the house was spotless. Calvo, perturbed by the commotion, took refuge in his workroom.

In the sisters' room, Samaritana sat calmly in her chair while Biancabella paced the floor, hands wrung together. They were each dressed in beautiful silk saris, Samaritana's jade green and Biancabella's the bright blue of the bay. Silk wraps, threaded with gold, covered their heads with face veil's dangling down ready to pin into place.

"What if he recognizes me?" Biancabella fretted for the thousandth time.

"I promise my spell will make you unfamiliar to him. Do not worry. All will be well."

Samaritana stood, took her sister's hands, and murmured the words to pull the glamour over them. A blanket-like cloud enveloped them. When Biancabella looked in the mirror, she gasped at her transformed face. Indeed, the king would never know her.

"Do you think the Brizia's will be able to convince them of our story? You have the coloring of someone from the East, though I don't look like myself; I still am too fair to pass for Persian."

"Fear not, I have an explanation for that if asked," Samaritana replied. The sisters and the Brizia's had rehearsed for weeks precisely what to say so everyone's story would match seamlessly.

The clap of wheels on stone rang out as the king's carriage pulled through the gate. They hurried from the room, securing the veils over their faces, and joined the rest of the family where they waited in the courtyard. Three horsemen led the way, one holding the standard of the king. Behind it followed a gilded carriage drawn by a team of six, whose tails swished proudly. The vehicle rolled to a stop in front of them, a sight Biancabella had been a part of many times in her old life.

A footman set out a step and opened the door. Dowager Finola stepped out, her graying hair pulled up in a neat bun, in a dress of black crepe. Biancabella suppressed a gasp and Samaritana put a supportive hand on her back. Finola looked exactly as Biancabella remembered her, the same wicked glow in her eyes. Renata, who emerged next, did not. She was frail, almost shrunken, her beautiful lavender gown hung from her emaciated shoulders. While the dowager glanced around her with calculation, her daughter barely lifted her head to regard the family.

"He mistook *that* for you?" Samaritana whispered with indignance.

Biancabella barely listened as King Ferrandino materialized from the carriage. Though dressed in the opulent attire of royalty, he was but a shadow of himself. His gaunt frame and hollowed eyes evoked the sense his spirit had been sucked out of him, leaving this shell of a man in his place. Biancabella thought of the handsome young man who had spoken to her in the snow at Monferrato, with his hearty good looks and his sweet, dancing eyes. The sight of him now cut her very core.

“Greetings, Signori Brizia and your family,” the king stated.

“Greetings, Your Majesty,” Calvo boomed and dropped into the bow he practiced all week. Beside him, the ladies curtsied.

“Rise, my new friends,” Ferrandino ordered. “We are pleased to meet our new neighbors and hope this is the beginning of a hospitable relationship.”

Formal introductions were made of Calvo and Lucia, who then took the royal party on a brief tour of the villa and grounds. The others went to wait in the dining room, where Samaritana held Biancabella’s hand to keep her from pacing. The daughters clustered around her protectively. The king’s group eventually joined them and the meal began. Servants bustled nervously about with food and drink in their most formal attire, Samaritana proud of their efforts.

“It was a pleasure to see your home, Signori Brizia,” Ferrandino commented once they were settled at the table.

“Yes,” agreed Renata, her voice barely audible. “It was empty for so long after the fever. I am glad such a beautiful home has new occupants.”

“We are new to this lovely city, Your Majesties,” Lucia replied. “But hope to stay and make it our home.”

“I understand you traveled from the East after a lengthy stay there,” the king said. “Please introduce us to the rest of your family.”

“This is my eldest daughter, Alessandra. She is skilled in herbs and hopes to find a healer to assist.”

Alessandra nodded at the royals. King Ferrandino and Renata smiled graciously, but Dowager Finola looked down her nose at the girl.

"This is my middle daughter, Ginevra; an accomplished embroiderer. And next to her is my youngest, Cecelia."

"And the other two?" Dowager Finola asked, her voice clipped.

"Ah yes," Calvo said smoothly. "Meet Amytis and Katana. They are the daughters of a wealthy Persian patron who wanted them to visit the West for a time. I offered to chaperone them."

Biancabella inwardly sighed with relief when Calvo repeated their alibi with perfect ease, the hours of practice had paid off. The king and queen smiled at the sisters, while the dowager studied them as though they were cockroaches, but no trace of recognition appeared on any face.

"How wonderful," King Ferrandino declared. "I am honored you chose my city for your stay. You beautify it all the more with your presence."

Biancabella had heard the king pay such compliments many times in the past. They always sounded sincere and full of good cheer. No more. Now they were but perfunctory comment, spoken prettily but with no heart behind them. The magnificent lust for life her Jaco possessed had been doused, leaving this sullen man in his place. Despite her hurt and anger, she admitted to herself that he had suffered in her absence.

"You must have many interesting tales to tell from the East," Renata uttered, even more the skittish fawn than Biancabella remembered. Her sleeve fell off her gaunt shoulder, and Biancabella noticed a blue bruise before the fake queen quickly adjusted her dress.

"Yes, Your Majesty, we have many," Samaritana proclaimed, her voice exuding charm. "We would love to share them with you sometime."

The meal drew to a close with more pleasantries and the family saw the royal party back outside to their carriage. The dowager boarded with barely a look back, but Renata nodded her head in appreciation before ducking inside.

"I insist on repaying your courtesy," Ferrandino told Calvo. "Let us show you the splendor of the castle and present you to your fellow noble families. We will hold a banquet at which you will be the distinguished guest."

"It would be our honor," Calvo answered with a bow, and Biancabella suppressed a smile. Poor Calvo. Today's meeting had been stressful enough on him, now he must deal with a banquet at the palace.

"And you ladies," the king addressed the sisters, "must promise to regale us with some exotic stories of the East."

"Of course, Your Majesty," Samaritana said and dropped into a deep curtsey.

"Again, it was lovely to meet you and your beautiful family," Ferrandino stated before climbing into the carriage.

With a rousing of the horses, the driver swept the royals out the gate. The moment it was out of sight, the daughters broke into a frenzy of screams, a banquet at the palace beyond their wildest expectations. While Lucia tried her best to calm them, Calvo merely shook his head and groaned.

CHAPTER THIRTY-FIVE

"That went well," Samaritana declared.

She smoothed out her skirt after taking a seat on a bench in the garden where Biancabella paced in front of her. A view of the city opened beneath them, Mount Etna standing sentry behind it. The balmy air brushed their cheeks in the late afternoon sun. A servant placed a tray with wine and cheese on a side table and scurried away.

"I suppose," Biancabella murmured, the faraway look on her face not lost on her sister.

"Was it hard to see him again?" Samaritana asked, pouring them each a glass of wine.

"At first, but he is so changed from the man I fell in love with, so much more solemn. He has lost his spark for life." A fact which dispirited Biancabella more than anything. Passing in front of her sister, she added with certainty, "He knows his wife is not me. He did not look at her or touch her lovingly once the entire visit."

Samaritana agreed with the assessment but still wondered, "Why would he go along with it then?"

"I don't know. And I don't know how he will react when he finds out I'm alive." She paused and sank next to her sister on the bench. "And I'm not sure if I even want him to find out."

"Whatever do you mean?" Samaritana exclaimed, unnerved by her sister's admission.

"He is no longer the man I knew. What if he is forever altered? What if we both are? What if the spark of love we shared never rekindles but was merely a passing phase of youth and innocence? I have found a measure of peace with the Brizia's. Perhaps I should accept that and move on with my life."

Samaritana knelt before Biancabella and took her hands. "It is true you are both changed—tempered by loss, pain, and grief. But true love becomes stronger in these trials not weaker. Jaco deserves to know you live and Dowager Finola deserves to answer for her actions."

Biancabella closed her eyes, and a single tear slid down her cheek. "What if he cannot get past the loss of the baby?"

Though she seldom allowed herself to think of the miscarriage, the hole it left in her heart forever anguished her soul. Until this moment, she never mentioned it to Samaritana, fearing the crushing weight of acknowledgement would break her. Now, she attempted to stifle her sobs. Her sister's arms wrapped her in a tight embrace.

"Alessandra told me about the baby. I'm so very sorry, Biancabella. Much was robbed from both you and Jaco. All the more reason you should have a chance at happiness again." She stroked her sister's golden locks. "All will be well."

The familiar words settled Biancabella's mind. Her sister was right. Jaco had a right to know the truth. How he reacted and what became of their relationship only time would tell. Biancabella need closure one way or another, and the sooner the better.

"So how exactly will I reveal myself?" she asked.

"I have had a plan in mind for some time. Our little dinner at the palace should provide the perfect opportunity." Samaritana smiled mischievously at her sister.

As the day deepened, the sisters sat with heads together while Samaritana explained what she had in mind. They sat Calvo and Lucia down alone the next day to tell them what they had planned and assured them if anything went wrong, the sisters would protect the family. As always, the couple worried more about Biancabella and Samaritana than themselves, but all agreed the truth needed to be exposed.

When the appointed day for the banquet arrived, fair and cloudless, a frenzy of preparation filled the house. Servants hurried from room to room drawing baths, laying out gowns, and styling hair. Cecelia hurtled like a boomerang in their wake. Lucia tried to calm her youngest, but even the family's matriarch composure cracked under the anticipation as the evening drew closer. Calvo, who hid in his workroom since the first rays of dawn, begrudgingly came out to dress when his wife's pleas became frantic.

The excitement of the Brizia girls gave Biancabella something to concentrate on other than her nerves. She spent to morning helping them select their outfits, accessories, and hairstyles. The enthusiasm of the daughters was contagious and she couldn't help but smile at their glowing faces. After all, dining at a palace with a king must seem like something out of a fairy tale them. While the servants worked their magic on the daughters, Samaritana brought Biancabella to their room to dress.

"I had these imported from the East for a special occasion."

She motioned to the bed where two elegant saris lay. Samaritana handed one to Biancabella, its deep purple silk threaded with gold felt softer than anything she had ever touched. Her sister helped her wrap the material around her, gracefully draping it across her shoulder. A pair of beaded slippers and an exquisite jewel-encrusted veil completed the ensemble. After her eyes were lined with kohl, Biancabella stared at herself in the mirror. Even without the glamour Samaritana would cast, she would be hard to identify as the past queen.

Her sister looked equally exotic in midnight blue threaded with silver. Whereas Biancabella hid her golden hair, long ebony tresses emerged from beneath her sister's veil. Outlined in black, her amber eyes sparkled like topazes. They stood side by side in front of the mirror, one a ball of excitement, the other a ball of nerves. Samaritana's delight at executing her plan that evening matched Biancabella's dread.

A servant came to announce their carriage awaited. Down in the entryway, the sisters found the rest of the party gathered. Calvo allowed his family to splurge on their attire for this evening and the results were well worth it. The daughters blossomed like colorful flowers in a vibrant garden. Lucia's stately burgundy gown lent her an air of nobility. Even Calvo shone in a newly purchased velvet doublet. Gasps of admiration greeted the sisters and after much fussing, everyone piled into the carriage.

While the others buzzed with excitement, Biancabella concentrated on the clap of the horses' hooves, trying to slow her heart. The small length of city passed between the villa and the palace. Other carriages clogged the road on the way to the banquet. Citizens lined the roadside in clusters to watch the procession. The onlookers talked and laughed with each other as the pageantry paraded by. Biancabella wished she could jump out and join them to escape the complexity her life had become. Sensing her unease, Samaritana squeezed her hand and smiled.

The palace walls rose before them, and they swept through the gates. Once their carriage made it to the front staircase, a footman opened the door to help the ladies exit with Calvo at the rear. Biancabella stepped out, last hit by a pang of nostalgia at the once familiar courtyard. Her mind drew back to the first time she saw it. She stared around at the ivy-covered walls, the travertine, and the fountain with its lazy trickle. Nothing had changed. Nothing, except her entire life. In a daze, she climbed the steps to where the royal family waited to receive them.

"And you remember my charges," Calvo declared, jarring her mind back into focus, "Amytis and Katana."

"Of course," King Ferrandino acknowledged them both with an incline of his head while they curtsied. "Please allow me to give you and your family a tour of the grounds."

He turned and led them into the palace; this man so familiar yet so foreign. Biancabella crossed through the main doors which loomed like portals of no return. When she passed back through them tonight, she would have the answers she so desperately sought, for good or for evil.

CHAPTER THIRTY-SIX

Inside the castle, rooms unfolded just as Biancabella remembered them with little change.

The same tapestries lined the walls, the same portraits of long gone Ferrandino's hung in place, all in stark contrast to the changes Biancabella underwent in her absence. The ballroom and throne room evoked memories of happier times, which now clung to her like a faded dream. The gardens, which bloomed in full beauty, only reminded her of the days spent with her dear Tessina, lost to her now. While Lucia and her daughters gazed about them in awe during the length of the tour, she felt nothing but the emptiness of the lost innocence for the naïve girl who first sent foot here. Samaritana watched her with curiosity.

"And now, dinner awaits," King Ferrandino announced and led them up a terrace into the dining hall."

Renata, the imposter monarch, met them at the door. Dowager Finola loomed behind her with a hand firmly on her daughter's back, a menacing shadow dressed in black.

"And here again is my lovely wife, Biancabella," Ferrandino said.

"Whose beauty is spoken of throughout the world," Samaritana declared while the family curtsied to the queen.

An awkward silence followed the proclamation, now so decidedly untrue. The true Biancabella watched the king escort

Renata to the main table, his hand placed lightly on her elbow. The royal couple gestured for the others to follow. Biancabella studied Renata, wanting to find a hint of greed or complacency, but saw only bleakness in her eyes. The poor good-hearted girl acted as her mother's pawn in the dowager's lust for power, likely under threat of death should she speak out. Her job was to produce an heir and ensure their line—a feat she had yet to accomplish and the weight of this failure showed on every inch of the fragile woman. Where she looked to find vengeance in her heart, Biancabella only felt sympathy for Renata.

Calvo, Lucia, and the daughters sat in a row beside the queen. Biancabella and Samaritana sat on the other side with only the dowager between them and the king. Other guests of importance filled out the remainder of the head table.

The king engaged in conversation with Calvo, the usually reticent man taking the opportunity to praise the skills of his daughters, which both surprised and pleased Biancabella. She hoped the city held bright futures for them regardless of her own fate. While Ferrandino listened politely and complimented when expected., the actions appeared more automatic than the sincere interest and emotion of the man Biancabella married. The eyes of all in the room studied the guests of honor, a new family of nobility always an interesting subject and, of course, fodder for gossip.

Servants brought out platters heaped with cheeses, meats, nuts, and olives. They distributed the antipasto amongst the diners with the same precision and grace Biancabella recalled from her days here, ensuring all plates and wine glasses remained filled. Renata only picked at the plate of cheese and nuts in front of her. Once Ferrandino saw everyone served, he turned his attention to the sisters.

"Tell me, young ladies, where are you from?"

"Persia," Samaritana replied, after delicately wiping her mouth with a napkin.

"Ah, an exotic place from the tales I've heard. You grace my court with your beauty," he complimented.

"Katana, is it?" Dowager Finola asked, fixing them with a harsh stare and Samaritana nodded. "Interesting that you have the dark complexion of the Persians, while your *sister* Amytis does not. Such a mystery."

Biancabella froze. *Did the dowager already suspect something amiss with their story?*

"In truth, we are half-sisters," Samaritana replied smoothly. "Both daughters of a pasha from his harem. Her mother was sold as a slave from a conquered land. That accounts for the differences in our skin tone."

All mouths gaped at the casual mention of harems, and Biancabella suppressed a smile at her sister's cleverness. Ferrandino gave the dowager a withering glance for the rudeness of the question. While she continued to stare at the girls non-plussed, he sought to change the subject.

"And what do you think of my fair city?" he asked.

"It is lovely, indeed. Truly a jewel on the bay as described. I've heard many stories of its beauty and must say it surpasses them all," Samaritana complimented, and Biancabella was grateful for her sister's charm.

The meal progressed with more elaborate courses. Beef, veal, and lamb, tender and juicy from the bone, platters overflowing with vegetables, rich pasta dishes and warm bread straight from the oven. Wine continued to flow freely. With each glass served by the girl who stood behind him, King Ferrandino relaxed a bit more and Renata's burden lightened on her face.

Biancabella almost envied them—the escape of intoxication—but she and Samaritana needed clear heads and drank only sparingly, but Biancabella felt a hint of familiarity about the servant girl. The dowager did not imbibe much either, her hawklike gaze always returning to the sisters.

Dessert arrived; a mountain of pies, puddings, and clotted creams. Along with the sweets, musicians entered the hall, lutes, and flutes in hand. They played lively tunes and some of the guests rose to dance. Next, one man sung a ballad of a heroic king who saved his people to return home to his true love. His voice held a mournful edge, eliciting a smattering of applause upon his completion.

"How lovely," Samaritana praised, and Biancabella sensed their moment was near.

"Did you find it enjoyable?" the king asked, his head leaning around the dowager, who had remained silent after her earlier remark.

"Yes, very much. Music is an art felt in the heart. The commonality of it bridges all cultures."

"What a delightful way to explain it," Ferrandino responded, with the first genuine smile Biancabella had seen on his face.

"We have many stories told through song in our land as well," Samaritana informed him.

"I would love to hear one sometime."

"You can hear one right now if you like, though I will require a lyre and some pillows to sit upon."

With a clap of his hands, the king summoned the requested instrument. Biancabella stiffened as the first part of their plan unfolded. Samaritana walked to the front side of the table where servants laid pillows on the floor in front of the king's spot. She settled herself among them, arranging her sari in an elegant drape around her legs away from the lyre. With a flick of her hand, she strummed a few tones and sang. From the first note, her rich, haunting voice captivated the room.

Once there lived a wise Maharajah, beloved by his people
His empire was his jewel, eclipsed only by the beauty of his wife
One day the call of war fell on him, and he marched out to defend his realm
Though he triumphed in battle, he returned to find his domain ravaged by plague
His dear wife was ill, she looked not familiar to him and he anguished at the sight
But palace walls are not deaf and blind and some knew the truth
His true wife was murdered, betrayed by one close to the Maharajah
This betrayer installed an imposter on the throne in the queen's stead
Yet such lies cannot be forever hidden, vengeance coming swift and hard for the guilty
Though he could not have his beloved wife, he had justice for her
His heart, still broken to this day, beats with the satisfaction of this restitution

Samaritana's voice faded, the last poignant notes of the lyre echoing off the stone walls only to be replaced with stunned silence.

CHAPTER THIRTY-SEVEN

As one, the room looked toward King Ferrandino, except for Biancabella whose eyes remained glued to her hands in her lap. After an expectant hush, the king clapped his hands, and the room broke into cheers from the crowd. Samaritana stood and bowed her head in acknowledgment before returning to her sister's side at the table. Biancabella could feel the penetrating stare of the dowager burn on them.

"That was an interesting song," Ferrandino ventured, the shaky grip on his goblet belying the calm in his voice. "Is it an old tale?"

"Yes, quite old," Samaritana replied, "though the sentiment endures. The desire for power and betrayal are not strangers to court life, are they?"

"No, I suppose not," he faltered while the servant refilled his hastily drained glass.

Biancabella dared a glance and saw the king's pale face behind Dowager Finola's sharp glower. Renata's nervous eyes darted everywhere but on the sisters, and the Brizia's all sat with countenances frozen in polite smiles. At the other tables, she watched courtiers talk behind their hands casting suspicious glances at both the dowager and Samaritana.

"I do not think that an appropriate song for entertainment," Finola huffed once she found her voice.

"My dearest dowager," Samaritana crooned, "the tale seems to have resonated with you."

Dowager Finola rose abruptly, glasses and platters clattering on the table. "I do not know what passes for manners in your country, but they are certainly not the norm here. Come, Biancabella." She motioned to Renata. "I've lost my appetite."

With a forlorn glance back at King Ferrandino, the phony queen exited in her mother's wake while the room watched in rapt silence. Carlo and Lucia shared a concerned glance. The flustered king regained his composure and ordered the musicians to play once more. The guests returned to their conversations while a happy tune rang out. Samaritana simply picked on some sweets left on her plate as though nothing unusual had happened, but Biancabella noticed more than a few surreptitious eyes on the main table.

"My apologies for my stepmother," King Ferrandino said to the sisters. "Her behavior is inexcusable to guests in my palace."

"My apologies for offending her. I seem to have struck a chord," Samaritana replied slyly.

"She lost both of her daughters to a fever last summer. Talk of death bothers her," he explained.

"Talk of death or talk of betrayal?" Samaritana looked the king squarely in the eye.

"What exactly are you trying to say?" Ferrandino bristled.

"Nothing your heart does not already know."

The king blanched but said no more. He turned his concentration to his plate. The servant came forward again to fill his wine glass. From her vantage point, she surely overheard the conversation. Biancabella felt the woman's eyes on her and her sister. Biancabella met the brown orbs piercing hers searchingly. *Aurelia*, her former maid, a bit more mature, but no doubt the same sweet girl who served with Tessina. She seemed to want to say something to Biancabella, but instead returned to her post against the wall.

The evening continued with stilted conversation. Everyone at the head table shifted in their seats through one clumsy attempt after another at reviving pleasant conversation. Only Samaritana was at ease, sampling the dainty cakes in front of her. The king asked Calvo about his carvings yet remained unable to focus on the answer, a distracted crease in his brow. Biancabella recognized the mark of his temper and worried Samaritana pushed too hard with her song.

Finally, he turned to Samaritana, "I would like a word in private with you and your sister."

"Of course, Your Highness, we would be honored." She rose as though this was a most natural request. Biancabella stood rigidly, her heart hammering away.

A guard escorted them out of the dining hall, inquisitive gazes following their every step. Calvo watched them go, worry painted on his face. If the king did not believe the girls, his whole family may suffer the consequences.

Ferrandino led them to a small receiving room, brightly lit by sconces despite its lack of windows. A small desk sat in the middle with two upholstered chairs in front. Biancabella knew it was for used for his most private discussions. He motioned for the guard to leave and the man shut door with a hesitant glance at his sovereign.

"What exactly was the meaning of that song?" he demanded, anger lacing his voice.

"Did it hold some special meaning for you, Your Highness," Samaritana inquired with a complacent edge.

In an instant, Ferrandino's expression turned from one of fury to one of despair. He looked around the room as if to make sure no one else could hear them, his breaths shallow. He sank into one of the chairs, head in his hands.

"My wife is not my wife," he whispered. "She is the daughter of my stepmother. Her name is Renata but we all pretend she is Biancabella."

"Why would you go along with such a charade?" Biancabella exclaimed, unable to keep the hurt out of her tone.

"When I returned from Tunis, Finola tried to convince me it was Biancabella. The girl was so wasted by fever, I hardly recognized her as anyone. Even so, I felt sure it was not my Biancabella." He leaned back in the chair and stared blankly ahead.

"So, you did not care enough to find out what happened to your real wife?" Samaritana accused, not moved by his misery.

"I was told both the dowager's daughters died. There were two bodies removed from her chamber. My servants confirmed it. I knew the dowager always wanted me to marry one of her daughters and guessed she replaced Biancabella with Renata. That meant my beloved wife had gone to her death, and with it, she took my heart, my soul, my reason to live." A sob came from deep within him. "But I am king; I had no time for grieving in a city ravaged by fever and a crisis of war only narrowly averted. So, for the greater good, I went along with it, not wanting to rob the city of its queen with all the other loss it suffered.

"I thought I did the right thing. After all, I could not bring Biancabella back from the dead. I numbed my heart and mind to the loss. But tonight, your song woke something in me, makes me wonder if I overlooked a far more heinous design than I have accepted all this time.

The women stood silent while thoughts turned over in his head. He raked his hands through his hair and asked with desperation, "Was my wife murdered?"

"No," Samaritana proclaimed and relief filled his face until she continued, "but someone tried to murder her."

"You know this? How?"

Samaritana raised her hands and whispered a few words in her sister's direction. Biancabella felt the glamour lift. She removed her veil and her golden hair cascaded down her back. Her whole body tingled as the king stared at her, his mouth agape.

"Biancabella?" he muttered, white as a man who has seen a ghost.

"Yes," she confirmed.

He stood and took a tentative step toward her. Eyes filled with wonder, he reached out to touch her arm as though to confirm she was a corporeal form. His fingers drifted to the golden rings around her neck. "How can this be?"

"Dowager Finola hired an assassin. He brought me deep into the woods to murder me. He failed when my sister killed him instead, saving me."

"Biancabella, you had no sister," the king said, pulling back his hand as though tricked.

"Yes, I do. A magical one. One I told you about long ago. One you dismissed as the imagination of a lonely girl."

At these words, Samaritana transformed into a green snake which slithered out of the pile of silk from her sari and up Biancabella to rest perfectly in the golden circles around her neck. King Ferrandino sank back into the chair. He sat for several minutes, his gaze becoming more focused but also more skeptical.

"Clearly, you are both gifted with magic. How do I know what you're saying is true and not some deception of the mind?"

Biancabella knelt and took his hands. She looked into his handsome eyes, so burdened now than when they first met. "When you proposed to me in the library, you swore to me that my heart completed yours and you only ever felt whole when we were together. I feel that wholeness now, don't you?"

Tears filled his eyes. "Yes, my Biancabella, I do."

He pulled her into an embrace and flower petals flowed from her palms like raindrops onto the carpet.

CHAPTER THIRTY-EIGHT

The king's disappearance with the foreign ladies caused a stir in the dining hall, the courtiers ever on high alert for juicy gossip. Calvo fidgeted in his seat, his foot tapping the ground. He watched the doorway where the three had disappeared, all sorts of scenarios running through his mind. As much as he wanted the king to know the truth, he worried for his family. Lucia placed a hand on his in an effort to calm him.

In the private room, King Ferrandino remained overcome with emotion at the homecoming of his true wife, equal parts joyful and infuriated by both the return and the deception. While he embraced his wife, Samaritana had slithered to the floor and reverted to human form. The king opened his arms to include her, even more petals scattered to the floor.

"I am sorry I did not believe you all those years ago, Biancabella. Your sister saved you. She is dearer to me now than all others but yourself." Ferrandino appeared a changed man, the life and vigor back on his face.

Samaritana bowed her head at the pronouncement.

"The dowager will pay for what she did to you," he promised.

"There is a bit more," Biancabella informed him. "Tuccio, the man who tried to assassinate me, told me I was not his first job for the dowager. She hired him to poison your father. That is the reason he died."

"How could I have been so blind for so long?" he muttered to himself, before shouting, "Guards!"

The door flung open and two of his personal guards stepped in, one a bit taller than the other, like mismatched bookends. Both took in the scene, their eyes widening at the sight of the queen as they remembered her. One's jaw visibly gaped while the other muttered to himself about the petals all over the floor.

"Fetch Dowager Finola straight away. Bring her to the throne room," the monarch ordered.

"Yes, Your Majesty," answered the taller one. "Right away."

The king led the sisters back to the dining hall, the shorter guard trotting alongside. Upon their entry, a hush fell over the room, the chatter extinguished at the sight of the trio. Ferrandino went directly to Calvo, whose face was a study of worry. He nervously stood; Lucia rising as well, her hand on his arm. Whatever the consequences, they would face them as one.

"My dear man," the king exclaimed, "how can I ever thank you for all you have done for my wife? You and your family have my eternal gratitude."

Calvo's shoulders relaxed, and he smiled at his wife and daughters, who gathered around Biancabella and Samaritana. From around the room, audible gasps rose as one courtier after another recognized their queen as she had once been. Murmurs began, with pointing fingers, and the king held up his hands, startling the room into silent disbelief.

"My citizens, I have both happy and evil tidings," the king announced. "As you can see, my queen, the lovely Biancabella, has returned to us. My happiness at this cannot be measured. However, an attempt was made on her life which left her near death, until this wonderful family nursed her back to health. She returns to us now with her sister. Those responsible will pay the price for their betrayal."

A buzz of conversation filled the room, people stammering amongst themselves while they looked at the royal couple. Biancabella smiled at a few of the familiar faces, but the returned smiles were strained. It was one thing to convince the king, quite another to convince a kingdom. Ferrandino's chief advisor, Tebaldo, came forward and pulled Ferrandino aside.

"I do not mean to be indelicate, Your Highness, but how can we be sure this is not some trick. This woman did not look like our beloved Biancabella earlier, yet now she does. Could it not be some glamour meant to deceive you? To manipulate the most wounded part of your heart? Is there any proof her claim is real?" He pulled nervously on his graying beard, caught between trying to protect and trying not to upset his king.

Before the king could answer, Aurelia, who still stood on the dais, strode purposefully from her spot against the wall. "If you please, Your Highness, I have something to say which may be helpful."

"Yes, of course, Aurelia, long have you been in our service. What have you to say?" he inquired.

"One day during the sickness, I brought fresh sheets to the queen's room. She was there with Tessina, both perfectly healthy. To help her combat her boredom during the quarantine, I brought her paper and charcoal. The queen drew this picture which she both signed and dated." She reached into the pocket of her dress and pulled out a folded square of parchment, every eye in the room glued to it.

Aurelia's ingenuity and composure impressed Biancabella. Her story rang across the room of guests further stunned that the testimony of a maid was now part of the equation

"When I returned the next day, I was told the queen was wasting away from fever. The woman in the bed did not look anything close to the how the queen appeared just the day before. In my gut, I felt something was amiss, so I grabbed this picture and have kept it ever since. If this woman is truly our queen, she will know what the drawing is."

"It is a drawing of my childhood home in Monferrato—the castle on the hill with the Alps in the background," Biancabella stated, tears in her eyes at the thought of her last day with Tessina, of all that was taken from her. "The dowager had me taken that night."

Aurelia handed the parchment to the king, who carefully unfolded it to reveal a neatly sketched castle with snow-covered mountains in the distance. He held it up for all in the hall to see. Nods and smiles filled the faces of all, even Tebaldo.

"My dear queen, what you must have been through. Forgive me," the elder councilor apologized. "And Dowager Finola was behind it all?"

All ears craned to hear the drama on the dais, and the king turned to face them.

"As you hear, Dowager Finola attempted to murder our good queen and placed her daughter on the throne in Biancabella's stead. I have been blind to her evil but I assure you all, she will pay dearly for her crimes. If you will excuse us, we must see to this matter immediately."

He took his wife's hand and led her out of the dining room down the long hall to the throne room. Along the way, he ordered several more guards to follow. Tebaldo came as well, his brow furrowed in thought at the severity of the situation.

In the empty room, Ferrandino led Biancabella to their thrones. The sentries, who guarded the doors all night, looked in wonder at the couple and shot questioning glances at their comrades. Once settled in their seats, the king took a few deep breaths, steeling himself for the encounter. Steps rang out in the hall, the echo off the marble growing with each successive footfall. The taller of the king's guards hurried into the room out of breath.

"Your Highness, I'm sorry but we have looked everywhere. The dowager and her daughter are not in the castle. They have escaped."

CHAPTER THIRTY-NINE

A frenzy of activity filled the night. King Ferrandino shouted orders from one person to the next. The palace, awash with rumors of the return of the true queen and the guilty dowager, did not settle until the wee hours of the morning. By then, one of the dowager's servants revealed where the woman and her daughter fled—Monferrato.

"She goes to your cousin Piero for aid," the king informed Biancabella, "though how she expects to fool him, I do not know."

"What of my parents?" a confused Biancabella asked.

The king's face grew somber. "We have much to discuss." He took her hand and told Tebaldo, "My queen and I will return to my chambers. Send any word to me immediately."

"Yes, Your Majesty," the contrite man said, eager to obey.

He led her down a hallway, where Calvo paced, while Alessandra, Ginevra, and Samaritana sat. Lucia helped Aurelia hand them mugs of warm ale. Only Cecelia, asleep on her mother's cloak, found any rest from the events of the evening.

"Take your family home. Biancabella is quite protected here with me. You will be rewarded handsomely when this is over," the king told the woodsman.

"No reward is necessary," Calvo replied, "so long as Biancabella is safe and happy."

Biancabella hugged him and Lucia. The family left, tired but happy the truth had come to light, Cecelia propped up between her sisters, with rumpled gowns and heavy eyes. Samaritana came to stand next to her Biancabella.

"Go to my chambers," Biancabella told her. "I will join you there in a while."

"I'll take her," Aurelia volunteered, and they departed down a corridor to the left.

Ferrandino locked hands with his wife and they walked to his chamber. Two guards stationed at the door opened it and stepped back. His room was exactly as Biancabella remembered—the stately bed, the simple but elegant décor, and the smell of pine and sandalwood. A large portrait of her hung on the wall, commissioned when she had first arrived in Naples. She surveyed the image of the happy, naïve girl who believed in love and goodness so fiercely. A pang stabbed through her at the memories of all that had transpired.

"So much has happened since we last stood here together." Her husband echoed her thoughts.

"Yes," she sighed, a realization dawned on her. "My parents are dead, aren't they?"

"I'm sorry to tell you they are. The fever reached as far north as Monferrato. They died only moments apart, according to Piero. He was next in line for succession. I sent a delegation to pay my respects shortly after I returned from Tunis. Your cousin is young but seems to have a sensible head on his shoulders."

Biancabella mourned the news of her parents. Sorrow mixed with guilt. She had not ever thought to worry for their well-being, considered them constants in the background of her life. Now they were beyond her reach. And poor Piero. She remembered her childhood playmate, so stern all the time. Her parents acted as his since his early days. Now he bore the heavy burden of leadership after being orphaned for a second time.

"Why would the dowager go to him, I wonder?"

"I suspect to continue passing off Renata as you. She will try to convince him I have been tricked and enlist his help to defend them. And I was tricked—by her! Oh Biancabella," he groaned, a guttural noise from deep within. "How could I have been so foolish? I knew Renata wasn't you, yet my broken heart accepted defeat. I did not even challenge the dowager. Will you ever be able to forgive me?"

He sank onto the edge of the bed, his head in his hands. Biancabella knelt in front of him and lifted his chin.

"I was angry and hurt, I admit it. Yet I see now that you truly believed me to be dead and how it broke you. How could you have ever guessed the depths of the dowager's treachery?"

"But I should have!" he insisted. "Especially after all the rumors she poisoned my father. I should have done more. I should not have given up."

"Jaco, you and I were the same in our belief in the goodness of the world and the kindness of the people in it. Neither of us could imagine the profound evil in the dowager's heart. Perhaps we were ingenuous and idealistic before life stole the notion from us. I, too, gave up. I hid my identity and let self-pity overcome me. But we must not surrender our love for life, for each other. The world needs people like us, ones who have been shown unimaginable wickedness and still choose not to abandon the idea that goodness is more powerful than evil. If we cannot do this, then the dowager and everyone like her will prevail."

"My sweet love, you who have been through so much are now strong enough for both of us." He pulled her onto the bed beside him. "Now, if it isn't too difficult, please tell me what happened that last night."

The king listened, wavering between horror and anger, while the story unfolded. Biancabella recounted the murder of Tessina, the abduction by Tuccio, her wounds and his eventual death with the appearance of Samaritana. When she paused, the king asked the painful question she expected.

"And the baby?"

"I lost the baby," she sobbed, emotions welling for the unspent grief of her miscarriage. "I'm sorry. There was nothing I could do."

He swept her into his arms, and they laid back on the bed. She rested her head against his chest, where the beating of his heart and the solidness of his form brought her a comfort she had forgotten existed.

"Never apologize for what that bitch did to you." The harshest words she ever heard him utter. "And I want you to know, I have never lain with Renata nor has she tried to get me to. We are husband and wife in name only."

He gently stroked her hair, combing his fingers through her long blond locks. Several small gems bounced onto the mattress along with some flower petals from her hands. For a moment, they stared at them silently before sharing a smile.

"There is one more thing," Biancabella said. "My sister. When I first told you and you didn't believe me, I denied her existence for fear that you would not accept me if you knew about her. That is a mistake I can never undo. She is part of me as I am part of her, and I can no longer disavow her importance in my life and the importance of honoring our gifts. To love me fully, you must love her as a sister, as the part of me she is. Our gifts set us apart from others and will continue to do so."

"I will love her like family, for that is what she is. Never feel the need to hide anything from me again. I am sorry I rebuffed your original attempt to tell me of her," he apologized. "But know, there is nothing that could change my love for you."

Ferrandino rose and called for his guard. He ordered him to bring Samaritana to them. She entered shortly thereafter with a hopeful look at the couple.

"Samaritana, this is Jaco, my husband and my love," Biancabella introduced. "Jaco, this is my twin, my dear sister, a gifted healer."

King Ferrandino bowed. He took Samaritana's hand and placed a kiss. "Biancabella told me about you once and I thought it the imaginations of a lonely girl. I am grateful I was wrong. Thank you for saving her."

"She is more important to me than anyone. I will always be here to protect her. We are not meant to be parted from each other. When we are together, fate smiles on us."

"Your bond is a special one," the king proclaimed. "I understand this now and have no intention of trying to break it."

The sisters hugged, more petals raining from the queen's hands. Once again, Ferrandino embraced them both and Biancabella's heart burst with happiness.

"You have both been through so much suffering. But now, you are with me and we will never be parted," he asserted. "It is time to find the woman responsible for our anguish and punish her accordingly."

CHAPTER FORTY

Biancabella paced her room, her mind a jumble of thoughts about the dowager and her cousin. The balcony doors framed a magnificent sunrise, and the bay rippled in a circle of pink where the orb kissed the horizon. After spending the night with Jaco, she returned to her room in the pre-dawn hours to curl up with her sister. Her reunion with her husband, both sweet and passionate, brought a smile to her face, before her immediate worries crept back in.

Coming to terms with the death of her parents would take time. Parents seem immortal beings to the young, wise councilors who know all the answers. Now, her poor cousin was thrust in the middle of the dowager's scheming. To what length would she resort to continue her deception? Would she put the boy's life in jeopardy?

"What will Piero think? Do you suppose he will believe Dowager Finola?" she asked her sister, who sat calmly on a tufted chair picking at the remnants of her breakfast on the table before her.

"I think once Piero sees you, there will be no question the dowager lies. Now, please come and eat something before you wear a hole in the carpet."

Biancabella did as bidden and sat across from her sister. Samaritana buttered a sweet roll and placed it on the empty plate in front of the queen. She added some strawberries, then poured a glass of juice. Biancabella nibbled on the roll absently.

"Jaco does not want me to go to Monferrato. He thinks the dowager is too dangerous. But how else can we convince my cousin?"

Aurelia knocked to announce her entrance. She surveyed the sisters, one the picture of relaxation, the other with hands wrung together. A younger girl with eyes as big as saucers entered behind the maid. They both curtsied to Biancabella, who bid them to rise.

"This is Isotta. She served the dowager and overheard her last night when that accursed woman hastily packed to escape."

"Isotta, did the dowager say anything other than where they were going?" Biancabella asked the timid girl, who looked everywhere but directly at the queen.

"As I told the head of the guard, Your Highness, all she said was Piero would help them. She seemed quite certain of it. The queen . . . I mean, Renata begged to be left behind but her mother would not hear of it."

While Isotta spoke, Aurelia changed the bedding and straightened up the room, but stopped in surprise at this tidbit of information. Samaritana appeared astonished.

"So, Renata wanted to stay behind and face charges of treason?" she asked.

"I'm not sure she thought about that. I think she just wanted this all to be over."

"What does Renata want over?" Samaritana asked, eyes narrowing.

The flustered girl's head bobbed between the queen and her sister, and Aurelia came to put a comforting hand on her back.

"It's all right to talk to us. You are not in any kind of trouble," Biancabella reassured.

"May I speak freely, Your Majesty?" Isotta inquired. After a nod from the queen, she continued, "I have served the dowager since I arrived in the palace. Renata was never a willing participant in her mother's charade, not like Lisabetta would have been, God rest her soul. The dowager threatened to kill her daughter if she tried to expose the truth and she beat her regularly to keep her in check. Honestly, Renata was so ill when you were kidnapped, she did not know the full evil of her mother's plan. She believed you died of the fever like her sister. If she had known you lived, perhaps she would have done more to stand against her mother."

Biancabella lowered her fork to stare empty-eyed at her plate. "So many lives ruined in Finola's quest for power. Renata always showed me true kindness. To have your own mother threaten to murder you, to beat you, how unthinkable!"

"We will see that all is made right. Do not worry," Samaritana said and reached for her sister's hand across the table.

"Thank you, Isotta, for both your honesty and your loyalty. I would be honored to have you serve me and my sister from now on."

The girl's face broke into a broad smile as she stammered out words of gratitude. Aurelia scooped up the dirty bedding and told Isotta to remove the breakfast tray. Once the servants left the sisters, they sat in contemplative quiet, until another knock on the door. This time a page boy summoned them to the king.

They joined Ferrandino in the throne room, where he sat at a large table flanked by his advisors. Biancabella remembered these sessions with his council and now noticed a few empty seats, like missing pieces from a board game. From his position at the head of the table, the king motioned the ladies to sit. Silence followed while they took their places among the grim countenances.

"Dowager Finola's treachery runs deeper than expected," Ferrandino informed them. "She had many guards and even some council members loyal to her. They have escaped with her and will uphold her story to your cousin."

"What story?" Biancabella asked, filled with guilt that Piero would be another of the dowager's pawn.

"She told many of us that a sorceress has bewitched the king into believing an imposter is his wife," an older gentleman explained; Lord Beltramo, if Biancabella remembered correctly. "Many deemed her story credible and fled before they too could fall to the influence of the sorceress. She was quite convincing in her distress for our safety."

"Did no one suspect her lies when she first tried to pass Renata off as Biancabella?" Samaritana uttered in dismay.

"A few, who are with her now, were either bribed or blackmailed for their propagation of her lies," the lord added, running fingers through his thinning gray hair. "With so many to corroborate her account, it was difficult to push back."

"So, the rest of you just went along?" Samaritana retorted, accusation dripping from her words.

Most of the men dropped their eyes to their lap, but Tebaldo spoke, "More should have been done at the time. We are all culpable."

"No," King Ferrandino contested, "the fault is mine." He turned to his wife, "Biancabella, news of your illness crushed me, but when I realized it was Renata and not you, I remained silent. I thought you were dead, and I wanted to be dead too. In my weakness, I failed my council, my kingdom, and most importantly, you."

"Jaco," Biancabella spoke softly and took his trembling hand, "you were blinded by grief, and I by despair. We all played a part. But now that we know the truth. Let us not dwell on the past but plan the way forward. Let us defeat this woman who used us all to her evil ends. How many guards have gone with Finola?"

"About one quarter of them," replied another council member, his voice oddly deep for his small frame.

"So many?" Samaritana exclaimed.

"Finola bribed many soldiers as did the council members who went along with her," Lord Beltramo affirmed.

"Those men coupled with that of Monferrato's will be a formidable foe," the deep-voiced man declared.

"Lord Magazza is right," the king agreed. "Yet we have no choice but to march on his lands and try to get him to see the truth."

"I hate to see bloodshed on either side," Biancabella lamented. "Poor Piero will think he is doing the right thing by protecting the false me."

"Indeed, we wish to avoid combat at all costs, but there is no guarantee that diplomacy will work," the chief advisor admitted.

"We may have another choice," Samaritana's voice rang out, her glance went around the table and stopped at the king. "If you can get Biancabella and me to the castle in Monferrato, I am certain we can convince him the truth of this matter."

"How?" Ferrandino asked

Samaritana took her sister's hand. "I have a plan."

CHAPTER FORTY-ONE

The trip north took several days. King Ferrandino, not wishing to appear overly aggressive, took only fifty men. This enabled them to travel far more quickly than a large army. Back in the Naples, the greater part of his forces mustered for the call if needed.

Every accommodation was made to make the trip easy for Biancabella and Samaritana. They had a large tent filled with a bed, which a horse pulled in a wagon, along with other supplies at the rear of the group. Biancabella argued they needed no special treatment, but Ferrandino insisted, a fact she secretly appreciated each night on the comfortable mattress. Yet, she managed to talk him into letting her and her sister ride horses instead of being drawn by a slow carriage.

Fair weather helped speed the way and early on the fourth day, Monferrato came into view, looking just the way Biancabella remembered it. In the light morning mist, red roofs climbed the hill to the castle, the lofty snow-capped Alps rising in the background. Fraught with nerves, she had not noticed much on the trip, but the sight of her old home took her breath away. Across a dewy field, the gates of the city stood open, beckoning her.

The king halted on this open plain just shy of the gates. Wind swept gently across the grass, the air far lighter than the salty humidity of Naples. The sisters dismounted taking in the scene.

Rays of sunlight pierced the mist with slanting beams, and birdsong stirred in the nearby trees. Biancabella gazed up at the castle, the standard of the marquis, rippling on the highest tower.

"It is as if nothing changed," she commented, but knowing the pennant now represented Piero, the new marquis, added "but in truth, everything has."

Samaritana put an arm around her shoulder, and they stood as one. Biancabella recalled their meeting in the garden, all the shared secrets from their youth. How safe their existence had been until she upended it all.

"I should have listened to you all those years ago. I should have obeyed you and never left. I should never have denied your existence to Jaco and should have been proud to call you my sister. So much misery could have been avoided."

"No, I was wrong to make you choose me over all others," Samaritana reflected. "When I discovered our fates spoke of suffering if we were separated, I tried to protect you by keeping you my prisoner. My unreasonable demands and stubbornness caused our woes as well."

"It seems we have learned that the trials of life cannot be avoided, they can only be faced," Biancabella declared. "Instead of bemoaning the past, let us use the adversity we overcame to our advantage, by realizing our true strength stems not from denying or punishing each other, but by uniting to become our best possible selves."

While they shared a tearful embrace, King Ferrandino approached. "I ordered the bulk of the men to remain here. The three of us will go up with eight guards and try to speak with Piero civilly."

"And if that doesn't work?" Samaritana questioned.

"Then we will try your plan."

They remounted and rode through the city walls. No one stopped them but a sentry at the gate hurried up the hill at the sight of them. The road crisscrossed back and forth up the slope of the hill; the hooves clapping on the cobblestones. Residents in the middle of their morning tasks halted to stare at the party, some pointing fingers and whispering. A few went inside their homes and shut the doors tight as though expecting trouble. Some adventurous folk, including a number of children, followed behind, the prospect of what may happen too tempting to miss. At the castle walls, the gates were closed, soldiers standing in front of them, more appeared on the parapet above.

"Halt!" A decorated officer stepped forward. "Announce your name and the purpose of your business at once."

"I am King Ferrandino of Naples. I seek to speak with Marquis Lamberico regarding his harboring of fugitives."

The man walked back the gates where he whispered through a small grate. The lock clicked, and the gate ground open just wide enough to let one person exit. Dressed in the robes of a priest, the stout man with a tonsured scalp walked to Ferrandino, who dismounted to meet him after motioning Biancabella to join him.

"Greetings, I am Father Bessimo. We harbor no fugitives here and we ask that you remove yourself and your men immediately." His kindly voice held no hint of threat, only the polite sternness mastered by the clergy.

"Do you see this woman here?" the king gestured to Biancabella. "This is my wife, Biancabella, the rightful Queen of Naples. Dowager Finola tried to have her murdered. If you give her sanctuary, you are indeed harboring a fugitive. One who deserves to pay for her crimes."

The priest regarded Biancabella with scrutiny, his gaze fell to Samaritana, still on her horse, and came back to the king. "Might I have a word with you alone, Your Highness?"

"No. Anything you have to say can be spoken in front of my wife."

While the priest hesitated, more citizens and soldiers ringed the group, straining to hear the conversation, their murmurs and gossip silenced for the moment. A small herd of goats scrambled between the party and the wall, its young shepherd's mouth agape amid their bleating and clapping hooves. He hurried the animals in the direction of the open pastures.

"Dowager Finola is here," Father Bessimo confirmed when the noise died down. "She told us a number of . . . concerning things and asked for our protection."

"And what are these concerning things?" the king asked, his patience fraying.

"That you, Your Highness, have been bewitched by a sorceress who poses as the queen but is really an imposter."

"That is a lie!" Ferrandino bellowed, causing both Biancabella and the priest to jump. "I demand to see the marquis at once!"

At the outburst, the guards from the gate slipped forward to assist the befuddled cleric. The mutterings from the crowd grew louder, people arguing whether the dowager or the king spoke the truth. Many stared openly at Biancabella, a sad longing in their eyes for the beautiful young girl who once graced the city, their wildest hope to find it was truly her. She scanned the mass of faces in search of anyone familiar, but to no avail. The decorated officer placed himself between the king and Father Bessimo, who rushed back to the safety inside the castle gate.

"I must ask you to leave," he ordered. "Return to your home and leave us in peace."

King Ferrandino's eyes bulged with fury, but Samaritana came and put a hand on his arm. They exchanged a meaningful glance. The gathered citizens again turned their attention to the confrontation. In the quiet that followed, only a baby's cry was heard. Biancabella smelled burning meat from an unoccupied stall while all waited for the king's response.

"Very well," he said after a deep breath.

Everyone watched intently as three remounted and slowly turned to depart. Most of the assembly, including the officer, trailed them all the way down the switchbacks to the main gate. The sun burned brightly on the king's party across the plain to where the remainder of the retinue waited. Wind blew the scent of the poplars from a small copse, reminding Biancabella of happier times here.

Once inside the privacy of the tent, King Ferrandino turned to Samaritana. "Our attempts at diplomacy failed. Now is the time for your plan."

CHAPTER FORTY-TWO

"Are you sure I will be able to hold the transformation long enough? I've only been able to manage a second or two on my successful attempts," Biancabella asked her sister.

She sat in the tent with Samaritana and the king. A brazier lit in the center threw off a pleasant warmth against the night's chill, its flames casting dancing shadows on the canvas walls. A few hours earlier, the sun set across the plain where the men hunkered down awaiting further orders near the city walls. They sat around fires in the makeshift camp, roasting several hares an industrious soldier trapped in snares near the forest's edge.

"Yes, remember our practice, on how to hold the energy." Samaritana had explained the plan to her sister and the king back in Naples, but now that the moment had arrived, they needed reassurance. "As I told you, it is a matter of tapping into your power. I will take care of the rest."

"And you are sure it won't hurt her in any way?" Ferrandino interjected, worry carved over his fine features as he gripped his wife's hand.

"No, it won't harm her. You have my word," she confirmed. "After all, do you think I would do anything to harm her?

"It may be our only way into the castle undetected," Biancabella conceded and though dubious, released herself from her husband's grip.

After a tense glance between them, Ferrandino kissed Biancabella on the forehead and petals scattered from her palms. A log tipped in the brazier, setting off a shower of sparks, and the couple jumped. They chuckled in unison at their apprehension. Biancabella knew they could trust her sister above all others. She crossed the space between them.

"Are you ready to try?" Samaritana asked.

"Yes," was the firm reply.

"Try to imagine the energy that runs through you when you produce the jewels or the flowers, just like we practiced." She gestured at the petals on the ground. "Take my hands and repeat after me."

Biancabella did as instructed and her sister began to chant words. They made no sense to her, yet they felt natural rolling off her tongue, almost familiar now after reciting them for the last several days. When Samaritana took her hands, she concentrated on the warmth that filled her center and the accustomed tingling, which preceded her petals or gems. The sensation of falling filled her along with a rush of hot air. Eyes squeezed shut, her hands released from her sister's, and a wave of panic flooded her, but only for a moment, because all went still.

Her eyes opened to a new world. The tent, now massive, soared far above her, not as focused but colors were reinvented, mostly shades of blue and green. Next to her was the king's foot, large enough to crush her with one stomp. The roar of the brazier, no longer crisp pops, sounded as though she heard it from underwater. Samaritana slithered to her side.

"How do you feel?" she asked, forked tongue flitting in and out.

"Different but balanced."

She moved, the supple grace at once peculiar and luxuriant. Her body flowed in sinuous curves across the carpet laid out on the tent floor, the feel of it reverberating through her whole form. Her tongue moved in and out without thought, like breath into one's lungs. Acute smells emanated from all around—burning wood, the flower petals, even the scent of Jaco. He knelt by the snakes and she could hear his heartbeat.

"Biancabella, are you all right?" he asked, his voice sending down a shower of hot air.

"Yes," she hissed in a sibilant voice. "I think it is time to execute the plan."

The king scooped them both up and hid them in the pocket of his doublet. Biancabella enjoyed the warmth of his body and the softness of the velvet lining. She entwined herself with Samaritana and a sense of wholeness filled her. Ferrandino strode from the tent where the guards snapped to attention.

"At ease, men," he told them. "I just need to relieve myself."

He walked to a dark area against the city walls, the guards' eyes on him ever vigilant. The sisters scouted this area with him earlier, choosing this place specifically. Gently, he reached into his pocket. After removing the snakes, he laid them on the cool ground. Biancabella smelled the roasting hare so strongly, her stomach turned, but the vast sky above stole her attention, dotted with hundreds of stars, twinkling like diamonds. She stared in awe. Samaritana glided to her side.

"Good luck and be careful," Ferrandino whispered, while Biancabella trailed her sister through a small gap in the stones.

Once inside, they faced the journey up the steep hill to the castle. Biancabella worried the climb would take hours, yet they moved at a speed which astounded her. Light and lithe, the constraints of ascending as a bulky human were removed, and she felt almost as if they were flying. Keeping to the shadows and the edges of buildings, they rose ever toward their destination unnoticed by anyone. At the castle gates, they slipped by two guards who chatted softly.

"This whole business is strange if you ask me," the heftier one said to his cohort. "That woman here this afternoon was a dead ringer for Queen Biancabella is all I'm saying."

"Witchcraft can do that though, right?" the thinner man countered. "Who's to say what the truth even is at this point."

"Well, we ain't paid to figure out the truth, only to fight for the marquis, but I for one will be damned if I'm gonna take orders from any of those dowager's men," Hefty Guard asserted.

"Agreed," Thin Guard huffed.

Samaritana nudged Biancabella in the direction of the castle, who was fascinated by the ease with which her sister found cracks and crevices to travel into the building itself. Sconces lit the hallways, but their beams did not fall all the way to the floor, leaving the edges in shadow. It mattered little as most corridors they traversed remained empty where they slithered on the chilled stones.

Never could Biancabella have imagined returning to her childhood home in this manner. Despite the years which had passed, she remembered every inch of the place, its design engraved into her memory like one of Calvo's carvings. First, they came to the door of Biancabella's old bedroom. Muffled voices emanated from within, as well as the cloying scent of Dowager Finola's perfume. The snakes slunk underneath the door into the dimly lit chamber, where the dowager stood over the bed scolding her weeping daughter.

"Enough of this! Act like a queen, not some simpering child!"

"But King Ferrandino is here. He knows the truth," Renata stammered between stifled sobs. She folded back onto herself on the mattress, a pathetic lump, whose shoulders shook with each whimper.

"Bah! He can prove nothing. Do not worry, I have the marquis petrified about witchcraft and what spells could be cast on him and his city. He is quite under my thumb, and his army along with it. Now sit up and wipe off your face, for heaven's sake," the evil mother demanded, no patience left for signs of weakness.

The dowager grabbed her daughter's hair and yanked her up. After a cry of pain, Renata sat with legs dangling over the side of the bed, a face of utter despair.

"Your job is to produce an heir which you cannot do by avoiding the king's bed. Remember that," the mother scowled, a slap to Renata's cheek for good measure.

"I'm so tired," she spluttered, earning her an eye roll from the dowager.

"You can rest when those women are dead. Now clean yourself up and keep this with you, in case we need them," Finola huffed, shoving a small dagger into the girl's hand. Patting her sleeve, the dowager stomped into the adjoining room. *Tessina's room*, Biancabella thought sadly.

"Tired of this lie," Renata whispered to herself while fat tears spilled onto her lap. She made no attempt to brush them away, but did throw the dagger out of reach on the mattress.

Samaritana prodded Biancabella back under the door. They slipped down the hall to her parent's old chamber, now presumably, her cousin's. In the more brightly illuminated room, they found the shadows in the corner. A plump, older woman cleared dishes off a desk onto a tray, her body blocking its occupant, with movements slowed not by age, but by a certain sadness in her posture.

"I will leave this," she indicated a nearly full plate, "in case you are hungry later."

Pomma. Biancabella remembered her voice, her round face always so full of laughter when Piero and she were children. The maid remained with him even after all this time. This gave Biancabella a measure of comfort for the poor man who endured so many tragedies already in his young life.

Pomma picked up the tray and carried it to the door. On her way out, she turned to say, "You really should try to eat something, my dear boy. You need to keep up your strength."

Piero, who now was in view, merely nodded blankly as the maid left. Pity filled Biancabella at the sight of her cousin. He sat unmoving, a forlorn shade in his unfocused eyes, long legs stretched out in front of him. A bright fire burned in the hearth, but no warmth radiated from Piero, only melancholy.

"It is time," Samaritana told her sister.

The snakes wound together, and she intoned the spell, Biancabella repeating it. Once again, heat engulfed her followed by a dizzying spiral upwards. The two maidens now stood in front of Piero, whose mouth hung wide open at the sight of them.

CHAPTER FORTY-THREE

Piero jumped to his feet, the chair toppling to the ground behind him. The tray of food clattered the floor, its contents scattering across the dark blue rug in globs and sprays. His eyes shot to the door estimating his chance to escape, a shout for help already forming on his lips. Samaritana held up her hand.

"Wait, please! We mean you no harm," Biancabella assured.

He bit off his cry, but remained too startled to utter a coherent phrase. Without taking his attention off the ladies for a second, he backed up against the wall to brace himself. Biancabella felt his penetrating stare as he scrutinized every inch of her. The boy she remembered had grown into a lanky, young man, who possessed the nervous air he carried as a child. He still did not hold up well when alarmed, as his wide-eyes and tremors confirmed.

"Piero, it is me, Biancabella, your dear cousin," she reassured. "Dowager Finola deceives you. She tried to have me murdered, thought me dead, and put her daughter in my place. You have seen Renata. You know she is not me."

Piero nodded slowly, suspicion lacing his face. He took a step forward, his eyes now on Samaritana, who he regarded with wariness. Neither woman spoke while he sorted through the multitude of thoughts hurtling across his mind.

"Dowager Finola also spoke of deceit . . . and witchcraft," he said at last. "How do I know where the true deception comes from? From all of you perhaps?"

"You have a scar on your left knee," Biancabella replied calmly, and Piero eyes jerked to hers. "You fell in my secret garden when we were little. You were spying on me and saw me talking to a snake. The snake healed you, and I told you she was my sister, but you were frightened and ran away."

When she spoke these words, Samaritana shifted back into her snake form. She wound her way up Biancabella and slid into the golden circles around her neck. Piero crossed the distance between them with tentative steps. He reached out to touch his cousin's arm; satisfied she was real, he extended his hand to her neck and stroked the snake. Tears filled his eyes.

"Biancabella," he whispered and threw his arms around her.

Flowers sprung from her hands, happiness filling her along with relief. Samaritana slithered to the floor and returned to her human self. While they helped him clean up the mess from the tray, he told them how he tried to convince himself that he imagined that encounter in the garden, but in his heart, he always knew the memory was authentic.

"I can't believe you are here now, and yet I can. I knew from the moment the dowager arrived, something was amiss. Rumors spread even as far as here about how changed you were after the fever. Once I realized the queen wasn't you, I assumed you died and Dowager Finola tried to pass off the woman as you. The thought that you were gone, along with both of your parents was unbearable."

"I heard they died from the fever," Biancabella said.

"Yes, but please, come sit so I can tell you the story."

After adding a new log to the fire, he brought two chairs to the small table and righted his fallen one to join them, pushing the tray of smashed food and broken china to the side. He raked his fingers though a mass of black curls and began his tale.

"Your parents went most of the summer without catching the fever, but toward the end of August both became gravely ill. The physician brought in every healer he could find, tried every suggested remedy, but to no avail. When your father grasped what fate held for them, he asked to be with his wife, so I ordered her carried to his bed. They died in each other's arms only minutes apart. Their final words to me were to tell you they loved you. I am so very sorry, Biancabella."

Biancabella wiped tears from her cheeks, touched that at the end, their thoughts had been with her. Thankfully, they never learned of the evil perpetrated by the dowager, who had her kidnapped around that time. At least, they left the world wrapped together their minds at peace. The fireplace behind Biancabella blurred to a haze of yellows and oranges to her wet eyes. Samaritana clasped her hand, stroking it lightly.

"I have done the best I can in their stead. There was much loss of life, nearly all in the march were affected. Even now, we are not fully recovered, both economically and spiritually," he commented, sadness thick in every word.

"Oh Piero, how alone you must feel," Biancabella cried.

"But my troubles sound quite little in comparison to yours. Tell me everything you went through."

Biancabella recounted the story, with Samaritana filling in details here and there. The actions of the dowager horrified Piero, and she had to assure him several times that her hands were just fine now. He brightened at the description of the Brizia family and Biancabella's subsequent reunion with Ferrandino. By the end of the account, the three held hands across the table, happy to be with each other again until her cousin's countenance turned dark.

"The dowager must pay for her crimes," Piero asserted and rose. "I will summon the king to my throne room immediately."

He led them through a tunnel that joined his chamber directly to the throne room. The startled guards jumped at his orders, one running out the door to fetch King Ferrandino, another leaving to gather reinforcements. Extra men marched in just ahead the king, who brought a small contingent with him as well. Piero strode to meet him, arms open.

"I was overjoyed to learn that my cousin is well," Piero stated. "And I apologize for not meeting with you earlier. Unfortunately, I fell for the trickery of the dowager, who I have ordered be brought before us with her phony queen."

"No apology is necessary," Ferrandino declared. "We were both unwitting victims of her malice."

No soon had he uttered this sentence, the doors pushed open. Dowager Finola strolled in, chin high, shoulders back. Renata crept in her wake. At the sight of Biancabella and Samaritana standing with the men, something between doubt and fear flashed for the briefest second on her face. She stopped in front of them, her daughter cowering in her shadow. The guards formed a loose circle around the room, every ear craning to hear what transpired.

"Dowager Finola, would you care to explain this?" Piero asked, pointing between the real and fake queens.

"I already told you, *this* is the result of witchcraft. Please tell me they have not entranced you as well," she scowled with all confidence.

"I do not think sorcery played any part in this. Nor does King Ferrandino. The deception here is yours. She is not

Biancabella." He pointed at Renata, who tried to disappear behind her mother.

"And how can you be so sure she is?" Finola countered, no trace of panic in her, even though she did not deny Piero's claim.

"She has proven herself to me. I remember the gold rings around her neck—a mark she's borne since our childhood together."

"Artifice, I am sure. Likely drawn on with a little gold powder."

Something about the glint in her eyes made the hairs on the back of Biancabella's neck rise. Knowing her scheme unraveled seemed to make the dowager even more dangerous, like a trapped animal. The guards took a collective step inward.

"Check for yourself," Ferrandino growled. "I assure you they are quite real."

The dowager moved closer, and Biancabella raised her chin the slightest bit to reveal the golden birthmark. Quicker than anyone could react, the dowager pulled a dagger from her sleeve and attempted to plunge it into the queen's exposed throat. Ferrandino, Samaritana, and Piero leapt forward, each knowing they would not stop her in time. Just before the blade made contact, the dowager arched backwards with a howl of pain and crumpled to the floor.

A knife protruded from the middle of Finola's back, who now lay face down on the marble. Behind her, Renata collapsed to her knees with a sob, bloody hands covering her face.

CHAPTER FORTY-FOUR

A split second of silence passed, everyone frozen in place, before Samaritana grabbed Biancabella and checked her neck for injuries. Guards rushed forward to check on the safety of both Piero and Ferrandino, who each demanded to know how the dowager snuck a weapon into the room, before issuing a flurry of orders. All the while, Renata wept on the floor, her dead mother's blood pooling ever closer to the folds of her skirt. Biancabella gently brushed away her sister's hands and walked around the body to Renata's side.

"You saved my life," she managed in a hoarse whisper.

"I had to stop her," Renata choked. "It was all too much to take, the deception, the threats."

Biancabella stroked her sister-in-law's hair. The others gathered close behind. Two guards who were tasked with removing the dowager marched over. They rolled the body onto a stretcher and took it from the room. A few shocked servants entered with buckets and rags to clean the blood off the floor. Renata did not even move when they started mopping next to her, she stayed down with her head in her hands. Though relieved the dowager finally paid the price for her betrayal, pity filled Biancabella for her daughter whose hand struck the fatal blow.

Renata dropped her hands and looked bleakly at the true queen. She smoothed her blood-soaked skirt and rose to face King

Ferrandino. "I am guilty of deceiving you, Your Highness. I accept any punishment my actions justify."

The king's expression softened at her word. "Renata, you were as much a victim of your mother's evil as the rest of us. That in itself is punishment enough. In the end, you came to the defense of your queen and saved her life. For that, I will be eternally grateful."

"I do not deserve such mercy, Your Highness," Renata wept. "I will spend the rest of my days living up to it."

The sisters comforted the shaken woman. Biancabella ordered Pomma, who had crept into the room with a number of other inhabitants of the castle, to tend to Renata. The elderly maid ushered her out of the room with an arm around her shoulder and gentle words of comfort. Ferrandino hugged his wife, who thanked him for showing Renata clemency. Piero and Samaritana joined them, and the four shared a happy embrace before leaving the throne room together.

It took several days to sort out all that had happened. For Renata's sake, Finola was buried quietly to avoid any public spectacle. Ferrandino issued an official statement declaring Dowager Finola guilty of treason and executed for said crime. He asked all to celebrate the return of their dear queen, Biancabella. Word spread quickly from Monferrato to Naples, a mixture of rumor and fact as is usually ascribed to such extraordinary news. Piero, thrilled to be reunited with his cousin, hosted the king's party for a week. At their parting, he embraced Biancabella warmly.

"I promise to come to Naples before the end of the year. I cannot wait to visit you there," he told her and helped her into the carriage where Samaritana awaited.

"Be sure to bring Renata with you," Biancabella said.

After years of threats and abuse at the hand of her mother, her sister-in-law chose to stay in Monferrato for a fresh start. Indeed, the change of scenery and softer mountain air already brought color back to her cheeks.

"I will." He kissed her hand, and the door shut.

"He will most certainly bring her," Samaritana affirmed to Biancabella, who settled on the plush velvet seat. "Have you noticed the way he looks at her?"

"Yes, I have. I even saw them walking alone in the gardens yesterday. Hopefully with time, she will be ready to return his feelings. Goodness knows, they both deserve some happiness in their lives."

The roads were lined with well-wishers the entire way back to Naples, excitedly cheering for the reunited king and queen, their story something only heard in fairy tales. They arrived home to festooned main gates and streets adorned with banners and streamers. Citizens packed every street, balcony, and window to hail their king, who led the procession. With its top down, the sisters leaned over the sides of the carriage to adoring shouts. People threw flowers in their path and a touched Biancabella added her own petals to the delight of all. A jubilant city welcomed back its monarchs, who both endured so many trials. The populace sensed a new era awakening, one of blessedness after a long darkness.

In the courtyard of the palace, the Brizia family greeted them. Calvo gave Biancabella an extra-long hug, elated that truth won out against evil.

"I'm so happy you are back in your rightful place," he told her on the way to the waiting feast, "and without that evil woman to worry about anymore."

"It's all thanks to you," Biancabella proclaimed. When he demurred, she grabbed his hands firmly. "You saved me, not even knowing who I was. You welcomed me into your home with no thought of compensation. You are a rare soul, the antithesis to the dowager's evil, and meeting you and your family is one of the greatest blessings of my life."

"I am blessed to have gained not one new daughter, but two." Calvo placed a kiss on her forehead and drew Samaritana over to kiss her head as well.

The celebratory feast went well into the night. The royal chefs outdid themselves with course after course of delicious food and a large orchestra's music filled the air. After hours of dining and dancing, the evening showed no indication of drawing to a close. While the rest of the crowd partied, the royal couple remained close to each other. On the dais, Biancabella lounged against the comfort of her husband's side, their hands interlocked.

"It's like waking from a bad nightmare," the king commented, as if reading his wife's mind.

Biancabella nodded and took in the scene. Samaritana stood on one side, a line of courtiers waiting to make her acquaintance. Calvo and Lucia danced a sprightly tarantella, years seeming to melt off their smiling faces. Cecelia joined them, her peals of laughter ringing sweetly across the room. Alessandra and Ginevra accepted dozens of dance requests from eager young men, who fought for their attention. Naples held a bright future for the Brizia family.

Samaritana excused herself from the courtiers and came to sit at her sister's side. Biancabella entwined the fingers of her free hand with hers.

"How fortunate I was that Biancabella's imaginary snake sibling was not so imaginary after all," the king stated.

"Yes, fortune smiled on me when I was given this amazing sister," Biancabella agreed. "Now let us call an end to this wonderful night before I fall asleep right here in a most un-queen-like fashion."

Ferrandino rose to make his rounds of the room and say his goodnights. Biancabella and Samaritana lingered a moment longer.

"What?" Samaritana asked at the enigmatic smile on her sister's face.

"It is as you always said—if we are together . . ." Biancabella began, and her sister joined her to finish the sentence.

"All will be well."

OTHER WORKS

A Prophecy of Wings

The Stewartsland Chronicles:
Not Every Girl
Unexpected Rewards
A Betrayal Exposed

ACKNOWLEDGEMENTS

Once again, I am blessed by a great team of people who help me get my work out into the world. To my editor, Chelsea Lauren, thank you for your expertise and guidance in polishing my words. To Keylin Rivers of *Fantasy Book Cover Designs By Keylin Rivers*, thank you for your beautiful cover art and the time and care you took with it. To Angelique Bosman of Ctrl Alt Publish, thank you for your formatting knowhow and your spot-on suggestions. To my beta reader, Jill, thanks not only for your time and input but for your incredible friendship. To my houseful of boys, thank you for supporting me and giving me the time and space to fulfill this dream. Finally, to my readers, thank you for allowing my stories into your lives. I hope you enjoy reading them as much as I enjoy writing them.

ABOUT THE AUTHOR

Reading was always a big part of Jane's life. Creating her own stories developed out of this love. To date she has published the *The Stewartsland Chronicles* trilogy, a YA Fantasy Adventure and *A Prophecy of Wings*, a retelling of the classic fairy tale, *Thumbelina*. Her latest work, *A Maiden of Snakes*, is also a retelling of the Italian fairy tale, *Biancabella and the Snake*. These books represent her goals as a writer—stories of adventure for teens with strong, yet relatable, female protagonists.

She lives in New Jersey with her husband, two sons, two extremely spoiled cats and a feisty German Shepherd. When she is not running around with her family or writing, she can be found curled up with a good book and said cats.

You can visit her at: www.janemcgarrybooks.com.